FRAGMENTS

DRAGONFIRE STATION BOOK 2

ZEN DIPIETRO

PARALLEL WORLDS PRESS

COPYRIGHT

FRAGMENTS (DRAGONFIRE STATION #2)

COPYRIGHT © 2016 BY ZEN DIPIETRO

This is a work of fiction. Names, characters, organizations, events, and incidents are either products of the author's imagination or used fictitiously. Any resemblance to actual events, business establishments, locales, or persons, living or dead, is coincidental.

All rights reserved. No part of this publication may be reproduced, stored in a retrieval system, or transmitted in any form or by any means (electronic, mechanical, photocopying, recording, or otherwise) without express written permission of the publisher. The only exception is brief quotations for the purpose of review.

Please purchase only authorized electronic editions. Distribution of this book via the Internet or via any other means without the permission of the publisher is illegal and punishable by law.

ISBN: 978-1-943931-06-4 (print)

Published in the United States of America by Parallel Worlds Press

DRAGONFIRE STATION SERIES

Dragonfire Station Book 1: Translucid
Dragonfire Station Book 2: Fragments
Dragonfire Station Book 3: Coalescence

Intersections (Dragonfire Station Short Stories)

Selling Out (Mercenary Warfare Book 1)
Blood Money (Mercenary Warfare Book 2)
Hell to Pay (Mercenary Warfare Book 3)
Calculated Risk (Mercenary Warfare Book 4)
Going for Broke (Mercenary Warfare Book 5)

Chains of Command Book 1: New Blood
Chains of Command Book 2: Blood and Bone
Chains of Command Book 3: Cut to the Bone
Chains of Command Book 4: Out for Blood

To stay updated on new releases and sales, sign up for Zen's newsletter at www.ZenDiPietro.com

1

Four months' worth of days stretched out across the starlit expanse, yawning away from Fallon in a disheartening oblivion of time and space. She stared out the porthole of her quarters, watching the darkness mock her.

In the amount of time it would take the *Onari* to reach Earth, she could have upgraded Dragonfire Station's entire surveillance grid, or instituted new security protocols. But then, Dragonfire wasn't her responsibility at the moment.

She turned away from the non-view that made the *Onari* seem like the only dot of life in the universe. No sense in looking out at an illusion. Not when a powder keg of reality needed her attention.

She paced a tight circle around the small two-seater couch, her arms crossed tightly. The trouble was, every time she thought about what had been done to her, it infuriated her. That was no good. Excessive emotion led to mistakes. She needed to crush her anger under the weight of her duty and loyalties, then hone it into a tiny, laser-sharp blade. Once she'd done that, she could use that edge to excise the rotten flesh from Blackout. She had no idea how far the disease went, but she and her team would remove every bit.

So much to be done, yet for now, she could only wait. She let her arms drop to her sides and blew out a slow breath. At the moment, she needed to check on Hawk. Jerin—as both the ship's captain and chief medical officer—had released him from the infirmary only because she'd known that keeping him there would have been nearly impossible. That meant that it fell to Fallon, as the leader of their team, to keep an eye on him.

Fallon strode out into the corridor, running her hands down her torso to smooth her fitted black jumpsuit as she went. Her fingers brushed over her comport and stinger. Although the *Onari* wasn't a Planetary Alliance Cooperative ship, it operated primarily within PAC space and complied fully with all the cooperative's protocols. As such, the crew was accustomed to armed security officers, which worked well for Fallon. She always felt better with a weapon or two on her person. Better yet, five or six, since she liked to keep her throwing knives handy.

Hawk's guest quarters were conveniently located two doors down from her own. She rang the chime, but got no answer. She tried again. Sighing, she turned on her heel, following a hunch.

She found Hawk in the bar, palming a huge green drink of something-or-other and chatting up the server, who looked all too pleased about it.

She slid onto a stool next to Hawk, glancing at his menuboard. "Zerellian ale. On his board," she said to the server, effectively dismissing him. The guy moved off, looking disappointed. He probably assumed she and Hawk were together. Hah.

She sized her partner up. His color was good, his breathing even. Good posture, no apparent balance issues.

"Here to send me to my room?" He lifted an eyebrow that said he wished her luck with that.

"Maybe. We'll see." She followed his sweeping gaze around the bar, taking time to note the precise position of the single entryway in relation to her seat. Business in the bar was light so far, but the *Onari*'s day shift hadn't ended, and more people would soon fill the empty seats. "You were supposed to be resting. Get bored?"

Hawk shrugged his bulky shoulders and scratched at his beard. "Not really. I just felt twitchy about being on a ship without mapping it out. I like to know where I am."

She knew what he meant, as she always felt the same about unfamiliar surroundings. "And the schematics on the voicecom weren't enough for you?"

He grinned, reminding her, as always, of a cherubic lumberjack. "You got me. Yeah, I checked out the schematics. But I like to see it all with my own eyes, too."

"Especially the bar," she concluded dryly. Her drink arrived and she accepted it with a nod of thanks, but didn't invite the server to remain to take part in their conversation. He slid away, sneaking occasional looks back at Hawk.

Hawk's blue-gray eyes twinkled at her. "Of course." He raised his glass to hers and barked, "Blood and bone!"

Apparently their team motto also worked as a toast. She touched her glass to his. "Blood and bone."

He tossed back a hearty drink, half draining the glass. His gaze roved past her again, eyeing up the other patrons of the bar. She noticed Dr. Yomalu, talking and making big waving gestures at a Trallian lab tech.

"Don't even think about it," she warned. "The only person you're taking back to your room tonight is me."

He leered at her, almost convincingly. "If you think you're up to it."

She snorted. "You're lucky you're not in the infirmary right now. I'm the one keeping an eye on your sorry ass."

He let out a loud half-sigh, half-groan. "Fine. Tonight only."

"As many nights as it takes until Jerin gives you a clean bill of health."

"Argh." He shifted in his seat. "You're killing me."

She had to laugh. "You'll survive. We'll be here for four months. That's plenty of time for you to make the rounds of the *Onari* crew. At least I'm letting you have a few drinks, right?"

That seemed to mollify him somewhat, though he did mutter, "I bet Peregrine's already found someone."

"It's not a competition." Fallon wrapped her fingers around her glass and peered into it. She'd downed more ale than she'd thought. Oh, well. Her purchase of another drink would only further improve the *Onari*'s financial standing. She felt a twinge of satisfaction, knowing how many cubics Raptor had already transferred to Jerin as payment for their passage. A staggering number, and none of it their own. As Avian Unit's hacker extraordinaire, Raptor had ensured that their team would have all the currency they needed to get their job done, courtesy of the very people forcing them to do it. Poetic, as far as Fallon was concerned.

Yes, another drink could only help everyone. She didn't need to be on high alert right now. She never let herself get stone-cold drunk in any situation, but she could afford a pleasant buzz tonight. She drained her glass, caught the barkeep's eye, and pointed to it.

Hawk shoved his glass against hers, causing them to clink, and indicated another drink for himself as well. "Like old times."

"What, Peregrine off with someone and you and me having drinks in the bar?" Fallon had no idea where Raptor was. She needed to have a long conversation with him about things they hadn't had time to discuss before. But that would wait until tomorrow.

"Believe it or not, you and I are old drinking buddies." He grinned at her, and his odd combination of massive size and impish, twinkling eyes made her laugh.

"I do believe it, actually. This feels...comfortable." She still hadn't recovered any memories from before her shuttle accident, but she had certain instincts that felt *almost* like memory.

"Always has been. Well, until I ditch you for some hot guy, anyway." He paused. "Or woman. Whatever."

Which made her wonder about her own hookups. "Don't I ever ditch you for someone?"

His expression became calculating, as if he was measuring his answer. "Not often. You tend to be more long-term about that sort of thing."

That was interesting to know. "Do you think that's why I got married?"

His answer was immediate. "I sure as shit don't know what you were thinking by getting married. I keep hoping it was a tactical move, not a personal one, though that seems unlikely at this point. Truth is, when I think about it too hard, it makes me want to smack you around a little. I mean, *what the hell*?"

He did, in fact, look irate, as if her choosing to marry while on an extended assignment had been a personal slight to him. Or perhaps to Avian Unit as a whole. If she'd known why she'd done it, she'd have said so, but thus far she'd been unable to unravel that bit of her recent past.

"If it makes you feel any better, she dumped me hard when she realized she didn't even know my real name." Fallon shrugged. "And it's not like any vows I took could be an actually legal thing—given that a BlackOp agent doesn't technically exist, outside of highly classified files within Blackout."

She reached for her glass, but he caught her hand, staying it. He stared hard into her eyes. "You made a commitment, though, and that means something. That gives you a responsibility to someone. Which puts the rest of us at risk because you, Raptor, Per, and I are a no-matter-what scenario. Whatever you take on, we take on. So if you marry, essentially, all of us do." He let go of her hand. "If you don't remember anything else, remember *that*."

Which was kind of a mean dig at her memory loss, but she

didn't mind. She much preferred the straight, brutal truth over tactful inferences or polite restraint.

She thought about her partners in Avian Unit, and their rejection of serious relationships. "Well, like I said. We're done. She packed up and ditched me. I didn't even say goodbye to her when I left Dragonfire Station."

His fingers played over the rim of his glass. "Because you wanted to keep her at a distance, right? Better if she hates you. Keeps her safer."

"She doesn't hate me," she argued. Then she had to admit, "But yeah. Better for her if she's not involved with me. Better for all of us."

He nodded. She began to understand why Hawk was her drinking buddy. He was deeper and more perceptive than she'd realized.

"Still love her?" he asked.

"She's...special." She couldn't quite meet his eyes, instead looking off to his right, where a pair of crew sat, eating their dinner.

"Must be, if you married her, however legal it was or wasn't." He sighed. "I'm sorry. It must suck."

"What do you mean? Her leaving me? Like I said, she's better off." Fallon picked up her glass and took a long drink. The spicy burn shocked her palate, but settled down to a warm, smooth finish. Mm. Zerellian ale. Her instincts had guided her true on that choice, as they usually did.

"Right, she's safer. But the first sign of trouble and she ditches? She's not like us. *Her* commitment is something that she can take back. And she did."

Putting it that way made her feel like shit. "Thanks," she muttered, gripping her glass.

"I'm just saying put it in perspective. Use that perspective to cauterize anything that's still bleeding." He fell silent, watching her in a tough-love sort of way that felt oddly comforting.

"Right. Thanks." This time, she said it without the sarcasm.

"Talk to Raptor about it."

Her hackles went up. "Why Raptor?" She already had questions about her past with him, and intended to find the answers very soon.

She couldn't read anything from Hawk's expression. He looked cool and unconcerned as he met her gaze. "You two have always been close, ever since the academy. And you'll be more likely to find him during the long, lonely nights ahead." He winked at her.

"Fine. Whatever." She finished off her glass and waved for another. So far, no buzz. Maybe she needed to dedicate herself more completely to the cause. The more they talked, the more she could use a nice tipsy haze.

But with the heavy topics out of the way, the tone of their conversation shifted. Hawk began telling somewhat-sanitized-in-case-of-curious-ears versions of some of their previous exploits. She wondered if certain details might be exaggerated, but he had her laughing and holding her stomach with his descriptions of both near misses and bang-on successes.

She stopped counting their drinks, but when she felt just beyond buzzed, she made a slashing hand gesture toward the barkeep, then closed out their tab on the menuboard. Hawk protested, but without enthusiasm. More for the principle of it, she guessed.

They finished the drinks they had, and Fallon decided it was time for them to go before they made asses of themselves by getting too loud. The bar had filled up considerably, with plenty of people standing about, waiting for a table or stool.

"Let's get out of here," she said. "I'll walk you home." She grabbed the menuboard, verified the expenses, and held it up for Hawk to authenticate. He was paying, after all. She slid off the stool to follow him.

The doors whooshed open and she failed to completely clear

the opening, awkwardly brushing against it with her hip. He pulled her to his side to steady her, and she returned the favor by tightening her arm around his waist when he stumbled over some invisible obstacle on the deck plate. They had it under control by the time they strolled into his quarters, but she was *tired*. As if the few minutes of walking had sapped all of her energy, bleeding it off into frigid space.

His quarters were a mirror of her own. No kitchenette, just a bed, a small living area, and an adjoining necessary. He led her right to the bed, where he began unzipping his jumpsuit. Oddly, she felt perfectly at ease with that development.

"I guess you're sleeping over?" He pulled his undershirt over his head and dropped it to the floor, exposing a wide expanse of very hairy chest.

"Why, is that normal for us?" she asked through a yawn. It would certainly be convenient. The short walk back to her quarters seemed longer than it should.

"Yeah. And don't worry, I've seen your panties before." He was too tired to even affect one of his bogus leers, which she never believed. The two of them had as much sexual chemistry as a chopstick and a teacup.

So she peeled off her own black jumpsuit and got into bed beside him wearing her undershirt and panties. "You don't snore, do you?"

"No. But you do." He turned his back to her, adjusted the blankets, and let out a long sigh.

"Do not." Wren would have told her so, if she did.

"Only when you're really drunk." His voice was muffled.

"Shut up and go to sleep."

"You first." He sounded exhausted, but amused.

They fell silent, and Fallon stretched her leg out, touching the back of his knee with her toe. "Hey, Hawk?"

He half turned his head to look back at her. "Yeah?"

"Thanks."

He settled back into his pillow. "It's nothing. You've done the same for me."

She smiled into the dark and closed her eyes.

———

THE DOOR CHIMED, jolting Fallon out of a pleasant sleep. She felt Hawk leaping lightly to his feet and moving away. For such a huge dude, the guy could move like a dancer. With him gone, she was free to sprawl out in the middle of the bed and appropriate his pillow, too. *Ahh.*

"On your feet, soldier. We have company." Hawk's voice broke into her doze.

Sighing, she kicked off the blankets and sat up. She ran her fingers through her haphazard hair and hauled herself out of bed.

"I see you two have picked up right where you left off." Raptor's wry smirk failed to bother her. His little eyebrow lift at her undershirt-and-panties combo didn't, either. Her team didn't get too precious about inconsequential things like nudity. Just as well, since these small quarters didn't have separate bedrooms.

She grabbed her jumpsuit from the floor. "I'm taking a shower. Whatever you want, it's too early for it." She shot Raptor a sour look. "We're not exactly on the clock here."

"Aw, well, I guess I just missed you guys." Raptor made a smoochy face at her and Hawk. Hawk punched him on the shoulder before sitting on the edge of the bed, not bothering to get dressed. Raptor staggered back a step, but didn't stop grinning.

"We'll wait for you." Hawk made a dismissive gesture toward the necessary.

Fallon was on her feet before he could change his mind, letting the door swish shut behind her. She shoved her clothes into the processor and stepped into the cramped shower. No water. Only a sonic pulse. She sighed. Four months without a hot, steamy shower would feel like a very long time. But at least she could still get clean. If sonic showers were her only complaint, she'd be doing incredibly well.

The lack of water made the shower more of a rugged necessity than a pleasant indulgence, though, and she got done before her clothing did. A quick inventory of the room's contents did not reveal a bathrobe. After a moment of debate, she wrapped a towel around herself and tucked it, turning it into an unfashionable tube dress that went down to her knees. At least the towel was big. And soft.

She wet her hair down in the sink and used a smaller moisture-wicking towel to dry it. Short hair had turned out to be more work than she'd expected, but the asymmetrical style suited her well. It gave her an edge that her somewhat plain, Japanese face didn't have all on its own.

She stepped into the small living area. "My clothes will be a few more minutes. Your turn?" she asked Hawk, who stood at the voicecom with Raptor.

"Yeah. Per's not answering. But she doesn't usually get up before noon unless she's on the job. We'll catch up with her later."

Hawk strode to the necessary and the door closed behind him, leaving Fallon alone with Raptor.

"You okay?" Raptor studied her.

"I'm fine. Why?"

"Just checking." He stepped away from the voicecom and sat on the small couch.

She joined him, settling on the other half. Her conversation with Hawk drifted up from her thoughts, along with a comment or two that Peregrine had made.

"What's our relationship?" she asked. "Something between the two of us is different than the dynamics among the rest of us."

He didn't seem surprised by the question. "I'm not sure I have a definitive answer to that. We've never fit into a tidy category."

"Were we a couple before I was assigned to Dragonfire?"

"A couple of what?" he asked. The words should have made him sound like a smartass, but he seemed genuinely frustrated.

"A romantic couple."

He made a sound of profound suffering. "Can't I just punch you in the head and see if that knocks some memories loose?"

"You tried that already, the night you broke into my quarters on Dragonfire."

"Oh. Right." He looked wistful, as if recalling good times long gone.

She snapped her fingers to get him focused on her actual question. "Romantic couple. Were we?"

"No." He leaned back and put his feet up on the small table.

She could have done worse. Raptor was a good-looking guy, with light-brown hair that seemed to want to go wavy, and big brown eyes fringed with thick lashes that she envied. There was nothing feminine about him though. He had wide shoulders and a narrow waist. Nothing like Hawk's hulking muscularity, but toned and defined in a way that most guys never achieved. If she had to, she'd admit that she found him very hot. But not while he was listening.

"Have we ever *been* a romantic couple?" she persisted.

His face did a squinchy thing that gave her an answer before he found the right words. "You and I found each other soon after starting academy. By the time we were halfway through, we were sharing a dorm."

She wanted to be clear on the details. "So we were what, in love? Best pals? Just enjoying a bountiful sex life?"

He smiled reluctantly. "All of those. We had everything in common, so we just fit together."

"What happened to change that?"

"Before we left the academy, we found out we'd been tagged

for Blackout. We got our unit assignment and our new names. It changed everything."

"Ah." He didn't need to explain that for her. Of course Blackout had changed things. They were meant to bond together as a group of four. Having a couple among them would be a distraction and a shift of power dynamics. Never mind that being on an elite squad tasked with literally unspeakable things would be hard on a relationship.

He nodded at the understanding he saw on her face. "Yeah. Being together while belonging to the same unit wouldn't have been smart, or safe, or fair to the rest of our team. When given the choice between us or Blackout, we both chose Blackout."

"I see."

That explained some things. It also meant he knew a whole lot more about her than she'd realized. Intimate things that she used to know about him, too.

"Is my lack of memory hard for you?" she asked.

He looked surprised. "I hadn't thought about it that way. But... no. We're past all that. Don't worry. You're not going to get any tortured crap from me about you getting married."

Oh, and there was that, too. She hadn't even gotten around to considering that part yet.

"Well, good." She had a lot to re-learn about him, but she knew she would. She took great comfort in knowing that he, along with Hawk and Peregrine, would stick with her no matter what.

"We're going to figure everything out." His voice was reassuring, as if he thought she needed it. "Your memory, and who's pulling the strings to try to bring down Blackout. Or whatever they're doing."

That caught her attention. "You think someone's trying to dismantle Blackout? From the inside?"

He pressed his hands out in front of him, as if trying to distance himself from what he'd just said. "I don't know. Maybe. I think it's either that, or someone's trying to get control of something that no one person should have control of. I don't think it's a simple power play within the organization."

Hawk rejoined them, clean and mostly dressed. He hadn't zipped his jumpsuit up above his waist, instead letting the top hang down over his hips. "What did I miss?"

She straightened to her full height. "Raptor was telling me about our sordid past, and previously very inventive sex life."

Raptor snorted, but Hawk nodded appreciatively. "Good. Glad I don't have to dodge that topic anymore."

Fallon had to laugh about the part of her statement he'd found noteworthy.

Hawk looked puzzled. "What?"

"Nothing. How about we get some breakfast while we wait for Per to wake up? If we have time, we can visit the infirmary." The sooner Hawk had a clean bill of health, the better, as far as Fallon was concerned.

"Why? You feeling sick? Can't handle a couple drinks anymore?" Hawk sat on the arm of the couch and nudged her with his elbow.

"Hah. Try me."

"Oh, you don't want to say that." Hawk nudged her again and she slapped at his beefy arm.

Raptor let out a long-suffering sigh. "If I didn't know that Fallon had a big hole in her head, I'd never guess it by the way you two behave together."

Fallon fixed him with a pointed look. "About that hole in my head. Since there are things I should know but don't, I was hoping you could give me some details. Starting with the size of your—"

"*Gosh*, I'm starved, let's go!" Raptor declared, bolting out of the room so fast that the doors almost didn't open in time.

She and Hawk followed at a much more sedate pace, laughing.

Peregrine joined them at midday, looking well rested. Hawk had received a clean bill of health from Jerin, which relieved both him and Fallon. Now they were ready to make plans for their long journey.

Avian Unit sat together in Hawk's quarters. The space was tight for four people, but they made it work.

"So what's the plan?" Peregrine asked. Fallon had learned to appreciate her abruptness.

Raptor and Hawk glanced briefly at Fallon, and she again felt the oddness of them continuing to defer to her as the unit leader. As far as her memory was concerned, she hadn't known any of them just a couple weeks ago. Why should they accept her authority? But Hawk, Per, and Raptor had insisted that was the way Avian Unit worked. So, fine. She'd lead.

"Long-term plan remains the same," she answered. "We lay low on the *Onari* and let our trail go cold. After four months, Blackout will have no idea where to even start looking for us."

She got three nods in response.

Fallon continued, "Raptor will be pulling whatever data he can along the way, though some of the planets we'll visit only receive basic communications with no access to the major datastreams. Those certainly won't have any chance of intercepting point-to-point transmissions, so we may not turn up much. Once we arrive at Earth, we infiltrate the PAC intelligence base in Tokyo. Its setup and public areas make it the perfect target for us. If we do it right, we should have the information we need to figure out who tried to kill us. Once we know that, we can determine how we approach PAC command at headquarters."

Fallon focused her attention on Peregrine. She could never decide if Peregrine's hair was honey blonde or light brown. Her brown eyes and thin, often-frowning lips were pretty, in a strong way. Fallon envied Peregrine's thick, but still feminine, physique.

Peregrine was all kinds of muscular, in ways that Fallon's body could never be. "Per, you and Raptor will run the infiltration. There's no way he can slip into a PAC base's high-security area unnoticed without you fronting him. You two will have a lot of time to work out your strategy."

Peregrine nodded. "A clean mission?" Meaning that their presence at the base would remain undetected, even after they got out.

"Highly preferable, if we can manage it. We don't want to give Blackout a beacon to bring them right to us, after all that time spent getting them off our trail."

"Right."

"What about the short-term plan?" asked Raptor. "What are we going to do here for months on end? We need to train to keep our skills up, and there's no gym or targeting room here. Something to pass the time would be great, too."

"We also need to resupply," Hawk added. "We're going to need casual clothes and equipment."

Fallon looked toward him. "I'll need to talk to Jerin. Hawk, if you and Per can figure out what supplies we need and where along our flight path we can get them, I'll see what I can do to arrange a stop." She hesitated. "Going back to the long plan. There's another thing I'd like to do."

Three pairs of eyes watched her expectantly.

"One of the things I'd like to grab from PAC intelligence is my birth identity."

Peregrine's mouth pursed thoughtfully, while Raptor and Hawk frowned. "How's that going to help?" Raptor asked. "Whoever you were back then, you haven't been that person for a decade."

She'd expected some puzzlement, if not outright resistance to the idea. "It could jog my memory. But even if it doesn't, reconstructing my past would at least help me better understand who I am."

"Does ancient history really matter?" Raptor pressed. "You haven't changed—you're the same exact person you were before. Why go digging into a past that hasn't been relevant to you in years?"

His comment stung, for some reason, but she replied calmly. "The first fifteen years or so of your life might feel irrelevant to you, but that's because you have the luxury of taking them for granted. It's all just a big blank spot to me, and somehow that makes it very relevant. I can't describe what it's like to lose your past, so you'll have to take it on faith that it matters."

His expression softened, and he looked contrite.

"It's a side detail, though. If there's time and opportunity, only. If it jeopardizes us or our mission, it's off the table. The primary objective is getting what we need to figure out who we're fighting." She searched their faces, trying to read their thoughts. Did her interest in her past make them doubt her decisions?

Peregrine leaned forward and touched Fallon's elbow. "We want your memories back, too. Whatever might help, we'll give it our best."

"Thanks, Per." Knowing her team would back her up eased a pressure on her she hadn't realized she'd felt. "I'm also going to try hypnotherapy with Jerin and Brak. We'll be giving it a shot in about an hour, actually."

"Why didn't you try it on Dragonfire? They had a therapist, right?" Raptor asked.

"They did. But at first, he didn't think it would be helpful. And when I realized that my head is full of classified info, I knew I couldn't talk to him about any of it, anyway. Jerin and Brak already know parts of what's happened to me. Brak's even got top-secret clearance for the work she's done for the PAC, so she knows the risks. I know we can trust them."

"Is there any risk to *you* in doing hypnotherapy?" Hawk asked the question, but the same concern showed on Raptor's and Peregrine's faces. "Like, it's not going to convince you that you're a mime or something, will it? I mean...nobody likes a mime."

The tension broke and they all chuckled or smirked.

"No," she answered. "Jerin said it either helps or it doesn't. It won't harm my big, dumb brain."

"Good," Hawk said. "All that flailing around and walking down invisible stairs would get annoying. Besides, if we're going to pull this mission off, we need our Fury."

She shook her head, wrinkling her nose at her private code name within Avian Unit. In ancient Greek literature, a Fury was a spirit of punishment. That struck Fallon as overly fanciful, and she preferred to think of the name as simply meaning intensity. Actually, she'd have preferred to ditch the secondary code names entirely, but the others seemed quite attached to them. Some bonding sort of thing. Whatever.

As for her teammates, Raptor was Ghost, for his ability to hack into systems and get in and out of places unnoticed. He had certainly made short work of her security system on Dragonfire, which still irritated her to no end. He also had some impressive field-medic skills. He'd practically brought Hawk back from the dead after extracting him from the moon that Blackout had exiled him to.

She particularly liked Hawk's second code name: The Machine, for his strength and great fortitude. Now *that* was a cool name, and fitting for an extraction expert. Perhaps if he'd been the one getting himself off that Zerellian moon, things would have gone better. But any escape you survive is a good one, so Raptor had ultimately done okay.

As well as being the extraction expert, Hawk had the dubious distinction of having contacts in unexpected places. Raptor teased him sometimes about missing his calling as a Rescan trader, but his connections would prove useful in getting the supplies they needed.

Finally, Peregrine had earned the name Masquerade in honor

of her talent for disguises and impersonation. Fallon had experienced that skill set firsthand while extracting Peregrine from Sarkan. Peregrine had quickly and convincingly changed their identities more than once on their race off the planet. Peregrine was also an expert with surveillance technology and "spy gadgets," as Hawk liked to call them. Per wasn't a mechanic or an engineer by any stretch, but she was damn good at using tech to give them an edge, and they could certainly use any advantage they could get.

"Right. Fury." She didn't like the name, but didn't hate it either. Fortunately they didn't normally use them. Her own secondary skill was piloting. Of course, she had a third duty as well. As their leader, she was also responsible for the lives of these three. It was a lot to live up to.

"We could change it to Brainstorm, which I always thought was better, if you'd rather," Hawk offered helpfully.

"Uh, no." That was way worse. She shook her head, but his comment had broken her somber train of thought. Which had no doubt been Hawk's intent.

"So what do we do tomorrow? And the next day? We have a lot of hours ahead of us," Hawk pointed out.

She gave him a squint. "Mostly we just keep our heads down and stay out of trouble. The crew thinks we're here for long-term medical treatment while on our way to Earth. Jerin says her people will mind their own business. Of course some of them know me from Dragonfire, so they might be curious, but Jerin assured me that confidentiality is sacrosanct here. We don't appear on any travel manifests or records, and no one will mention us in any communications."

Peregrine looked skeptical. "How can we be sure?"

Fallon had asked the same thing, prone as she was to suspicion. "We can't, really, but Jerin was adamant. Her crew either adheres to the standard operating procedure for a hospi-ship, or they get dumped at the nearest outpost, however wretched, and blackballed from ever working in any healthcare position involving the PAC or Bennaris."

"You buy that?" Hawk asked.

Fallon lifted a shoulder noncommittally. "Frankly, she was pretty scary when she said it. I liked that. Made me feel more confident in her ability to properly intimidate her people."

Raptor said, "We'll keep our eye on things, just to be sure." Then he looked from Fallon to Peregrine to Hawk. "So which one of us is supposedly being treated? It's Hawk, right? For his massive ego complex?"

"No, it's you, for your severely kicked ass," Hawk retorted.

Fallon ignored them both. "The official story is that Peregrine is the daughter of a high-ranking official, and suffers from a chronic illness. The three of us are here to ensure her safety, which is of diplomatic importance."

"Ah. Good story." Hawk squinted at Raptor. "I'll still kick your ass, though."

Raptor grinned. "You're always welcome to try."

Peregrine closed her eyes, looking like a long-suffering mother. "Shut up, or I'll kick both your asses."

The men smiled, but shut up.

Fallon had to marvel at her change of circumstances. Two weeks ago she'd been married and living aboard Dragonfire as the chief of security and second in command of the station. A straight-arrow PAC officer, right out of the recruitment vids. Now she led this group of rogue BlackOps. A group that someone at Blackout wanted dead, and that spent as much time teasing each other as they did talking actual strategy.

As much as she missed Dragonfire, it still seemed like a pretty good trade.

2

Fallon left Hawk's quarters as her teammates began working up a shopping list. She had more time than she needed to get to the infirmary for her appointment, but she welcomed the chance to get out of the tight space.

As she stepped out, she saw Brak down the corridor at the door of Fallon's own quarters. She joined the Briveen, who had become a good friend back on Dragonfire, when Fallon had been struggling to reconcile her sense of self with her false identity.

Brak shifted to face her. "I was just on my way to the infirmary and thought I'd see if you'd like to walk down together. I can give you a quick tour along the way."

In just a short time, Fallon had come to think of Brak as something of a kindred spirit. They both struggled with unique circumstances. Not only did Brak shun the lengthy rituals the dinosaur-descended Briveen were known for, she had run away from her home planet to become a cybernetics doctor. Fallon hadn't asked too many questions about that, knowing it to be a highly sensitive subject, but she'd gathered that Brak's caste did not allow for a scientific career.

"I'd love a guided tour, thank you. I memorized the ship's schematics to orient myself, but that's nothing like the real thing."

Brak clicked her teeth with amusement, and her blue-green scales glinted in the daylight brightness of the corridor. "Right, that eidetic memory of yours."

Fallon fell into step next to Brak as they walked away from the aft of the ship, where Fallon and her team were housed in empty crew quarters. Being so near the engines, these were the least desirable quarters, but Fallon found the constant hum of the machinery comforting rather than grating. She slept better when she couldn't hear every tiny sound.

"Not eidetic," Fallon corrected. "I do forget stuff. But I remember most things, especially if I specifically make note of them."

"Sounds handy," Brak remarked as they walked down the golden-cream-colored corridor of Deck Two, with its evenly spaced doors.

"Sometimes," Fallon agreed. "The irony never escapes me though, given…" She pretended to rap on her head with her knuckles.

Fallon smelled the warm baked-bread scent of agreement. She appreciated the eloquence of Briveen scent communication.

"Of course, Jerin and I will do whatever we can to help with that," Brak answered. She pointed to a break in the uniformity between the doors. "This is where the family quarters begin. They're larger than those for singletons."

When they reached the bow of the ship, Brak gestured at the areas contained there. "Here you can see maintenance conduit entryways, the lift down to Deck One, and the stairs. Since the lift is below at the moment, do you want to take the stairs?"

"Sure." As they started down, Fallon thought that "stairs" might be overstating the steep descent. She recalled that ancient sailors had called stairways on ships "ladders." Sure, *that* she could remember. Pointless minutiae.

Instead of dwelling on her shortcomings, she said, "I'll have to revisit the stairs for some exercise later."

"You can use the therapy rooms to work out after hours, but the physical therapists work a wide range of schedules and it can be tricky to arrange." Brak gracefully picked her way down the narrow stairs ahead of Fallon.

When she got to Deck One, Fallon took a hard look at the doors leading to systems ops and ops control. She ignored the nearby nursery—diapers and rattles were of no use to her.

"I can show you around the crew-only areas later, or someone else can," Brak offered as they began walking away from the nose of the ship. She pointed out the different types of therapy rooms, as well as her own cybernetics lab.

Deck Two had been simple and fairly unadorned, but a tasteful effort had been made on Deck One to create a comfortable atmosphere. The walls of the corridor were the same warm, golden-cream color, but artwork hung here and there to enliven the space. Fallon didn't recall having been on a hospi-ship before, and was a little surprised by the lack of the efficient sterility she'd unconsciously expected.

But then other hospi-ships might be completely different. The *Onari* could be as unique in its décor as it was in its philanthropic mission. Other Bennite ships worked solely for the profit of Bennaris, whose entire industry was rooted in healthcare. Maybe those vessels would be blandly institutional inside.

"And here's the infirmary," Brak concluded when they reached the doorway.

Beyond it, Fallon saw guest quarters, and beyond those, she knew she would find the airlock and the double-level cargo bays. She'd survey them later. Right now, she had her uncooperative brain to deal with.

She'd already seen the infirmary, so she had no need to take stock of the wide space, full of techbeds and apparatus she couldn't even identify. She'd made a point of memorizing the details of everyone on board, and therefore recognized both of the current patients. One was a man who had very recently endured back surgery and would need a couple more days for recovery and physical therapy. He didn't even seem to notice Fallon as he thanked the nurse and gingerly walked out.

The other patient was a crew member. Griggs. Zerellian male, ops control. He appeared to have a burn on his arm. A nurse slowly moved a dermal regenerator back and forth over the wound.

Next to him, Dr. Jorrid Yomalu frowned at the techbed controls. Fallon had only seen him in passing thus far, but people spoke highly of him. Word had it that he had a love for thrill sports. She'd never known an adrenaline-junkie doctor, but he certainly sounded like an interesting guy.

Dr. Jerin Remay had watched Fallon and Brak enter, and moved to intercept them. She double-teamed Fallon with questions immediately. "Have you and your team settled in nicely? Do you need anything?"

"We're doing well, thank you. Your ship is pleasantly homey, and well equipped."

Jerin's pride in her ship was evident in her smile. With her glossy black hair, golden-tan skin, and green eyes, the doctor was quite attractive. The red-jeweled stud on one side of her dainty nose suggested a certain aristocracy, though Jerin's attitude was always forthright and genuine.

"Should we get to work?" Jerin asked, and Fallon nodded.

"We've prepared a private room." Brak indicated one of the enclosed spaces with an elegant wave of her cybernetic arm.

Fallon took the cue and led the way. "Since you asked," she remarked to Jerin, "there are a couple things we're hoping you could help with."

"Oh?"

"First, we need some supplies. Hawk will let me know where we could get them without going off course."

They stepped into the room and Jerin secured the door behind them before answering. "There are some places we prefer not to dock, but if you let me know the destination, I'll do what I can. What's the second item?"

Fallon stepped back to let Jerin move past her. "Thank you. The other issue is that there's no place to exercise here, unless you count the stairs, or maybe the physical therapy rooms. But those already have intended purposes, so they're hardly ideal."

"That's true." Jerin's words came slowly, as she thought something through. "Actually, that's been a problem I've been meaning to handle for some time. I just haven't had the brute strength to get it done." A smile spread across Jerin's face. "But it seems that now I do."

"Uh-oh. What have I stepped in?"

Jerin laughed lightly. "Nothing too terrible. Hospi-ships are usually assigned to a much smaller region of space and spend as much time docked as they do traveling. That's why they aren't usually designed with a gym. But my crew's been making do with the physical therapy rooms for too long. I've been wanting to convert Cargo Bay Two into an exercise and rec area. It's not large enough for a track, but it could accommodate several treadmills and other equipment. Perhaps a climbing wall. I'll leave it up to you all to design something that makes the best use of space."

Fallon smelled a rush of fresh strawberries, causing her to glance at the source. Brak didn't show much outward pleasure, but the strong fragrance communicated her enthusiasm.

"Would you be interested in helping us with that?" Fallon asked her. "If you have time, I mean."

"I'd be delighted to help in my free time." Brak smiled, which Fallon appreciated, knowing it wasn't a natural gesture for her. "I've been wishing for something like that since I arrived."

"Kellis can assist you with anything mechanical you need," Jerin said. "She'll be the one to do any structural adaptations. She's well versed in all the PAC overhaul and upgrade codes."

"That's great." Fallon hadn't gotten to know Kellis very well yet. She did know that her legate of security on Dragonfire, Arin, had taken quite a liking to her. They were both Atalan refugees, so they had a lot in common.

"This will be Kellis' final project, which will earn her the necessary credits to complete her degree."

Fallon hadn't known that Kellis had not yet received her credentials. Fallon *had* heard many raves about Kellis' skills though, and had more than once wished that Avian Unit had a member with her kind of mechanical experience.

"Is there anything else you need?" Jerin asked. She seemed ready to finish their conversation and get to work.

Fallon was slightly less eager to get started. "No, thank you. Mostly we want to stay out of the way and not cause you any problems."

"Don't worry about that," Jerin assured her. "We take care of ourselves very well here. Now, if you'll lie down?" She indicated the techbed.

"Right." Fallon sat, then swung her legs up and settled back. Time to get to work.

"You've recovered no memories since the surgery I performed?" Brak moved to the techbed controls.

"No. Well, I did say something which my team told me was a phrase we use, but I think it was probably a coincidence." She'd blurted out their team motto while Hawk was suffering from serious injuries. But it was really just two words tacked onto something she'd already heard. Probably nothing.

"Did you say it out of context?" Jerin asked.

"I suppose it was in context. But it didn't feel like a memory."

"Hm." Jerin joined Brak at the head of the bed.

After a minute of silence, Fallon asked, "Should I be doing something here?"

"Just relax," Jerin answered, the smooth melody of her voice a calming thing all by itself. "We're going to administer a light sedative. You know how you start dreaming sometimes, just as you're dozing off?"

"Sure." Fallon stared up at the ceiling.

"That's because when you turn off active thought, the brain begins functioning on its own. Your brain works much harder when you're asleep than when you're awake. Once you're in a semiconscious state, I'll talk to you while Brak monitors your brain activity."

"Okay." Fallon hoped she wouldn't say anything too sensitive or embarrassing. The idea of talking in her sleep with no filter did not sit entirely comfortably. But she'd lick the exhaust manifold on a Rescan freighter if she thought it would bring back her memory.

"Administering the sedative now," Jerin murmured. "Just relax and let your thoughts roam."

Let her thoughts run free. Sure. She closed her eyes and tried, but intentionally becoming dreamy did not seem to be her strong suit. So she stared up at the ceiling again, visually measuring it in centimeters, meters, and millimeters in width, height, and on the diagonal. Each measurement flowed into the next and she felt increasingly relaxed.

She wondered if measuring the ceiling might be an old habit of hers, perhaps a strategy against insomnia. She tried to imagine herself as a child, doing the same thing, and couldn't. She tried to imagine herself as a child at all. She might have been a cute kid. Had she worn dresses, or preferred pants? She willed any childhood images to appear.

"How are you feeling?" Jerin's voice pierced through her.

Fallon jolted and sat up. Infirmary. Jerin and Brak. No imminent danger.

It was a bad feeling, though. The last time she'd bolted awake in an infirmary, she hadn't even known her own name. Okay, well, technically she still didn't know the name she'd been born with, but her Blackout name was plenty enough for her. She'd earned that name.

Fallon pressed a hand to her chest, as if she could still her racing heart that way. "Did I fall asleep?"

"Not exactly." Jerin came around the side of the bed. "Everything went as planned."

"Did you find out anything?"

"You said many things. Some definitely not real, and some things that could possibly be real. But none of that is what matters. If we managed to reach any real memories, those neural pathways have been reestablished and those remembrances should return to you."

"So we wait. Again." Scrap. Not the result she'd hoped for.

Brak stepped to the other side of the bed. "Yes. Three days, then we can do this again."

"How many sessions before you declare me hopeless?"

Jerin chuckled. "Probably more than you'd be willing to do. This is all at your direction. If you want to keep going, we will. If you want to quit, we will."

"Fair enough." She twisted herself around, putting her feet on the ground to stand. "I guess I'll let you know if I recall anything."

"Don't be discouraged," Brak advised. "Hypnotherapy is not something that often works the first time. Or the second. It's a slow and gentle, long-term kind of thing."

"I'd be fine with quick and brutal," she admitted, "so long as it worked."

Jerin's eyes held sympathy. "I wish there were such an option. Memory is a delicate thing."

"Yeah." She shook her head to get herself refocused. "So when can we start on this new gym?"

―――――

FALLON HAD new appreciation for the jumpsuits she and her team wore. Throughout an entire day of picking stuff up, piling it onto anti-grav carts, and moving it all into Cargo Bay One, the suits had stood up to the rigorous bending, lifting, and sweating beautifully, while providing perfect comfort. Well, other than a couple of sneezes caused by dust.

"Guess we can count this as our workout for the day." Hawk placed a huge bin on the cart without any apparent effort.

"Only if you work up a sweat," Peregrine answered. "You need to step it up."

"Oh, I wanted to leave a little for you all to do. You know, so you can feel like you've contributed." He stacked another bin on top of the first.

Raptor snorted out a laugh. "If you worked as much as you talked, we'd be done by now."

"I'm pretty sure Kellis' opinion of us is getting lower by the hour." Fallon looked to the engineer, who had taken numerous measurements and now sat on the floor in one corner, drawing out plans on an infoboard.

"Nah, I think you guys are hilarious," Kellis piped up, not lifting her eyes from her infoboard.

"Well, damn, that's not at all what I was going for." Hawk bowed his shoulders in comedic dejection. "I was hoping for powerful. Impressive. Maybe even heroic."

"Sorry." Kellis' unapologetic apology caused both Fallon and Peregrine to grin.

"How are the plans looking?" Fallon asked, adjusting the cart's controls for a heavier load.

Kellis finally looked up. "Good. I'm working at maximizing the space to provide the different types of activities you guys suggested. I think this is going to be great for the ship. We don't exactly have a lot of rec areas, and our quarters don't provide much space for socializing, either."

Her tawny curls framed her face, hanging just below her jawline. The color of her hair set off arrestingly vivid turquoise eyes. A visit to the salon on Dragonfire must have resulted in the new golden highlights. Fallon liked the addition. It complemented Kellis' tan skin, which shone like sun-bleached sand.

"We're sure you'll create something great," Raptor assured Kellis, who smiled at him.

"I'll do my best. Finishing off my degree would be a relief. I've been doing double shifts, between work and school, ever since I joined the *Onari*."

"How long ago was that?" Fallon asked, testing the load on the cart to make sure it wouldn't shift as she pulled it to the other cargo bay. She already knew the answer to her question, but she wanted to get to know Kellis better in the conventional way.

"About a year ago now. A little less."

"That's a long time to pull double shifts!" Hawk stopped stacking for a moment, rolling a shoulder. Fallon suspected he might be working harder than he let on. "What will you do with all that extra time?"

Kellis laughed. "Work a little less. Sleep a little more. Start working out here. I've been using Trin's physical therapy room when it's not in use. The treadmill is great, but I've had to be creative with strength training."

"I haven't known too many engineers into strength training." Peregrine paused between bins too, to join the conversation.

Kellis looked down and her hair shifted to cover part of her face. "I got an injury in the war on my planet. Not from fighting or anything," she qualified hastily. "Wrong place, wrong time, is all. But I was in a wheelchair for a while, and since getting better, I make sure not to take my body for granted."

Fallon found that highly admirable. Kellis must have worked very hard to escape her beginnings and establish a new future for herself. She surely had some luck on her side, too. Many Atalans still remained trapped on their world, caught between opposing factions bent on domination. Fallon was glad Kellis and Arin had managed to get free of it.

She grasped the cart's control handle and gave it a small twist, putting it into glide mode. "All right. I'll move this one over and then we can clear up the little bit that's left."

"And then lunch!" Hawk called after her as she guided the cart into the corridor.

Lunch sounded terrific. A long lunch sounded even better. Would it be wrong to have some Zerellian ale at midday? She knew perfectly well that afterward, they'd be unloading everything they'd moved into Cargo Bay One and getting it organized neatly. Assembling was always harder than tearing down, and she wasn't looking forward to that part. An ale or two might make it more pleasant. Her back was already feeling the effects of their labors.

Not that she was going to let on. Hawk would never let her hear the end of it.

Two more days of grunt labor had Cargo Bay Two ready for its refit and Cargo Bay One organized. In the infirmary, Fallon was ready for another crack at hypnotherapy.

"You haven't had any hints of memory?" Jerin's dulcet voice settled over Fallon like a warm, silky blanket.

She shifted, getting comfortable on the techbed. "Nope. Not a thing."

"Altogether expected," Jerin assured her, then moved out of sight to join Brak at the techbed controls. "We'll proceed just as we did last time."

An hour later, Fallon drifted up from what felt like a momentary loss of concentration. She turned her head to look back at the doctors, only to have a sharp pain slice into her back. She sucked in a breath through her teeth.

"What's wrong?" Brak suddenly stood over her, and Jerin moved into view as well.

"Muscle spasm in my back. All that lifting in the cargo bay is catching up to me."

Jerin returned to the techbed controls. "Yes, I see a rather nasty little spasm there. We'll get that sorted for you right now. Lie very still, please."

Fallon forced herself not to move, even though the stabbing sensation in her back made her want to slide right off the bed.

The pain bled away, and she found herself relaxing.

"Better?" Jerin asked, a smile in her voice.

"Much."

"It was only a strained muscle. I've repaired it, as well as a few others, just to be sure they won't bother you. Brak, would you mind getting a cup of biogel?"

"Not at all." Brak bobbed her head and moved to a cabinet near the door. She returned holding a clear cup full of a thick, transparent liquid.

Fallon downed it. The sharp tang of its aftertaste echoed in her mouth. She handed the cup back to Brak.

"That will help keep you in good shape," Jerin said, moving to face Brak on the other side of the techbed. "How are things going in my new rec center?" Humor crinkled her eyes.

Fallon sat up. She hadn't been about to complain of the soreness that had built up over the last couple days, as it had been so minor, but she did feel better now. More energetic, too.

"It's going great. Kellis completed her plans for the refit, and we have the bay cleared. After she's done working on something in ops control, we're going to start laying down new flooring."

"Ops?" Jerin raised an eyebrow. "I hadn't heard of any issue. I'll have to talk to Demitri about that."

Fallon hopped off the table. "So, we'll do this again in three more days?"

Jerin nodded. "I'd like to fit in two more sessions before we make it to Levana Prime. We're expected to be there for a week, so nearly all the medical staff will be boots on ground for the duration."

"Gotcha." Fallon arched her back, enjoying the stretch. "Well, I'm going to get down to our rec center in progress and get started a little early, since I'm feeling so spiffy."

"Let us know when we can see it," Brak said. "I'm really looking forward to having a place to work out every day."

"I will." Fallon felt particularly gratified to be doing something that would please the friend who had done so much to help her. She went back to work with a boost of enthusiasm.

FALLON HAD GROWN STEADILY MORE IMPRESSED with Kellis as the days wore on. The engineer thoroughly researched every detail as she worked through the project. Each day she showed up with a plan, confident and ready to work. With her direction, they'd installed shock-absorbing floors and two-way soundproofing for the walls. In Cargo Bay One they'd created a new, more deliberate organization system, including clever built-in storage units that spanned the double-decker height of the bay. The ship wouldn't suffer for storage space.

Which only left them with outfitting the rec center. Kellis had built five basic-but-sturdy treadmills. Fallon had no idea where she'd gotten the parts for them, but as long as no one came looking, she didn't care. Kellis had also borrowed some auxiliary equipment from the physical therapy department for the short term, but Jerin would need to procure some actual resistance machines.

Jerin had resoundingly vetoed a sparring ring, making it clear that the *Onari* was in the business of healing injuries, not creating them. Kellis had engineered a fantastic climbing wall that went right up to the upper hull of the ship, though. Until they got some anti-grav vests for emergencies, climbing was restricted to the highly experienced only. Jerin had eloquently announced to the crew that anyone sustaining a serious injury would answer to her as soon as they were patched up. The woman could be downright menacing when she chose. Which made Fallon like her even more.

They'd managed to scavenge some furniture from storage, as well as other locations throughout the ship. Some people had even loaned their personal items, which impressed Fallon. That kind of generosity was hard to find. Jerin would get the rec center properly furnished and equipped as soon as she could, but Fallon and her team didn't mind these little deficiencies one bit.

Fallon was pleased that Brak shared their enthusiasm. Day shift had ended, and the cyberneticist was due to arrive for her first look at the completed work any minute. Kellis had retired to her quarters, and Peregrine and Hawk had gone for food and drinks. Only Fallon and Raptor had remained, wanting to admire their creation a little longer.

Funny how the time had gone by with something to focus on. Nearly two weeks had passed since boarding the ship. It had felt good to just determine a goal and keep working at it until it was done. Especially with her team, as well as Kellis, alongside her. If only all work could be so straightforward.

Two more hypnotherapy sessions had produced no results, and the *Onari* was due to arrive at Levana Prime late tomorrow, after the end of the day shift.

The opening of the door interrupted Fallon's musing. Brak entered, giving off the delicious scent of strawberries. She took a slow tour of the new rec center before announcing, "You all have done a remarkable job."

Brak's obvious pleasure pleased Fallon. Clearly, Brak saw past the mismatched furnishings to all the potential.

"I can't wait to get started on that wall." Brak eyed the apparatus with great interest.

"But will you? After Jerin's warning?"

Brak smiled. "Of course I will. It's not easy to break one of these bones." She gestured at herself.

Fallon wished she believed in Second Life—the idea of her soul being reborn into another body after her death. If she had, she could've hoped to be reborn as a Briveen. Exceptional strength and dexterity, greater hearing and sight, and gorgeous scales to top it all off.

"I'd challenge you to a race to the top, but I'm guessing that racing goes past risky and into reckless." A shame, because Fallon would have loved to see how she stacked up against Brak at climbing.

"Wise." Brak tilted her jaw upward and Fallon smelled the sweet musk of amusement.

Raptor hung midway up the wall as they approached. His broad shoulders and long, muscular limbs meant that he could brute force his way up using primarily his arms, while she'd have to use every centimeter of her body to make it happen. Ah, well. At least she got to admire him while he did it.

Brak glanced at her in a knowing way. Though she said nothing, Fallon had a sense that her friend had scented her appreciation. There was no hiding one's feelings from a Briveen.

She shrugged. "So?"

Brak held her palms up in a display of innocence. "I didn't say anything."

"You didn't have to."

Brak let her hands drop. "He's very good-looking, what's not to admire?" Her head tilted as she watched Raptor, and it made Fallon wonder about her.

What the hell. She decided to ask. "Do Briveen ever get romantically involved with non-Briveen?"

"Only ones who leave Briv for good, and not usually, even then. So the answer's pretty much no, with only a few exceptions." Brak sounded very matter-of-fact.

"Hm. Well *you've* left Briv. What if your perfect match ended up being human, or Rescan, or something? Would you be willing to give it a try?"

Brak made a soft chortle of amusement, which sounded a lot like a growl to Fallon. But an amused growl. "Far be it from me to pass up the perfect guy."

"Actually, now that we're on the subject, I met a Briveen you might like. He had a great sense of humor and I felt like he didn't care for the rituals any more than you do. He performed the basics, but no more. I sensed that he only did that much because he was an ambassador and felt responsible for upholding expectations." Fallon had quite liked him.

"Who?"

"Honorable First Son Gretch of the House Arkrid." He'd visited Dragonfire soon after Fallon had lost her memory.

"Arkrid. A respectable house. I don't know any of them personally, though."

"If all the stars line up, maybe someday I'll get a chance to introduce you two. Wouldn't that be something?"

Brak's teeth chattered in amusement. "That would definitely be something."

Fallon hoped they got the opportunity to give it a try. She looked up at Raptor nearing the top of the climbing wall and wiped her hands on her jumpsuit to ensure they were dry. "Shall we show him how climbing is really done?"

Brak didn't even wait, leaping up to grab a handhold. "I thought you'd never ask."

―――

Levana Prime hung far below the *Onari*, with a single orbital elevator stretching across the space between the two. Fallon had been pleased to discover that Levana Prime's docking station had a certified maintenance crew. A systems check would keep the ship in compliance with the PAC's stringent requirements while hiding its recent undocumented visit to Dragonfire Station.

She and Raptor would descend to the surface later for a basic supply run, after all the medical crew had gotten their turn on the orbital elevator.

In the meantime, Demitri Belinsky and Endra had joined Fallon and her team in the sparsely populated bar. Demitri had the responsibility of commanding ops control, much like a captain would on a PAC ship. Endra worked in sys-ops, ensuring that the ship's many systems worked flawlessly. She also happened to be the best friend of Fallon's former wife, but Fallon had brokered a relative peace with Endra when she came on board.

Since neither Demitri nor Endra performed any sort of medical care, they'd both remain on the ship unless they took some leave time to visit the planet.

"I'll have a day and night down there halfway through," Endra said, taking the last sip of her wine. "Then I'll be right back up for duty. I like to get planetside as much as I can, but I spent most of my leave days on a visit home."

"Will you visit Levana Prime?" Peregrine asked Demitri. She'd talked to him more than anyone else that evening, and Fallon suspected she fancied him. Demitri was a little on the young side, maybe twenty-two or so, but definitely fair game. He had pale skin, dark eyes, and dark hair. The contrast between light and dark was attractive, but he wasn't Fallon's type at all. She did wonder about his story, though—how such a young person came to work the bridge of Jerin's ship. He seemed genuine and bighearted, so he certainly fit in among the crew of the *Onari*.

Demitri smoothed his napkin over his lap before answering Peregrine. "Nah, there's nothing down there that interests me. It's just a nice little farming planet. To tell the truth, I always sleep better on board a ship."

"What's it like commanding the *Onari*?" Peregrine asked.

He seemed surprised by the question. "It's great. Great people, doing great things. You know. Great."

"Well, great," Endra answered with a laugh, causing the others to laugh too.

Demitri's cheeks turned pink. "I mean I like it here. I get to do all of the flight, navigation, and operational stuff, while Jerin handles the big decisions and the healthcare side of things. It's a perfect scenario for me."

"I see." Peregrine sat back, her long ponytail swinging before settling behind her. "You like the flying stuff, but are more comfortable in a supportive role than being the head tomato."

Demitri looked puzzled. "Head tomato?"

Peregrine nodded. "You know, the lead person, the one whose ass is on fire if something goes wrong."

"Oh. Right. There's still plenty that can light fire to my ass, but I like being able to focus on caring for the ship. I'd rather not have all the additional responsibilities of a tomato head."

Fallon couldn't help it. She snorted. And once she got going, her snorts turned into guffaws, which became all-out laughter.

Hawk and Raptor laughed right along with her. Endra chuckled, though with more restraint.

"It's not you," Fallon assured the blushing Demitri. "Sometimes I don't understand Per either. The other day, I was lifting a bin and she told me it had gone all kerbity-glop."

"No," Peregrine protested. "I said 'curdy-got' and it's a perfectly good phrase for when something's filthy dirty."

"Where?" Hawk demanded. "I know tons of Zerellians, and I've read plenty of Zerellian literature, but I never heard that. Ever."

"Well, it's an old-fashioned phrase," Per conceded. "I grew up watching all the classics over and over. I guess some of the more colorful phrases stuck in my psyche."

Fallon found that sweet, actually. Like Per was their very own generational throwback.

"So you really can't blame us for not knowing what the hell you're saying," Raptor pointed out.

"Fine." Per chuckled, then waved to the barkeep for another drink.

Fallon caught the smile that passed between Per and Demitri. She'd also noticed that Hawk and Endra created sparks whenever their eyes met. Sarkavians had a relaxed approach to sexuality, with most considering monogamy to be unnatural. Hawk and Endra might just be an ideal live-in-the-moment combination.

Fallon stifled a yawn. It wasn't that late, but she'd worn herself out the past few days. Busywork had occupied her thoughts nicely, keeping her from dwelling on bigger issues. At the moment, nothing sounded better than a good night's sleep.

After excusing herself, she took a quick shower, dressed for bed, and put her head to the pillow. Tomorrow she'd get a look at Levana Prime, as well as a chance to see the *Onari*'s crew in action, doing what they did best.

AN INVISIBLE WEIGHT forced itself down on Fallon's back, making even the air feel too heavy to draw into her lungs. She felt every bump and crevice of the dirt beneath her, from her cheek to her toes. From the corner of her eye, she saw two moons hanging in space, seeming to mock her.

She pressed her palms against the ground and struggled to shove herself up, only to find herself doing a push-up on her bed.

Soft sheets lay under her palms, not damp grass. The air in her quarters felt oppressive. Stale.

The image from the dream still seared her mind. It lingered like a real event, and she was seized by a desperate urge to look at the space outside the *Onari*. Immediately.

She bolted from the bed and right out of her quarters. Her bare feet raced over the deck plates with barely a sound. At the stern she flew down the stairs, then continued down the corridor. She threw herself at the door of the first physical therapy room.

Locked. Of course it was. The physical therapists had gone to the planet surface. She could get past the lock, but she wasn't about to break into a room on the *Onari*.

The bar, then. She pivoted and ran. Once there, she forced herself to take a breath and walk in like a sane person. If anyone noted her lounge clothes, they didn't say so. At this hour, the few patrons of the bar had probably imbibed to the point of not noticing much at all, or else had eyes only for their companion. That suited her fine.

No one paid her any mind as she walked to the bulkhead, her eyes locked on the moderately-sized porthole. She pressed herself to its cool surface and felt her heart bumping between the hull and her ribs. There. She saw Levana's Luna Major, and—closer—Luna Minor. Why had she dreamed about them? She'd felt like they were looming over her, getting closer. As if they'd been causing the pressure forcing her to the ground. As her gaze wandered over the pitted surfaces of the moons, her heartbeat gradually slowed. The intense feelings faded, like fog burning off under the glare of the sun.

Why would she dream about moons? Was it some sort of memory, struggling to reestablish itself in her mind? Or was it just a dream, inspired by the planet below?

She turned her back to the hull and let her head loll against it. Damn. Always more questions than answers, and Jerin and Brak were on the planet's surface.

She couldn't discuss it with them over the voicecom. She also couldn't go down to Levana's surface. Just thinking about being beneath the twin moons made her skin crawl.

Fallon hesitated as she passed Raptor's door, but kept going. Too complicated. She moved on to Hawk's door, then froze before she could touch the chime. He probably had someone in there with him and it would be awkward if she showed up.

Sighing, she went back to Raptor's door and pressed the alert chime.

He answered, wearing only a pair of lounge shorts and looking sleep worn but sharp. He stepped away from the door in silent invitation.

She began pacing around the tiny living area.

"What's up, Fal?"

"I need either you or Hawk to go with Per to the surface tomorrow." They'd agreed that if they had to split up, they'd only do it in pairs. Paranoid, sure, but paranoia kept them alive.

"Okay. Why?"

"I might have been there at some point. Someone could be watching for me." She chewed the corner of her mouth, trying to pull up more than just disjointed thoughts.

"Relax." He put his hands on her shoulders and guided her to the mini couch, then sat facing her. "Per will take care of disguises. In medical personnel clothes, it's unlikely anyone would recognize you."

True. She didn't have a rebuttal to his very logical argument. Even so, she wasn't about to set foot on Levana Prime.

He continued, "It's just a low-key farming planet. Small cities, booming commerce. No PAC presence. What's your concern?"

"I had a dream, or a memory, or something. Two moons. A weight pressing me down to the dirt. I don't know what it meant. Maybe it didn't mean anything." She turned to more fully face him. She wanted to look at his eyes, to see if he thought she'd cracked a gasket. "But I started thinking, maybe I've been on Levana Prime before. Maybe there's someone who would look for me there."

He rubbed a hand over his jaw. Still smooth, she noticed. He must have had a doctor apply hair-growth retardant. Which explained the smooth chest she'd seen a time or two, as well. "I've always been one to follow a gut instinct, even if it seems illogical. So I'll go to the surface with Per in the morning, but as far as I know, you haven't been here. Your dream, or memory or whatever, must have meant something else."

"Maybe. I don't know. I wish I at least knew which one it was. A dream is fine, it just means my mind is screwed up. We already knew that." Recovering a memory, though, would be a very big deal.

He reached over and smoothed her hair. "That's driving me nuts."

Oh, great. She realized her hair had been standing up in a wild, ratty mess. She ran her hands through it, trying to create some semblance of order.

"When I get down to the surface, I'll find Jerin and Brak and talk to them. Okay? We'll leave it to the experts."

For whatever reason, his calm approach loosened the knot that had formed in her stomach. "Yeah. That sounds good."

She glanced toward the porthole in his room and went to it. Situated on the same side of the ship as the bar, she could make out the moons if she looked hard to the left.

She didn't feel the same, looking at them now. The feeling of foreboding had gone. But the memory of it remained.

"Really spooked you, huh?" He stood right behind her.

"Yeah. It did."

He put a warm hand on her shoulder. She leaned into it for a second, then straightened. "I'll let you get back to sleep."

"You can stay as long as you want." He let his hand fall away.

"No. I should try to sleep, too." She about-faced. "Thank you." She gave him a long look, to let him see that she meant it.

"I didn't do anything," he said with a shrug.

She smiled faintly. "Then thanks for nothing."

"Hah. Right." He walked her to the door. "Good night then."

"Night." She took slow steps back to her own quarters, trying to let the entire experience drift away from her.

Back in her room, she retrieved the blanket, which she'd flung halfway across the small space. She visited the necessary, caught a look at herself in the mirror, and laughed. Her hair still stuck up in all directions. She wondered if Raptor had tried to tame it at all, or only made it worse.

She climbed back into bed, giggling. She closed her eyes, thinking of him just down the corridor, probably laughing at her.

She relaxed and let herself succumb to sleep.

3

Fallon slept later into the morning than usual. By the time she woke, scrubbed the crust out of her eyes, and mustered up the motivation to go find breakfast, Raptor and Peregrine had already boarded the docking station. They might even be nearing the surface.

She opted for light protein and a high-carbohydrate tango fruit. They'd provide her with energy for a good workout. It would be a welcome relief to get back into her routine of starting each day with a run. Afterward, she would come back to the bar for some blistercakes and tea.

When Fallon arrived at the rec center, she was surprised to see Brak, running on a treadmill set at a significant incline. Fallon chose the treadmill next to her friend and cued it to a warm-up pace.

"Good morning." Brak didn't sound the least bit winded, in spite of her speed.

"Morning." Fallon began to jog. "What brought you back to the ship?"

"As soon as I got to the surface, I had two unexpected requests and needed my lab. I figured I'd have a run before going back down. What about you? Getting a late start today?"

"Yeah. A strange dream woke me in the middle of the night."

"Ah." Brak didn't pry, but since they were alone, she might as well take advantage of the opportunity.

"I wondered if it might even be a memory. Do you think a memory would come as a dream?"

Brak tilted her head the barest amount to look at Fallon. With her greater range of vision, she didn't need to twist her neck as Fallon did.

"It's possible," Brak answered. "Can you describe the dream?"

Fallon increased her pace, feeling sufficiently warmed up. "Not very well. It seemed so vivid at the time, but it faded quickly. All that stayed with me was the feeling of two moons, pushing me to the ground. A dire feeling, like I was doomed."

"Did the feeling linger?"

"Briefly. It made me want to look at Levana's moons. I had to visit the bar to get a view. But by the time I got my eyes on the moons, the feeling had retreated. I just felt kind of anxious and edgy."

Brak clicked her teeth as she thought. "Memories are usually more concrete than what you're describing. A scene, hearing someone speaking, a recollection of having done something. And once you recover a memory, it tends to take root. Maybe even spur other memories. What you describe sounds more like an abstract manifestation."

"So not a memory, then?"

"Impossible to say. What you experienced might be some aspect of a memory, occurring as a sort of posthypnotic suggestion." Brak touched her treadmill's controls, slowing her pace to a brisk walk.

"Hm. So there's nothing to be done about it?"

"We can address it during your next therapy session. See if

planting some suggestions along those lines dredges up anything else. But it could have been just a dream."

"Right. Thanks." Fallon punched the speed up, falling into a quick rhythm of footfalls.

Brak's treadmill slowed to a stop. "Have you had any other possible memories?"

"No." Finally, Fallon's breathing and heart rate started to increase.

Brak pivoted on the now-still treadmill to face Fallon. "If anything comes up, let me know."

"I will."

"Want to race me up the wall before I go? I brought anti-grav vests up with me."

"Hell, yeah." Fallon could finish her run later. Next to the climbing wall she found six vests in a bin. "Nice."

"More supplies will be delivered later. The shopping on Levana Prime isn't bad, for a farming planet."

"Good to hear. Maybe Per will find some of the supplies we need." Fallon shrugged into a vest, clipping it securely down her front. She activated it, and a tiny screen indicated full power. If it detected a sudden loss of altitude, the vest would kick in, letting her drift to the floor rather than plummet. Fortunately anti-grav vests had become quite sleek in recent years, and this one would not encumber or inhibit her climbing at all.

Brak selected a larger vest and put it on. "Should one of us say 'go'?"

"Sure. Go!" Fallon grabbed handholds and swung her left foot up to a secure ledge. She shifted her left hand to stabilize herself, then launched to the right, grabbing a hold with both hands and swinging her legs up so that she was in a crouch. She leapfrogged her way upward, all the while keeping Brak in her peripheral vision. Brak was bigger, and not quite as agile, but she had greater strength. They fought to outdistance each other, with the difference seesawing a half-meter in Brak's favor, then in Fallon's.

In the end, they crested the top of the wall together. No winner, no loser. So unsatisfying. "Ugh," Fallon said.

"Nice match to you, too," Brak said, beginning her descent.

"Hah. Yes, nice race." Fallon started down as well. Descents were tougher for her than ascents. "You're really good."

"Thanks." Brak carefully picked her way down the wall.

Fallon set foot on the floor moments after Brak did.

"Did you climb when you were a kid? I've always wondered what Briveen childhood is like." Fallon had never seen a Briveen child in person, but knew that they still had their biological arms, which were short, three-fingered, and relatively weak.

"No. Juvenile arms can't lift a body's weight." Brak unclipped her vest and returned it to the bin. Fallon made a mental note that they'd need to put up some hooks for storage.

"Then it's great that you're able to climb now. Your cybernetics must have changed your whole relationship with the universe." Fallon stored her vest as well.

Brak looked uncomfortable, and Fallon felt a spike of embarrassment. She must have overstepped some line about discussing a Briveen's arms. "I'm sorry. That was inappropriately personal. Forget I mentioned it."

"No," Brak protested. "That's not it. My people are very open about our cybernetics. They're a rite of passage into adulthood and we're quite proud of them. It's just…I don't want to lie to you."

She ducked her head and lifted a shoulder, just as Fallon smelled a hint of ammonia. She felt bad for provoking such discomfort and contrition, but had no idea what had prompted it.

Brak straightened and went to the door of the rec center, locking it. Then she returned to stand in front of Fallon. "I consider you a very good friend. It makes me deeply uncomfortable to lie to a friend, particularly in light of the highly sensitive information you've entrusted me with."

"You don't have to—" Fallon shut her mouth, because Brak

had already reached her left arm to her right and removed the limb.

Fallon tried not to stare at the tiny, scaly arm Brak had revealed. Brak gently placed the false arm she'd removed on the ground, then reached her biological arm to her left and removed that one too. She lifted her arms and gave them a little wave.

"This is why I'm here on the *Onari*," she said. "My parents think my disgrace is that I ran away and became a scientist. The truth is, I ran away *before* my surgery. I like my biological arms. I didn't want to lose them."

Fallon floundered for something to say that wouldn't sound idiotic. "I'm honored you'd trust me with this information. Actually, I'm kind of overwhelmed by it."

For the first time since Fallon had met her, Brak looked unsure of herself. "Do they look awful?" She gazed down at her arms.

"No. Not at all. They look like you."

Brak's eyes turned shiny, as if flooding with tears.

Shit. She'd said the wrong thing.

But Brak murmured, "Thank you."

They remained silent a few long moments, simply being together in this communion of exposure and truth.

Brak took a breath. "Only Jerin knows. No one else on this ship, besides you."

"I don't know what I did to deserve such an honor, but I'm humbled by it." Fallon couldn't have meant her words more. She felt like Brak had entrusted her with a gift, and it bonded her closer to her friend. She felt indebted, in a way, by the endowment of such trust.

"And you're sure they aren't ugly?" Brak's voice had lightened, sounding almost amused, even. She lifted the small arms again, flexing the three clawed fingers on each.

"Not in the least. They're pretty, really, the way dainty, fragile things are." Fallon offered her hand.

Brak's head tilted in surprise, but she reached out and grasped it. The shine came back to her eyes. "No one's touched my real hands since I ran away from Briv."

"Really?"

"Yes. I immediately started hiding them. My earliest prosthetics were very rough. Barely functional, and they didn't look right, either. Not like real cybernetics, anyway. I kept refining them, and eventually came up with these." She nodded at the arms on the ground. "They're fully functional, and visually indistinguishable from cybernetics."

"Couldn't you create cybernetic ones that use your real arms, rather than hide them? Surely that would be more comfortable." Fallon couldn't imagine wearing those prosthetics all the time.

"I could. And they would definitely feel better. But then people would know about my real arms, and word would get back to my parents eventually. My mother would be humiliated beyond measure. I've done enough to disgrace her already."

"Wow. That's a big burden to live with. I'm so sorry." Fallon's heart broke for this beautiful, brilliant woman. At least Fallon had her team, who knew her better than she knew herself.

Brak gave Fallon's hands a squeeze and gently withdrew. "Don't be. I love what I do, and where I am."

"You are one amazing woman," Fallon declared. Brak had given up a lot to become a scientist and live her life on her own terms.

Brak snorted. "From you, I'll accept the compliment. Since I don't know anyone else who'd take on the PAC, much less a covert intelligence division of it."

"I guess we all do what we have to." Fallon hadn't intended to declare war on Blackout. They'd forced her into it when they tried to kill her and her team.

"Yeah." Brak picked up an arm and reattached it, then did the same with the other. "Well, I need to get to work. Let me know if you have any more strange dreams, or potential memories."

"I will. And let me know if you need anything, too."

Brak folded her prosthetic fingers into the shape of a stinger or a gun or something, and waggled them at Fallon.

"What's that?"

Brak laughed. "Trin's finger-gun thing. Thought I'd try it out. Apparently, I can't pull it off, at all."

"Oh. Right. I haven't gotten a chance to get to know him very well, but I remember seeing him do that once."

"We'll have to arrange an evening together once we leave Levana. You'll love him."

"Give me a day and time, and I'll be there," Fallon promised.

Brak tried the finger gesture again, then walked out of the rec as they both laughed.

FALLON HAD EXPECTED Raptor and Peregrine back that evening, but they sent a message instead and didn't return until the following morning.

"No offense, but four months of the same faces is going to be boring, so we figured we'd take our time," Peregrine explained.

The pair had procured more circumspect, casual clothing for them all, as well as some of the tools and electronics from the shopping list they'd compiled. They gathered in Peregrine's quarters to check out the new gear.

"These are nice." Fallon ran her hand over the cargo pants and soft stretch-knit shirt. They didn't suggest any particular affiliation or geography. Wearing those, she could be anything from a mechanic on a cargo freighter to a tourist from Earth.

"Thought they'd suit you." Raptor tossed her a pair of rugged black boots. "Those too."

He certainly knew her style. But the others' clothes weren't so very different from hers, so perhaps they all shared a certain esthetic.

"Speaking of the close-quarters thing," Peregrine said with an arched eyebrow. "Now that the rec center is done, I hope you all won't take it amiss if I don't join you in the evenings very often."

Raptor shrugged, while Hawk grinned. "Didn't expect you to."

Peregrine frowned at him. On her, it wasn't a negative expression, simply a thoughtful one. "Just giving a fair heads-up."

"It's a good idea," Fallon agreed. "Finding separate groups to socialize with, at least part of the time, will keep us from getting sick of one another."

"Of course it's a good idea," Peregrine answered. "Remember Darvon Four?"

Hawk and Raptor chortled, while Fallon raised an eyebrow, affecting a very sarcastic expression.

Peregrine grimaced, realizing her faux pas. "Sorry. Sometimes, for a second, I forget that anything's different." She tossed her ponytail back with an impatient twitch of her head. "On Darvon, we were stuck in an underground one-room bunker together for three weeks, with no other people to talk to. We were getting snippy by the time we finally got out of there. That was fairly early in our career with Blackout, and we learned our lesson about big personalities and small spaces."

"Makes sense." Fallon stuffed her new boots and clothes into one of the sacks Raptor and Peregrine had used to bring them aboard. "We'll be working together during the daytime, but we can deem evenings personal time, to do with as we like."

Nods indicated unanimous agreement.

"Unless we actually *want* to hang out," Hawk drawled. "It's been known to happen."

"On occasion," Raptor agreed, lips twitching.

Peregrine's expression remained cool, as if she didn't anticipate such a turn of events. The better Fallon got to know her, the more she liked her. A people pleaser, Peregrine most definitely was not.

Fallon didn't begrudge the *Onari* its very important work, but she was glad when the crew finally returned from Levana's surface so they could resume course to Earth. She felt better knowing that the space between her team and their objective grew progressively smaller.

They only had two more dockings scheduled. One was official hospi-ship business, but the other would be at a small moon base where Hawk had a friend who could provide some of the less mainstream items that Avian Unit needed.

Fallon had learned not to ask how Hawk knew these people, or what they actually did.

"Some things are better left unknown. But Hawk's sources deliver," Raptor had assured her. Or at least tried to assure her. She'd found the entire idea less than inspiring.

But back-end connections were a specialty that Hawk brought to the team, so Fallon would just have to get on board. As she apparently had in the past.

In the meantime, she developed a pattern. She liked the cyclical tidiness of a good routine.

She also decided to begin a concerted effort to get to know the *Onari*'s crew. She got herself invited to join Brak, Kellis, and Trin for dinner. As she joined them, she welcomed the chance to talk with the Kanaran physical therapist. She'd heard a lot about his good nature and sense of humor.

"I remember that finger thing you do," Fallon told him as they settled around a large, round table in the back of the bar. She tried to imitate the gesture, but the others laughed, so it seemed she had not done an accurate rendition.

"No, no, no, it's like this." Trin held his index and middle fingers straight out toward her while curling his other two fingers under. His thumb lay over the index finger, but he wiggled it to indicate some sort of firing action.

"I see." Fallon copied it correctly, but the others still laughed. "What?"

"It's just funny to see you doing Trin's thing," Kellis explained with a smile.

Kellis was too genuine to make fun of her, but Fallon wouldn't have minded. She had no problem with being the butt of a joke, so long as she could laugh along.

Trin smiled at Kellis in a way that caught Fallon's attention. Hm. Either Kanarans expressed friendly affection differently than she knew, or Trin had a thing for Kellis. A big thing. His muddy green eyes warmed like a pair of supernovas when he looked at her. She wondered if Kellis realized.

As conversation continued around her, Fallon idly speculated whether a relationship would work between Trin and Kellis. Were Kanarans biologically compatible with other species? Kanaran people only had a single gender, neither male nor female. But Trin lived as a male. Fallon hadn't had to spend much time thinking about what had brought him into Jerin's employ. Life on Kanar must have been difficult for him.

Well, his affection for Kellis was hardly any of her business. Fallon just hoped for his sake that he didn't end up spending years pining after her, only to find his feelings unreciprocated.

Love. She sighed inwardly. What stupid shenanigans. They'd all be better off without it.

"How's your new patient?" Kellis asked Trin. The *Onari* had brought along a client from Levana.

"Doing great," he answered. "Have you met her?" He tossed a look around the table, but they all shook their heads.

"Mara. Great kid. Gave me permission to talk about her case with the crew. Anyway, she's fifteen years old. An unusual allergy has diminished her lung capacity. She'd become bedridden. Jorrid repaired her lungs and immune system, but Mara has so much muscle waste that she needs some intensive therapy to get strong enough to work the fields again."

"Aw, poor thing. And she's here all alone? How long will you need to work with her?" Kellis furrowed her brow in concern.

"A month or so, I'm guessing. Her parents couldn't afford to leave the farm for such a long period of time."

"She'll get so bored. Maybe I could ask her to lunch or something?" Kellis picked at her Bennite stew without eating much.

Trin smiled. "I was hoping you would." He included the rest of them in his gaze. "All of you. Which is why I wanted permission to tell you about her." He seemed quite pleased with himself.

Fallon took a big bite of buttered bread while the others all nodded eager agreement to help the kid. Which made Fallon the only one not offering to help out. Oh, Prelin's ass. She didn't want to babysit a teenager. But she didn't want to be the only one refusing to befriend the farm girl. "Sure," she agreed, trying to sound upbeat. Sometimes a soldier made sacrifices for the good of the team.

"That's worth a finger gun!" Trin made the gesture at her, his eyes sparkling with humor. He was a good-looking guy, Fallon supposed, with his easy smile and close-cropped brown hair.

Fallon returned the finger gun, making everyone chuckle again. She wasn't above a little silliness to get a laugh.

Conversation took off again, covering a wide variety of topics and colleagues. The *Onari*'s crew was a tight-knit bunch. Chatty almost to the point of gossipy, but not quite crossing that line. Keeping up on all of the latest news without trampling on the personal boundaries that made tight living situations tolerable. Fallon respected that.

One by one, the others excused themselves. They all worked the day shift and had reason to want to be bright-eyed the next morning. Fallon had no such motivator. With the rec center built and the next stopping point weeks away, she had nothing but time and her self-imposed routine.

Left alone in the bar, she was faced with what to do next. She didn't want to return to her quarters. Exercising this late didn't appeal either. Getting her body all revved up would make it impossible to sleep. The rec center did have some spaces for playing games, reading, and socializing, though. She could go see who might be interested in a game of Go. Or chess, or cards. Something.

But she had no reason to hurry. She left the table and slid onto a stool at the bar. Her Zerellian ale arrived in short order, and she sipped it, wondering how she'd fill the next three months.

She needed something to occupy her hours. She rolled a spiral drinking straw between her fingers as she thought about it. It would be great if she had some medical skills to offer, but she didn't. She could improve security, but Jerin wouldn't want her crew to feel buttoned down with security protocols. Hospi-ships didn't get attacked or hijacked, anyway. Even pirates gave them the respect they deserved. Perhaps partly because the heavy penalties for being caught with hospi-ship supplies made them too risky to bother with.

So what else did Fallon have to offer? She thought about her primary skill sets. Shooting things. Throwing knives. Fighting. Piloting. None of those seemed like viable trades aboard this ship.

She was also good at investigating. How about that? She rubbed her thumb over her lips as she thought about how she could apply that skill to her current situation and objectives.

She could grill each of her teammates for details about their shared past. She could then research relevant details like locations. Maybe a memory would jiggle loose, but at the least she'd gain a better understanding of the life she'd forgotten. It would definitely be nice to have a personal history that went back more than several weeks.

But she hoped for memories. Hypnotherapy still hadn't given her any results, in spite of regular sessions. Maybe it just wouldn't work. She might have to simply accept the fact that her memory began the day she'd woken up in Dr. Brannin Brash's infirmary on Dragonfire after that shuttle accident.

She made a sound of irritation in the back of her throat.

"You okay?"

She looked up. The man two stools down regarded her with a friendly, curious expression. She recognized him and her brain immediately supplied his details. Ben Brooks. Age thirty-three. Human nurse. She'd seen him around but they hadn't talked.

"Yeah. Just trying to figure out what I'm going to do with myself for the next three months."

He made a sympathetic *hmm* sound. She eyed him as she sipped her ale. Handsome guy, for someone who liked broad chests and deep, dark skin with eyes and hair to match. Which she did.

"What would you like to do?" he asked.

"Good question. I don't seem to be good at downtime."

"I guess you could start with figuring out what you'd enjoy." He shrugged and smiled, as if apologizing for not having a better answer.

"Yeah. I'll have to work on that." She tilted her glass so that the amber liquid slanted. Then she gently rotated it, making the angle of the ale shift around. She looked back up at him. "Are you on day shift tomorrow?"

"Are you asking if I'm up past my bedtime?" His teasing expression made her smile.

"I suppose so."

"Well then, you're right. I should finish my drink and return to my quarters."

His expression didn't change, but she had the impression that he was calculating the odds of taking her with him. Which were, in actuality, nil.

"I should do the same." She tilted her glass up and drained it, then wiped her lips with a napkin as she stood. "It was nice talking to you."

"Name's Ben." He didn't rush to stand or finish his drink. He just nodded in a friendly way. She liked his cool composure.

"I know. Fallon."

"I know. Take care, Fallon. Good luck figuring it out."

"Thanks."

She decided to start on her research. She'd begin grilling Peregrine the next day about what she knew of Fallon, but tonight she could investigate how many planets with two moons there were in the galaxy.

On the way back to her quarters, she dropped by Peregrine's. Surprisingly, she was both present and alone.

"What's up?" Peregrine asked after letting Fallon in.

"Aren't you getting bored?" Fallon kicked her feet up on the table in front of Peregrine's couch.

"No. I'm fine." Peregrine sat next to Fallon. "You seem to have itchy feet, though."

"Yeah. I just feel so purposeless, you know? How are you dealing with all this time on your hands?"

Peregrine's mouth twisted in a wry sort of grimace. She had such an expressive face. "I've spent the majority of my adult life on the move. Busting my ass in OTS and security school, running missions for Blackout. Sometimes I forget what it's like to just exist and *be*. But that's what everyone does here. It's refreshing, and I plan to make the most of it."

Fallon tried to imagine approaching her time here as a vacation, and failed.

Per spoke again. "You should try just *being*. Accepting whatever happens to exist, at any particular moment."

"Okay," Fallon agreed. "But what, specifically, are you doing with all the hours between going to sleep and waking up? That's my real problem."

Peregrine barked out an amused, "Hah!" She propped her feet on the table too, copying Fallon's posture. "Well, I'm reading a lot. Watching holo-vids. Listening to music. Catching up on all the things that were going on in the universe while I was too busy to notice. And when a certain someone is free, then I see him." She shrugged.

"Ah."

"Maybe you could use a good fling," Per suggested.

"Nah. That would be a complication. I don't need that."

"Yeah, you were always more sentimental about that stuff." Peregrine lifted her hand to her mouth and nibbled absently at the pad of her thumb, lost in thought.

"Was I?"

"Sure. I had a good laugh when I found out you'd married a Sarkavian."

"Well, thanks."

Per nudged Fallon's foot with her own. "Not at you. Just at the irony that you'd chosen someone from a culture that's so carefree about sexuality."

"Fine. Ha, ha. Irony is freaking hilarious."

"Oh, stop pouting. So what's your biggest issue? Not having something marked out to do every hour of the day?"

Fallon crossed her feet. "Yeah. But I came up with one thing to keep me busy. Lucky for you, you get to help."

"Oh, great. I'm sure this bodes all kinds of good things for me." Per's lack of enthusiasm was underwhelming. "What do I have to do?"

"You've filled me in on vital statistics and resumé bullet points, but I want to get a better picture of my life before. I want you to tell me about every mission we ever went on, in chronological order. And any personal anecdotes that happened in between that you recall."

"Is that all?" Per's face was deadpan.

"Careful, your sarcasm is showing. But yes. I want to know my past. If it helps me remember, then all the better, but even hearing it secondhand is something."

Peregrine let out a long sigh. "When you put it that way, I'd have to be an ass not to do it. But that's going to take forever."

"You can squeeze a lot into three months, if we work at it."

Peregrine sighed again. "What about Raptor and Hawk?"

"They'll be doing it too. I just haven't told them yet."

Per barked out a real laugh this time. "Can I be there when you do?"

———

Hawk's long, swear-laden tirade the next morning no doubt turned out to be everything Peregrine had hoped it would be. She laughed in quick, snorting bursts that in turn made Fallon laugh.

"Can't you just wait until Raptor rips those records, then read them yourself?" Hawk complained.

"No. That's months away, if he can even get them. There's no guarantee." Fallon supposed Hawk had better plans than rehashing old history, and she almost felt bad about imposing on him. But then she remembered that his plans probably consisted entirely of throwing down with members of Jerin's crew in various horizontal ways. His love life was eventful enough that he could miss a date or two for the greater good.

"Well, bloody hell. Fine. But you can be sure I'm going to include every embarrassing thing that happened to you," he groused.

"Wouldn't expect anything less."

Peregrine spoke up. "I was thinking we might coordinate, to keep it chronological. Once we're done, Fallon will have a much better understanding of our work as a unit."

"Fine," agreed Hawk. "But daytime hours only, as previously agreed. Dinnertime and after are still my own. Deal?"

"Deal," Per and Fallon said together.

Hawk practically kicked them out of his quarters at that point, and Fallon went to see Raptor alone. His agreement didn't surprise her. Somehow she'd known he'd be the only one to be immediately on board with the plan. Not that Peregrine and Hawk were less supportive, or that they truly minded helping her. They just didn't seem to filter their thoughts from her as Raptor did. Like Fallon, he operated more internally.

"I think it's a good idea," he added.

"Good. Because I'd like to start with how you and I first met."

"Why?"

"I'm going for a chronological perspective, and from what I understand, that was the first any of us knew of one another," she explained.

"Oh. Well that makes sense."

Hanging out in her partners' quarters was beginning to feel weird, since all of them had similar quarters and similar couches. She pressed her feet against the edge of the table, pushing it half a meter away. Then she slid off the couch to the floor, resting her back on the couch. She patted the floor next to her, glancing toward Raptor.

He joined her, looking conflicted.

"What?" She didn't like the expression on his face.

"You used to do that, back in school. All the schools, actually. Academy, OTS, security school. You stopped when we became full-fledged members of Blackout. You said it was time you grew up and learned how to sit on a couch." Memories flared in his eyes. History that she'd once shared, but now existed only in his head. Strange to feel like an outsider to her own life, and even stranger that she'd begun to get accustomed to it.

"You think it's some sort of fledgling memory?" she wondered. "Or just a personal habit, coming back to me? I do seem to like all the same things I ever did."

"No clue. I understand computers, not brains." He watched her silently for a long moment. "I'd like to hope it's a memory, but I don't want to be disappointed."

"Does it mean a lot to you for me to remember?"

"Of course. As a unit, we'd be stronger if you had everything you're supposed to have. As your friend, I want to see you made whole again."

She could see exactly why she'd been drawn to him, in her previous life. She and Raptor had chemistry, though whether that was an inherent thing or something he generated through the power of his memories, she had no idea. For her part, he just appealed to her. She couldn't pinpoint any particular reason for it. She liked the way he moved. The tone of his voice and his particular way of gliding across the syllables. He had charisma.

He was right, though. She was definitely less than whole. She looked him in the eye. "I'm sorry I'm less of a teammate because of this. I really am. I don't want to fail you guys." The idea of letting them down haunted the dark corners of her mind during her less confident moments.

"You're not," he said immediately. "You won't. That's not what I meant. You're still everything you ever were, just minus the memory. And I've told you before, the four of us are bonded in a way that won't break."

"Like soul mates, and marriage, but without the romantic thing." That was the description Peregrine had once given her.

"I guess." He ran a hand through his hair. "I just mean that you never have to worry about us giving up on you, or being disappointed in you. If you went around biting babies and sucking their brains out, we'd assume you had a good reason and would back you up."

She laughed. "That's awful!"

He relaxed, smiling. "Not the first time you've said that."

She smiled back. "I like the idea of people who will have faith and back me up, no matter what. People I'll do the same thing for. So." She pressed her palms together and rested her chin on the tips of her fingers. "Tell me everything about how we met."

Raptor let his head drop back as he rubbed a hand over his jaw. "I guess there's only one place to start."

Drew walked across the quad, enjoying the sunshine and fresh air. Since starting the PAC academy six months ago, he'd spent much of his time indoors. He'd never minded studying hard, which he'd expected to do at the academy, but he did miss spending time outside.

Glad to have left his last class of the day behind him, he intended to get an early dinner before returning to his dorm for a long night of study. He had his sights set on finishing first in his class to ensure his acceptance into officer training school, or OTS as they usually called it. Being a PAC officer had been his goal for as long as he could remember. The uniforms, the technology, the adventure. He wanted to be part of something bigger than himself.

Before he even started the academy, he'd been recruited by the intelligence department. Quietly, of course, and he'd not been allowed to tell anyone about it. The possibility of becoming one of the elite had intensified the fire within him to excel. He'd vowed to himself that he would live up to their every expectation, and then some. He would be so good they *had* to select him to become an intelligence officer.

He noticed a hand-to-hand combat class going on at one end of the quad and detoured to get a look as he passed by. His favorite teacher spoke to a student, who wore the typical close-fitting pants and shirt for close-contact training. Commander Whelkin then gestured to another student, and the two faced off against each other.

It wasn't a bad match, skillwise, but Drew could see both of them hesitating. Trying to avoid taking a hit. Afraid of getting hurt. Whelkin shouted some corrections, and the students did try, but they clearly had no passion for hand-to-hand fighting.

Whelkin's frustrated gaze fell on Drew as he passed. "Drew!" he called. "Join us for a moment, if you have time."

Drew shrugged and closed the gap between him and his teacher. Whelkin's attention shifted to another student, who sat properly on her knees, back straight, brown eyes sharp. There was a certain edge to her, an intensity that set her apart from the others.

At the teacher's gesture, she leaped to her feet and crossed the makeshift sparring ring to join them.

Whelkin said, "Drew, this is Emiko. She's my best student in the afternoon class. Emiko, Drew is the best student from my morning class."

They bowed politely to each other, in perfectly equal measure. Emiko had a roundish face, average features, and hair she'd pulled back into a thin ponytail. Her eyes, though, burned with a fierceness that he recognized. She was here to win.

"I'd like the two of you to show the others how this is done." Whelkin gestured to the rest of the class, who sat watching.

Drew wore the cargo pants and T-shirt typical of academy students, rather than the usual sparring clothes, but he didn't mind. "Sure." He slipped his shoulder out of his backpack strap.

The girl just nodded, fixing Drew with a cool, observant gaze. He'd grown ten centimeters in the past year, and felt like he towered over her slight form. She didn't seem the least bit intimidated. In fact, she eyed him like he was beneath her.

They stepped into the space, facing each other. Whelkin shouted, "Begin!"

Neither of them moved. Drew waited her out, but she only watched him. She was the calculating sort, then. She'd take her time to figure out his strategy. He liked that. He took a step to his right, and she moved with him, keeping the space between them constant.

He struck. A light jab, to test her. She blocked immediately. So he tried again, faster. And again, harder. Each time, she turned his hits aside, as if they were nothing, until he was hitting his hardest. She had a way of moving that kept him from being able to get to her center mass. She was just...slippery, and his strikes always slid off to the side.

Just as he wondered if she'd ever launch any attacks of her own, she did. A punch to the face, then one to the sternum. He dodged the first but the second glanced off his ribs.

Surprised, he decided to get close and overwhelm her. He stepped into her space, ready to grapple, but after a rush of movement he found himself on his ass. He immediately leaped back to his feet. All right, then. Time to get serious.

He moved in again and let fly with the three-punch combination that Whelkin had taught him just that week. Block, block, a decent impact, and then his arm was in a vice, and his ass was on the ground again.

"Excellent," Whelkin called as Drew leaped to his feet again. "Thank you both."

Drew and Emiko eyed one another, each making sure the other had turned off battle mode before dropping their guard. He felt out of breath, and his butt no doubt had a large bruise or two, but other than a small pink mark on her cheek, she looked unaffected.

"You can't be afraid to take a punch," Whelkin lectured the others. "Sometimes you give up a hit to gain the advantage. The more hits you take, the better you'll get at it."

He turned his attention to Drew and Emiko. "Nice work, you two. Emiko, why don't you take off early while I teach your classmates some basics?" He gave her a wink.

She smiled, bowed low to her teacher, and went to retrieve her backpack. After putting it on, she gave Drew a shallow but proper bow, then turned to leave.

"Hey," he surprised himself by saying. "Are you up for an early dinner?"

Fallon enjoyed Raptor's storytelling. Mostly hearing his personal feelings and observations about school, and his initial impressions of her. His impression of the events was as important to her as the events themselves.

"That's it?" she asked.

"Yeah. You wanted something more dramatic?" Raptor shifted against the front of the couch, stretching his arm out on the seat cushion.

"Definitely. Laser beams and rampaging psychopaths. Or something."

"Sorry."

She shrugged. "So my name was Emiko?"

"Just the academy name the intelligence department hooked you up with when they recruited you. You never told me the name you were born with."

"Safer that way, no doubt, for both of us." The idea made her a little sad, for some reason. They'd been sixteen. Too young to be involved in the spy game. Yet they'd already started the long descent into Blackout. "Interesting that I went by Emiko at the academy, and Emé at Dragonfire."

He scratched his ear. "Yeah, we talked about your alias a little, back on Dragonfire. It was obviously a flare you were sending up for me to find. I did, eventually. Once I realized I should be looking."

"Why would Blackout let me use that name?"

He gave her a half grin. "No way they'd let you. No doubt they gave you a perfectly benign alias, and you changed it, and by the time they realized, it was too late."

"That would seem to indicate that I knew something was going on, from the very start of my time on Dragonfire."

He nodded, his lips drawn into a narrow line of deep thought. She didn't have anything more to add to that idea, so she tucked it away to ponder later and moved on to the next issue.

"Did we start dating right away?" She wasn't sure she wanted to know details, but there was no point in having these sessions if she was going to shy away from the uncomfortable parts.

"Not exactly." His eyes focused on some spot on the ceiling. "I mean, we didn't go about it in such a straightforward way. We saw each other as…I don't know, partners. We figured out pretty quickly that we were both on the fast track to intelligence. We weren't supposed to talk about it, and we didn't, other than a rare shadow of a reference. But we knew. It made sense for us to be together."

"That's mercenary." And far more clinical than she'd expected for a pair of teenagers.

"It wasn't, really. We were great together. We fit. We talked about our studies, we sparred. You taught me a hell of a lot about close combat. And you did a lot of crazy-ass flips and stuff back then, too. You taught me to do one of them, before I got too big to make it work. But we laughed, too. A lot. And we had trouble keeping our hands off each other. Like I said. We just fit."

Well, that sounded better, at least. More organic and reasonably hormonal. "Why was I so good at fighting?"

"You told me once that your father taught you. That he started training you as soon as you could walk. And then you refused to talk about it, ever again. I think you were mad at yourself for saying something about your first life."

"First life," she repeated. "Like we get more than one."

"Don't we? How many have you had by this time? The one you were born into, the academy, OTS, security school and Blackout, your new life on Dragonfire, and now this. Sounds like a lot of lives to me. A lot of names, too."

"I guess so." She considered all the names she must have used. "Seems like I wear names like hats. Just put on whatever one fits me at the time."

"We all do. It's not a big deal."

"Isn't it? Do you ever feel like you don't know who you really are?" She turned to her side, resting her head on the couch as she looked at him.

"Never. I've always known who I am and what I'm about. Who other people think I am has nothing to do with that."

She fell silent, thinking about his words. Finally, she said, "Since waking up without my memory, I've been living my life based on what people have told me about who they think I am."

"Not true. You've played out the scenarios you found yourself in, but you knew something was off. You were looking for answers before I even showed up at Dragonfire."

She liked his interpretation of events better. "Do I seem like the same person you knew before?"

"Absolutely."

"When did we meet Peregrine and Hawk?"

"You mean Poppy and Olag? We'd seen them around, since they entered the academy at the same time we did, but we started getting to know them halfway through our third year, when we'd been matched up with them for intelligence training in OTS."

"*Poppy* and *Olag*? You're kidding, right?"

A slow grin spread across his face. He hadn't dropped those names by accident. "Nope."

She snickered. "Oh, man. I can't wait to call them that."

"At your own peril," Raptor warned.

"No worries. Apparently, I was the top of my class in close combat."

He laughed. "Well, among them, anyway."

"What, someone surpassed me?" That was a little disappointing.

"Just barely."

"Who? I demand a rematch."

"Hawk."

"Oh. Well, Prelin's ass. I take back my challenge." She loved a good fight, but if she went up against Hawk, she'd have to fight to kill. He outmatched her too much in size and strength.

"You barely edged out Peregrine," he added. "And I tied her."

"Huh. I must have been a heck of a teacher, then."

He didn't answer. He just kept frowning up at the ceiling.

"What's wrong?" she asked.

He sighed and reluctantly met her gaze. "It's just...I always wondered how you and I would have ended up if we hadn't gone into intelligence. How different life might have looked, you know? Sometimes I think about what our kids would have looked like."

Her stomach dropped. Well, shit. This was not where she wanted things to go. She did *not* want to deal with soppy, leftover sentiments from the past. "Uhm... Really?"

He snorted. "Hell, no. Can't believe you fell for that." He laughed in delight.

Relief flooded her, followed by irritation that he'd gotten the better of her. "Do. *Not*. Do that again," she enunciated forcefully. "You nearly gave me a heart attack."

He laughed harder, dissolving into a hail of guffaws as he held his stomach. "You should have seen your face."

"Right. Well, I think we're done here." She crossed the room. "I'll catch you later." She paused when the doors opened. "Thanks, though, for helping fill in my memory."

He waved her off, still chuckling.

"Asshole," she muttered once the door closed. Then she smiled fondly and went to find Peregrine.

4

Fallon's routine filled her days nicely. Each morning, she started with a good hard run and a climb up the wall. Frequently she did so with Brak, since they'd adjusted their schedules to mesh. Afterward, she grabbed a quick breakfast, then did her hypnotherapy session if she had one that day. Still no luck with that, and so far, her teammates hadn't come up with connections to any two-mooned worlds.

Otherwise, she spent two to three hours with either Hawk, Peregrine, or Raptor, or sometimes a combination thereof, hearing her life recounted to her from their perspectives. She wondered how her own memories of those shared events would differ. She found it interesting to pay attention not only to the story, but to the specific details her partners found noteworthy. It gave her insight into them that she hadn't had before.

Each day she had lunch in the bar—sometimes alone, and sometimes with others. In the afternoons she researched places or other details from the stories that her teammates had recounted to her. If she had time, she went to the rec center and played some sort of board or card game with whoever happened to be there looking for an opponent.

The rec had caught on, and almost always had a few people in it. Trin's young patient Mara often visited, having little else to do when not with the doctors or having physical therapy. She'd turned out to be a quick study at playing Go.

Fallon's days were finally passing at an even clip, and she felt pleased to have found a proactive way of using the time. Before long, the *Onari* arrived at the moon base Hawk had directed them to so he could connect with one of his "associates." By this point, the ship was just a week away from Jerin's next stop, where they'd take on fresh food and administer whatever basic healthcare might be needed at a small outpost.

Hawk's destination looked awfully dubious to Fallon. But since Raptor and Peregrine seemed unconcerned, she pretended to be as well. The four had gathered in Hawk's quarters as he prepared for his mission.

The moon had no atmosphere and no orbital elevator. The *Onari* had edged up close and Hawk now awaited a small transport ship from the moon's surface.

"Who do you want to go down with you?" she asked Hawk while he rummaged around in a dirty backpack, taking some things out and putting others in. She considered asking for details about his plans, then decided not to. She just had to trust him.

He shoved a lumpy, leather-wrapped thing into the backpack and gave it all a good shake before zipping it closed. "Raptor. My guy has access to some datastreams that he might be able to jack into."

"So your guy's a data broker as well as a…trader?" Which was the most polite term she could come up with.

"That's right. Good guy. Long as you don't turn your back on him." Hawk grinned like it was a joke, but Fallon was sure it wasn't.

"All right. Keep us posted." She glanced from Hawk to Raptor.

"You got it." Hawk winked at her. He was entirely too blasé

about it all, but she supposed this was his schtick and he'd know if he should be worried. She knew he wouldn't put Raptor in unnecessary danger.

"I'll leave you two to prepare, then."

"Good luck," Peregrine told them, following Fallon to the door.

"I'm just excited to be going along on one of these adventures." Raptor looked quite pleased about the situation.

Hawk shot him a glare of disdain. "You wouldn't be going this time, either, if the PAC didn't want to smoosh us into space dust. So don't get used to it."

Fallon and Peregrine left them to bicker, and the door slid shut behind them.

"You're sure they'll be okay?" Fallon looked at the closed door, frowning.

Per shrugged. "No, but I have faith that they can get the job done. Hawk knows what he's doing."

Despite being prefaced by a negative, Peregrine's response actually made Fallon feel better. She turned from the door to face her partner. "Well, you're the only one left, so why don't you spend the rest of the morning telling me about the time we had to steal data from Zerellus. You mentioned that last time."

"Right. Your quarters or mine?" Peregrine had been a good sport about all of the recent storytelling. Much better than Hawk, who didn't actually mind the narrative so much as the responsibility of telling Fallon her own past. He always seemed far less comfortable than Peregrine or Raptor about sharing his personal observations of her.

"Doesn't matter," Fallon answered. "They're essentially the same."

HAWK AND RAPTOR returned hours later with the electronics Peregrine had wanted and some data for Raptor to rip apart, along with frustratingly closed mouths. Fallon had hoped for some details, but nope. Ah, well. At least they'd been successful.

The next morning, Fallon had her eleventh hypnotherapy session. Afterward, she asked Brak and Jerin, "So how long do we keep doing this? I've looked up studies on hypnotherapy, and they show that if a patient hasn't recovered any memories by the tenth session, the likelihood of success is less than ten percent."

The doctors exchanged a look. "That's true," Jerin agreed slowly. "But Brak and I are willing to continue as long as you wish. Less than ten percent is still a chance."

"I'm not just wasting your time? You both must have far better things to do." She felt increasingly bitter about her persistent memory loss, not to mention wasting the doctors' time. She didn't want to be a burden on anyone. Least of all her team. Maybe she should stop making them tell her about the past, too. Nothing she did seemed to help. An uncharacteristic feeling of negativity rose in her.

Jerin put a gentle hand on Fallon's shoulder. "It's never a waste of time to help a friend."

Jerin's warmth and caring deflated Fallon's poor mood, leaving her feeling merely empty. She rubbed a hand over her eyes, not used to so much emotional disarray. "I think I'm just tired."

"Fatigue is a normal side effect of the therapy. A nap is a good idea."

"Thanks. That sounds good, actually. I think I'll do that."

Back in her quarters, Fallon didn't bother to change into lounge clothes. She simply lay down on the bed, pulled a blanket to her chin, and plunged headlong into sleep.

A HANDSOME GUY smiled at her, but he looked weird. Like he was looking at her through a clear globe or something, making his face seem distant and distorted. His mouth moved, but she couldn't make out any words. It was like a slow-motion scene in a holo-vid.

She reached toward the sphere, but her touch made it cloud over. The guy disappeared, and she immediately missed him. He'd made her feel tethered to something secure, and now she felt she'd been set adrift.

The sphere became pitted and opaque. A pale bluish light glowed from it. It was a moon. And in front of it, another moon appeared. That felt familiar, like it meant something.

The first moon moved toward her until it collided with the smaller one, siphoning it up into itself. One moon now. Bigger. Brighter. And still moving toward her.

She tried to back away, but couldn't. The moon kept bearing down, filling her entire range of vision and burning her eyes with its glow. She could do nothing as the moon loomed, luminescent and beautiful, yet ominous. It began pressing the air out of her lungs as it crushed her.

FALLON WOKE, her breath rasping. She slapped the light panel to brighten the room and sat up. It wasn't as bad as the first time she'd dreamed about the moons. The images remained clearer, too. She could still picture the guy. A boy, really. Raptor, the way he must have looked as a teenager. As Drew. And those moons again.

Did it mean anything? Dreaming of Raptor-as-Drew didn't seem strange, given how many stories he'd told her about their academy and OTS days. She'd spent a good deal of time thinking about them. But the moons again. Why?

She lay back on the bed, thinking. She didn't have the sense of alarm like the time she'd gone running through the ship. She just felt frustrated. Her brain had begun to seem like her enemy. Like it was playing games with her. Why couldn't it just materialize the stories she already knew?

"Ahh!" she shouted in frustration. That felt really good and no one was likely to hear her over the engines, so she did it again. "AHHHHH!" She let loose a long string of creative swears, as if they were a magical formula for memory retrieval. They eased some of her aggravation.

"Dammit." She checked the time. She'd missed lunch, but she didn't care. She wasn't hungry. She needed to get out and find something to do though. She didn't want to be alone with her thoughts.

Maybe Mara would be looking for someone to play a game with. That, at least, her broken brain could manage to do.

Fallon followed her established routine and in no time, the *Onari* docked up to the outpost unimaginatively named PAC Outpost 346. It occurred to Fallon that this little installation marked the halfway point between Dragonfire Station and Earth.

Raptor bubbled with enthusiasm. This was his first opportunity since Dragonfire to tap directly into an official PAC datastream. He hadn't come up with anything useful from the data he and Hawk had bought from Hawk's contact. There might well be something of use there, but sifting through so much dreck without a real idea of what he was looking for had proved problematic.

Nobody even went aboard Outpost 346. Once the *Onari* docked, the outpost's small but efficient crew loaded the hospiship, thanked it for the offer of medical help, but declined.

Which unceremoniously put them back on their way to Earth.

"Your grip's a little off." Fallon adjusted Mara's fingers, guiding them to the right place on the knife. "Now. Step left, then right, and throw."

Mara did as instructed, and this time the knife flew in the right direction, crashing into the target Fallon had installed, then falling to the floor.

"That was better." Mara seemed encouraged. She'd filled out during her month on board, and though still a bit pale, she looked much better. She'd stayed longer than the originally projected month, but when the *Onari* arrived at its next stop, Mara would be taking a transport ship home.

"Yup. Try again." Fallon handed her another knife, which promptly thunked to the floor along with the other.

A couple people sat nearby at the gaming tables, watching, while others went on about their own business, pounding the treadmills or scaling the climbing wall. It pleased Fallon to see the rec center serving the ship's crew so well.

Mara didn't get discouraged or fatigued. She kept tossing and hitting the target, then retrieving the eight knives when she'd thrown the last one. Finally, one of the knives caught off-center of its point and hung for a moment before dropping to the ground. She let out a whoop. "It stuck!"

"It did. Good job."

Mara retrieved the knives again and held them out to Fallon. "Show me again how you do it."

"What, with all eight?"

Mara nodded.

Fallon shrugged. "Okay."

She took a few steps back to increase the distance. Last time she'd thrown a quick cluster of three knives. With eight she could be more showy. She slid six of the knives into the bandolier she wore on her chest—one of her prized possessions, along with her collection of exotic knives. She'd left the latter in storage on Dragonfire, though, choosing to bring only functional items on board the *Onari*.

With a knife in each hand, Fallon snapped her arms forward and watched as the knives landed in unison, perfectly aligned along the horizontal. She quickly grasped two more and made a trickier throw, firing them into place on a vertical line, creating a diamond shape on the target.

She went for an even harder shot, choosing to hit the top-left and bottom-right quadrants, then reversed that for the final two knives. When they slammed into the board, she'd created a circle of eight equidistant, perfectly aligned knives. She allowed herself a tiny, smug smile.

Mara's face lit up with such a sudden onset of hero worship that Fallon had to restrain a laugh. The two people on the climbing wall remained focused on their own activity, but ones at the tables and the three on treadmills at the other side of the rec clapped and shouted things like, "Wow!" and "Nice!"

The doors whooshed open and a young woman entered, carrying a baby. The pair sat at one of the gaming tables.

"I think that's enough for today. We don't want to be whipping knives around with a baby nearby." Fallon grinned at Mara. She wasn't worried about her own throws, but you never knew with a novice what might happen.

The girl nodded, then jogged to the target and began collecting the knives. She returned them to Fallon, then sat next to the woman and baby.

"Have you met Corla?" Mara asked while Fallon wiped the knives on a cloth and slid them into the bandolier.

"No." She smiled at the young mother, a mahogany-skinned Zerellian with her hair arranged in a multitude of tiny braids. "Nice to meet you. I'm Fallon. I'm surprised I haven't seen you by now."

Corla settled the baby in her lap, facing the child outward.

The tiny girl looked like a miniature version of her mother. Her head wobbled slightly, as if she hadn't entirely gotten the hang of holding it up. "I've been working night nursing shift while Daisy here has her days and nights all mixed up. No point in me working day shift when she's sleeping the whole time. So unless you've hurt yourself or gotten sick late at night, there's no reason for you to have seen me." The mother chuckled and gave the baby a tiny bounce, which made the girl's toothless mouth bloom into a huge smile.

Fallon laughed along with Mara at the baby's delight. "She's gorgeous." She took a seat next to them, leaning forward to watch the child. She had no idea whether she had any experience with the things.

"Is it tough to take care of a baby on board a ship?" Fallon asked.

Corla raised her eyebrows contemplatively. "I imagine the basics are pretty much the same. Her father's taking the night shift right now too, in ops control, and we just take the feedings and diapers day by day."

"So she stays in the nursery while you work?"

"Sometimes. Other times people watch her for us. The rest of the crew helps out a lot. Daisy has tons of honorary aunts and uncles."

"Can I hold her?" Mara asked.

"Sure. You know how?" Corla settled Daisy into Mara's lap.

Mara held the baby confidently. "Oh yeah. I have four younger brothers and sisters."

"Big family!" Corla made a silly face at the baby, who laughed.

Mara seemed to have an enthusiasm for all things baby, and she and Corla talked about sleeping, teething, and all manner of things that did not interest Fallon. Nonetheless, she looked on with a polite attentiveness for several minutes.

Finally she checked the time. "If you two will excuse me, I'm supposed to meet someone for an early dinner." To Corla, she said, "It was nice to meet you."

"You too."

Mara smiled up at Fallon. "Thanks for the throwing lesson. Can we do it again tomorrow?"

"I'm not sure. If not tomorrow, then the day after," she promised.

"Great! I can't wait!"

Throwing knives and babies. Mara's interests seemed to cover a broad spectrum, and Fallon liked that. Hopefully the girl would sample many things before she honed in on what to do with her life.

As she walked down the corridor to meet Trin and Kellis, Fallon wondered if *she'd* been given that kind of opportunity. Perhaps she'd always been destined to spy and kill. Her father had certainly started her training early, from what she could tell.

KELLIS AND TRIN went quiet as she approached, suggesting that Fallon had just been the subject of their conversation.

She slid into the chair across from them. "What's up?"

"Nothing. Just trying to decide on what to order." Trin studied his menuboard just a little too attentively.

"Right." She decided not to force the issue. "What looks good? I was thinking I might have a burger again. The one I had last night was fantastic."

Kellis ran a finger down her menuboard. "I was thinking about the carrot-corn bisque and some sushi."

Sushi did sound good. Burger and sushi? Why not? When the server came, she ordered it, along with a cold tea with lemon.

"I heard you're going to give knife-throwing lessons to Mara." Trin beamed at her. He'd been the one to encourage her to befriend the girl. Apparently Fallon had earned high marks from him for doing so.

"We just started, actually. She seems quite enthusiastic."

"Good. She was getting bored. The last stage of therapy usually happens amidst a wave of tedium. For the patient, that is. I love seeing them get to that point."

Fallon nodded, as there didn't seem to be much more to say on the subject. Belatedly, she added, "She's a good kid. I'm glad she's almost ready to go home."

"Next stop: Caravon." Trin's bright eyes sparkled.

"Really? I hadn't heard about that." Fallon would have to research the planet. She knew it to be a modern PAC world, highly industrialized and popular for corporate headquarters. As such, it could prove highly useful for her and her team.

"Jerin only got the request a few minutes ago. I happened to be with her at the time." Trin winked.

"You didn't even mention that!" Kellis sent him a dirty look. "But why would Caravon want our help? They have excellent hospitals."

Their drinks arrived, causing a pause in conversation. Fallon took a long slug of her tea, enjoying the sweet-sour flavor and the coldness snaking down her throat.

Trin held his glass of water but didn't drink. "Would you believe they had a case of Arburian plague?"

"You're kidding! How did that happen?" Kellis toyed with the handle of her warmed almond milk. Fallon found her fondness for the childish beverage rather cute.

"They're not sure. For now, they're guessing that a person had some tainted grain hidden away in their luggage, then ate it while on the planet. Of course, the microbe doesn't become the plague until lodged in the intestines of its unfortunate host. So the bioscanners wouldn't have picked it up." Trin set his glass down. "Once that person got digesting, though…" He wrinkled up his nose and grimaced.

"That's ridiculous," Kellis spat out.

Fallon agreed. "I don't feel that sorry for the person who smuggled it in. But it really sucks for others to get sick because someone else didn't follow regulations that are there for a very good reason. How many cases?"

"Only two so far, and Caravon is treating them in quarantine. But they don't have any Arbur-5, which is the quickest way to shut down an epidemic before it can start."

"Right," Kellis murmured. "They're lucky we were already headed that general direction."

"Yeah, they are," Trin agreed.

"What's Arbur-5?" Fallon asked. Unlike the crew of the *Onari*, who were all required to be certified as field medics regardless of profession, Fallon had little medical know-how.

"Technically it's a volatile compound. Short shelf life, which is why most planets don't stock it, unless they harvest grain. In tiny doses, it inoculates against the plague, and also prevents a patient already suffering from it from progressing in the disease. So long as the patients hang on until we arrive, they ought to make it."

"What's our ETA?" Fallon asked.

"At our previous speed, three weeks. But Jerin authorized high-speed transit, so we're looking at four days. The command crew is prepping the ship. We should get the announcement soon."

"Wow," Kellis breathed. "That's going to cost us a *fortune*."

Trin nodded. "We'll need a complete refuel, and we'll have to change out the transducer coils. They'll be completely fused by the time we arrive. But the Caravonians will compensate us."

Fallon was sorry for the cause, but didn't mind that their voyage had just been shortened by two weeks. She wished she could have paid Jerin to blast straight to Earth posthaste, but that would have been ridiculously suspicious without any medical emergency to warrant it. Caravon had inadvertently saved her some time.

She'd been in a perfectly fine mood before, but she suddenly perked up. When their food arrived, she dug in with gusto.

"Ahh, look who's happy." Trin winked at her.

She paused between bites. "Not about that plague. That's a shame, and I hope everyone's okay. But I'm not sorry to get to Earth sooner."

Trin and Kellis shared a look that reminded her of the way they'd stopped talking when she'd arrived.

"What?"

They became unusually engrossed in their food. "Nothing," Kellis said, spooning up her soup and putting it in her mouth.

Fallon put down her burger. "Right. That's twice now." She gave Kellis, then Trin, a no-nonsense look. "What's up?"

Kellis looked down at her plate. "We've just been speculating about what you're going to do there." She rushed on, her words coming fast. "I know, we're not supposed to, but it's just Trin and me. We wish we could help. That's all."

Fallon frowned at them. "Why would you want to help?"

Kellis peeked up for a moment, then stared down at her sushi. "We've gotten to know you. I mean, everyone on Dragonfire loved you, and we've seen how you are here, too. You're a good person. You've even helped out a lonely kid, when you surely have problems enough of your own. Whatever you're doing must be…" She trailed off. "Important."

Fallon took a quick look around the bar to make sure no one could overhear. She ducked her head forward and spoke in a hushed voice. "You're better off not even thinking about it. I'm not going to insult you both and insist we're just going to Earth to visit friends. But seriously, leave it alone. Don't think about it. Don't talk about it."

Trin looked sad, as if feeling very sorry for Fallon. "We won't. We don't want to add to your worries."

Kellis pushed a piece of sushi into her mouth and mumbled something mildly agreeable sounding.

The pleasure of their meal had leaked out, like oxygen from a depressurized airlock. They finished eating in relative silence, with only a polite observation here and there. Fallon was glad when the food had disappeared and she could excuse herself.

Back in her quarters, she felt unsettled. She didn't like that Kellis and Trin had been discussing Avian Unit's business, even just between the two of them, even when they could have no way of knowing anything at all. Curiosity could be terribly dangerous.

Her door chime sounded. Sighing, she answered it. Kellis wore a steely, determined expression.

Fallon peered at her in surprise. "Something wrong?"

Kellis glanced around before softly hissing, "Yes. And I want to help."

"What do you mean, you want to help?" Fallon frowned at Kellis, who'd refused to take a seat on the couch.

"I know something's up, or something's wrong. With the PAC, or maybe even PAC intelligence. I'm from Atalan. I know what it looks like when a government starts to go sideways. You and your friends show all the earmarks of things gone wrong."

Fallon opened her mouth to deny it, but Kellis held up a hand. "You don't have to explain anything to me, or give me any details. That's fine. But you're doing something big, maybe something that could affect the *Onari* or even my family on their new home planet. Brak and Jerin know a whole lot more than they let on, and they trust you and are helping you. I sure as heck trust them. And I want to help too."

Fallon stared her down hard, but Kellis stood her ground. She crossed her arms over her chest and refused to look away.

"You really don't know what you're talking about." Fallon

didn't want Kellis anywhere near her operation. Having an untrained person around such a delicate op could be a disaster for everyone.

"That's right, I don't have a clue, except that something smells stinky. But I still want to help."

"Even if you knew what you were talking about and I were on some big adventure, what do you think you could actually do to help?"

"You tell me. If you need anything mechanical done, I can make it happen." Kellis said it with such quiet authority Fallon didn't doubt her. Jerin had described her as an engineering prodigy more than once, as well. Fallon remembered how much she'd coveted the skills Kellis had, and wishing someone on her team had that kind of ability. But she'd been thinking of a trained operative. Not a completely green newbie. No, that would be too much of a risk. It would be a crazy thing to do.

"There's nothing you can do for us," Fallon said coolly. Then she put some steel in her voice. "Please leave, and forget we ever had this conversation."

Kellis narrowed her eyes. "No."

Fallon stared at the woman. She wasn't used to being disobeyed. "What do you mean, no?"

"I mean you're going to take me seriously. If you and those other three are good at whatever it is you do, then you can find a way to make use of what *I'm* good at doing. Just stop saying no and *think* about it." Kellis set her jaw. Something about her stance reminded Fallon of...well, herself.

"I—" Fallon's refusal and dismissal died in her throat. She recalled schematic after schematic of security systems, force fields, air-intake construction, and polaric diffusers. The truth was, if they'd been recruiting a fifth member for their team, Fallon would have been hoping like hell for a mechanical engineer right now. Raptor knew security and Peregrine understood surveillance, but that was nothing like being able to construct and deconstruct the systems they'd be fighting in the process of breaking into PAC intelligence.

Kellis saw Fallon's hesitation, and they both knew it. Scrap. It would be even harder to shake her off now.

"You don't like your life here? You want to mess it up by getting involved with stuff that isn't about you?" Fallon didn't want to risk an innocent person's life. She wanted to scare Kellis off. Make her forget about her offer. Which Fallon should *not* be finding so darn attractive. It was just too risky. But then, Avian Unit *was* the best, and if they couldn't protect an asset, then they wouldn't be the best, would they?

"I love it here!" Kellis countered, too loud. She continued, more quietly, but emphatically, "I love it. I love the people here." She licked her lips. "I told you a little about it, but until a year ago, I couldn't walk. I got shot in the war. For being in the marketplace at the wrong time. I sat in a wheelchair for six years." Her face creased with pain. "I was a burden to everyone. I was the reason we couldn't move to another village, with better access to food and water. My wheelchair wouldn't make it through the sand, and no one could carry me that far."

Kellis took a deep breath and forged on. "Then I lucked into the *Onari*. Lone survivor of an exploded Rescan smuggling freighter. Jerin fixed me. Trin became my friend. And suddenly I had a whole new life."

She squeezed her eyes shut for a moment, perhaps fighting tears. But her voice didn't tremble or waver. She spoke every word with absolute conviction. "Ever since I was able to stand on my feet again, I keep putting one in front of the other and going where they take me." She pointed down at her toes, then gestured at Fallon. "They've brought me to you. Now are you going to let me fight against whatever needs to be fought, or are you going to make me feel useless again?"

She glared at Fallon, as if daring her to try.

Fallon let out a slow, silent breath. Well, damn. Taking Kellis into the field would be crazy. But maybe it was the kind of crazy they needed. "I'll have to talk to my team."

"Absolutely not." Hawk looked at her like she'd lost her mind. "She's not even military."

"That's right," Fallon agreed. "Not PAC. No affiliations at all. We don't have to guess her loyalties. We know exactly what they are." The more she'd thought about it, the more she wanted to make it work.

"We'd be putting her life at risk." Raptor had been quiet about it, but he mirrored Fallon's own doubts, making them seem twice as big.

"Yes," she admitted.

"How does she even have any idea about us?" he asked.

Fallon rubbed her hand over the short side of her hair. She'd been thinking about that, too. "She watched her own government go sideways and fall. She might have heard something about the assassination attempt on me at Dragonfire. She's definitely noticed me leaving my post to travel across the sector with you three. I'd have to question her more in-depth to figure out her thought process, but whatever it was, she knows something's up. I'm sure she doesn't suspect how deep it goes."

"Even we don't know that. Yet." Peregrine chewed on the pad of her thumb. "She'd be incredibly useful. I could come up with some really good stuff, with her brain at my disposal."

Hawk grimaced. "That's a disgusting way of putting it. She's just a kid."

"She's twenty-seven," Fallon pointed out. "Just a year younger than me." The other three members of Avian Unit were only months from her age, and they all knew it.

"Yeah, well," Hawk grumbled lamely. "She seems younger."

True. Kellis had an earnest naiveté that made her more

youthful than her years, in spite of hardships that could have made her bitter and hardhearted.

"We don't have to give her more details. We could just give her engineering problems to solve," Fallon argued.

Hawk didn't answer, which was a good sign. She could force the issue, of course. As leader of their unit, she could make a decree. But this was too big. She wanted unanimous consent, even if it had to be grudgingly given.

"Why don't I bring her in for an interview?" Fallon suggested. "We can all have dinner in my quarters. I'll set it up nicely. And you can grill her." She hoped Kellis was up to that. If not, she was a poor candidate to help them, anyway.

Raptor and Per nodded. Hawk sighed and nodded too. "Fine."

A thought occurred to Fallon, and she wondered if it was time to talk about it. She'd been pushing off discussion of the future, of the restructuring she envisioned for Blackout. It was bad luck to plan ahead during dire circumstances. But maybe it was time.

"I have plans," she said carefully. "When we clean house at Blackout, I intend to establish accountability. Make sure some psycho admiral can't tear apart the PAC or risk interstellar wars by violating treaties. We're going to get inside and set Blackout and PAC intelligence right."

She might as well have set off a concussion bomb. She heard absolute silence as her teammates stared at her, eyes narrowed.

Finally, Raptor spoke. "How? We're just an ops unit. We're the sword, not the arm. Definitely not the head."

That was what it all came down to, wasn't it? They were the sword, not the brain. They'd been trained to run missions, not entire organizations. But she'd known ever since she'd realized what had been done to her that she would never be someone's sword again. She'd either become the brain, or she'd be nothing at all.

She met Raptor's eyes without hesitation. "We're going to take over Blackout."

Hawk muttered the filthiest thing she'd ever heard him say.

The ensuing silence stretched around her, warping the fabric of time as they all stared at one another. After seconds that felt like an eternity, they came out the other side of their emotional wormhole together.

"Damn right we are," Hawk growled. Per and Raptor nodded.

Fallon felt a slow, deliciously wicked smile spread across her face. It felt wonderful. And reckless. And just the right kind of crazy.

FALLON FELT as if Avian Unit had burst out of a chrysalis, transformed. Or, at the least, that their mission had finally kicked into gear with a clear goal. The means of achieving that goal remained murky, but no matter. One thing at a time.

They arrived at Caravon and delivered the needed medicine while the repairs to the *Onari* began. It would take about three days to get the ship back into shape, which left Raptor with plenty of time to do what he did best.

Peregrine worked her disguise magic on him and Fallon, turning them into a middle-aged couple. She gave both of them tips on moving slower and more cautiously, as older, less active people would do.

"Then there's this." She reached into her bag of tricks, as Fallon liked to think of it, and pulled out a thin, silver cuff bracelet. A plain piece of jewelry, like you'd find on any number of planets.

Per fastened it around Fallon's wrist. "There's a tiny button here." Peregrine touched the underside of the bracelet. "Now it's activated."

The bracelet vibrated against Fallon's wrist, like a humming throat. "What is it?"

"Proximity detector. A receiver for the transmitters in our tattoos."

"Ah." Fallon gave her wrist a shake. The bracelet felt like a regular piece of jewelry, other than the buzzing. She pressed the button, causing it to go still.

"I didn't have the equipment before to make something that could do both long- and short-range detection. But these should work nicely for now, until I can upgrade to something that can distinguish who's who." Peregrine looked quite pleased with herself as she handed a bracelet to Raptor.

"Hawk and I will have them too. We should start wearing them at all times, just to be sure we have them in case of emergency."

Peregrine removed her own bracelet and turned it over so they could see the back. She showed them how to decipher the tiny readout. "That's it." She snapped it back onto her wrist.

"Nice work." Raptor tucked the bracelet under the long sleeve of his tailored shirt. Fallon decided he'd make a very good-looking middle-aged guy, in another decade or so.

"It's nothing." Peregrine looked pleased, though. "Good luck."

"No problem," Raptor declared. "Easy in, easy out."

"Let's hope," Peregrine muttered.

Raptor reached out and gave the end of Peregrine's ponytail a gentle tug, which made her lips turn up into an almost-smile.

"Don't worry, Masquerade. Blood and bone."

She nodded. "Blood and bone, Ghost."

Fallon immediately loved Caravon. The buildings rose hundreds of floors into the air, all metallic-shiny and blinking with lights. Groundcars didn't even exist. Hovertaxis delivered people directly to upper-level platforms on the skyscrapers. A ludicrous expense. Clearly, Caravon had a point to make about what kind of planet it was.

Standing on the ground and looking up, Fallon saw the air transected by so much traffic that it looked like a swarm of many different types of bugs, all swirling around in chaotic patterns.

"You look too happy. Stop it," Raptor teased.

"I'm loving the fresh air. And the sunshine," she admitted.

"I can tell. That's why I didn't hire a taxi." He patted her shoulder in a way that was far too geriatric for a middle-aged man and she snorted at him.

"You'd make a cute grandpa," she teased as they walked across the large square that separated the transport station from the other central buildings.

He made a sound of disgust. "To be a grandpa, I'd have to be a dad first, and no way in hell I'd ever curse some kid or some woman with that burden."

She laughed. Not being parent material herself, she knew exactly what he meant.

"Here we are. After you, my dear." He gestured for her to enter the hotel ahead of him. "Restaurant's on the eighty-second floor. I hope it's as good as everyone says."

So they were in character now. Fallon walked into the hotel lobby, saying, "I'm sure it is. Everyone keeps telling us we have to try it."

While waiting in the lobby for a lift to take them up, they pleasantly debated the benefits of staying at a large hotel versus a small one.

When they arrived, Fallon took a long moment to admire the restaurant, which had not spared a single expense. Ridiculously costly laser-etched mosaics practically sprang out of the walls and sprawled across the ceiling. The chandeliers alone would have bankrupted some small planets. The effect was sleek, sparkling, and entirely decadent.

She and Raptor kept up their banal patter as they perused the menus, made selections, and waited for their meals. After the server brought their drinks, Raptor excused himself to use the necessary.

"Don't be too long, the food will be here soon," she called.

She got the boring job of doing nothing at all, while he did his magic. On the ninety-third floor, the hotel had a PAC-access dataport, hardlined into the planet's official datastream. The entire floor was reserved for PAC guests. Fallon didn't worry that Raptor might be caught. He was the Ghost.

She smiled, thinking of the name. It had begun to grow on her.

She just hoped that no one would blunder out of some room and somehow recognize him. It was their only worry. Raptor had already keyed into all of the hotel's security feeds and ensured that none of them would see him.

Fallon dug into her steak when it arrived. She wasn't about to let good food go to waste. She nearly swooned when the morsel touched her tongue and melted into a pool of pure flavor and bliss. Screw Raptor. If he didn't get back soon, she'd polish off her food and start in on his, too. The tender leeks and brussels sprouts put shame to all others she'd ever tasted.

Fifteen minutes after he'd left, Raptor returned. "I see you've started without me."

"You're lucky there's anything left." She put her last bite of steak into her mouth and chewed, eyeing his food meaningfully.

He grinned. "Don't even think about it."

She ordered dessert instead. Five-layer chocolate walnut cake with a fudge ganache. Seeing her order it on the tableside menuboard, Raptor requested one for himself, as well.

When they were both too full to eat another bite, they waddled out, heaping praises on any staff they saw. They weren't just acting either. Fallon didn't know if she'd ever had such a delicious meal. They rode the elevator down, casually walked across the square, and returned to the station.

"Twenty minutes to the next elevator," Raptor told her, after checking at the window.

Their priority now was to get off the planet. They hadn't said a word about what Raptor had done on the ninety-third floor, even obliquely. They just needed to get their asses back to the *Onari*.

Fallon liked it, though. The adrenaline. The excitement. This was her life, no doubt about it. She liked wondering if there was an ambush around the corner or a fight about to find her. She *almost* hoped there would be. Almost. The exhilaration of the game made her feel alive in a way that nothing else ever had.

Raptor eyed her knowingly and a rueful smile curled his lips. She raised her eyebrow at him, but he only shook his head. They took seats on the orbital elevator and waited out the long ride quietly, like a middle-aged couple who'd already had all of life's urgent conversations.

THEIR STOPPING at Caravon also meant Mara's departure. It was the perfect place for her to get a safe, reliable ride back to her homeworld, which Jerin had already arranged. The crew of the *Onari* gathered at the airlock to see the girl off.

Mara said many thank-yous and gave too many hugs to count. When she came to Fallon, she hugged her fiercely. Touched, Fallon hugged her right back. Then she handed her a small, rolled bundle.

"Here you go. So you can keep practicing. I expect you to get good and win some competitions."

Mara's mouth rounded around her "Oh!" of surprise when she realized what Fallon held. "Your knives? I can't."

Fallon waved a dismissive hand. "They're just a practice set. I have another. They're high quality, though, so take good care of them like I showed you."

"I will. Thank you!" She gave Fallon another, even more squeezy, hug and then Trin walked with her into the docking station. He'd ensure that she got on her ship safely.

"That was very nice of you," Jerin murmured.

"Not a big deal." Fallon shrugged. "I don't need two sets."

Jerin just smiled.

———

"I heard you're one hell of a knife thrower."

Fallon stared, nonplussed, at Dr. Yomalu. She hadn't had a proper conversation with the guy in the past three months, and here he stood outside her quarters with a game smile and a bottle of Zerellian ale. Quite a cheeky move. She'd been on her way to meet Brak for their morning run.

But there was no sense in turning down good ale. She accepted the bottle and tucked it under her arm. She didn't invite him in, though. She remained in the open door of her quarters.

"You heard right." No sense in false modesty, either.

"I've come to bribe you for some lessons." Yomalu was some mix of ethnicities she couldn't identify just by looking. She knew from his record that he'd been born in the Orestes cluster, but had moved from place to place ever since. He didn't have good looks, height, or an impressive physique, but he did have a winning smile that spread from ear to ear. And ale.

"Bribe?" she repeated.

"Enjoin." When she remained blank-faced, he tried again. "Entreat. Incentivize. Corrupt?" His light-gray eyes widened, as if the last option were his most favored possibility.

"How would you do that?"

He glanced to the left, then the right, and leaned forward conspiratorially. "Word has it you have an appreciation for that stuff." He nodded at the bottle under her arm. "I happen to be a collector. Three centuries' worth of vintages. What you have right there is a hundred-year bottle from the Devandor region. Super rare." He smiled pleasantly.

"Keep talking."

"If you'd be willing to give me some lessons, I'd be happy to gift you several bottles of your choosing."

An offer way more than worth her time. "Define several."

"Four lessons a week, a bottle upon every fourth lesson."

"My instruction is far more valuable than that. Two bottles," she bargained. "And this one doesn't count."

"Five lessons, two bottles. And fine."

She'd have done it for his original offer. Heck, she'd have done it for free. She had time on her hands, after all. "Deal."

He grinned, his forehead crinkling too much for a man of his middle years. No doubt he spent an excessive amount of time being exposed to solar rays. A doctor should know better. The wrinkles made him look amiable, however, in addition to his huge smile. She found herself liking him.

"Can we start this afternoon? During my lunch break, maybe?" he asked.

She mentally ran through her to-do list. "That works."

"Excellent." He gave her a jaunty salute. "See you then!"

She smiled as she went back into her quarters, letting the doors close behind her. She studied the ale bottle's label and, after a brief argument with herself, decided it was far too early in the day for ale. Too bad. She tucked it away for later. She had a workout to take care of.

AFTER FRESHENING up after her workout, Fallon's next stop was Hawk's quarters. He'd promised to tell her about their mission to Artelon Three, which had apparently been a messy one. She looked forward to hearing the tale.

After his initial grumbling about delving into the past, he'd settled into the storyteller role. She'd known he would, given how much he liked telling tales at the bar.

He handed her a tall glass of cold tea and palmed one for himself. He settled on the couch while she took the chair opposite him.

"So what are we talking about today?"

She knew he knew. Which he also knew. But she played along. "Artelon Three."

"Oh, right. Nasty business. One of our worst. Everything that could go wrong, did. No clean in and out on that one. We barely got out at all."

He tapped a finger on the side of his glass, ruminating. Fallon waited patiently, enjoying the anticipation of getting to see the action through his eyes.

―――

HAWK SMOOTHED his hands over his uniform. His palms always got sweaty during a job. Not from nervousness, but adrenaline. The feeling that he was about to do what he did best, alongside others who were the best at what *they* did. This was what he lived for.

"I'm in." In the corner of the huge room, Raptor had plugged in to the station's central processing core. The technology was the same as what the PAC used, but this dingy little station was anything but PAC. This place operated on the dark side of an unpopulated moon, and Blackout had discovered that it had become a hub of people trafficking.

Just thinking about it made Hawk want to tear someone apart. The idea of people capturing other people—mostly refugees of war, though the slavers weren't too particular if they thought they could pick off someone who wouldn't be missed... A rage grew up from Hawk's bones that threatened to shatter the room around him. He hated this room. Hated its bareness, hated the two security podiums he and Fallon were handling, and the core in front of Raptor, too. Hated the very existence of the station. Hated that he couldn't single-handedly eradicate slavers and exploiters from the universe.

He held it all in, though. He'd gotten good at that, thanks to the academy and OTS. Somehow, the academy had seen the good beneath the simmering wrath, and given him an outlet for both. Thank Prelin. He had no idea what he would have ended up doing if he hadn't been recruited.

"Almost done? Time's ticking." Hawk looked over his shoulder to Raptor and saw Fallon behind him, holding her palm to the identifier screen in front of her, just as he was. The security on this crappy little station was as tight as anything Hawk had seen outside of PAC headquarters. All three of them had to work in tandem to make Raptor's data-stripping program run. If they didn't get what they needed in the next thirty seconds, though, the room's periodic DNA scan would detect them and blow their operation all to hell.

"Seventy-three percent," Raptor called. Hawk and Fallon exchanged a worried look.

"Eighty-eight percent." Ten seconds.

"Ninety-three percent." Two seconds. Too late.

The air intakes hissed, adjusting the room's internal pressure for the scan.

"Off the floor!" Fallon ordered.

He lifted his hand from the screen and heaved himself up onto the small podium. His feet couldn't even go hip-width apart, but at least he could stand solidly. Fallon fit more comfortably on top of the other podium. Raptor gritted his teeth, balancing on the core's console with his toes.

The sweep began at the floor, and Hawk watched the cozy-looking orange light rise slowly, searching for life readings. The only way to turn off the sweep was out of reach—on the outside of the room's doorway.

"Catch me!" Fallon shouted.

She launched herself at Hawk, and he had barely enough time to brace himself before she slammed into him. He somehow managed to keep his inadequate toehold on the podium. There wasn't room enough for her to put her feet down with his.

"Now what?" He held her securely, her back to his front.

"Over there!" She pointed to a tiny ledge next to the door. The emergency door release, smaller than one of his feet. But the release wouldn't work with a DNA sweep in progress.

He put his left arm around her waist to hold her up to his shoulder, then put his right hand on her bum. Using his right arm and left shoulder, he launched her on what he hoped was the right trajectory, and not too hard, toward the emergency release.

She got her foot on it as if she had wings, but immediately slammed into the wall like a sack of potatoes. She didn't fall, though. Nobody had balance like Fallon.

She stood on the emergency release, leaning toward the door, and took a sonic decoupler out of her pocket. Nice. If she could disable the door, they might just make it out alive.

The door slid open, revealing six people holding stingers. Hawk was pretty sure they weren't the legal, usually-used-in-nonlethal-ways kind of weapon.

Prelin's ass. He stepped off and dropped behind the podium, reaching for his own weapons and hoping the people at the door didn't take Fallon out before he could even fire.

Knives appeared in her hands and she flung three in quick succession, hitting two of their opponents in the eye and the last one in the forehead. She dodged a stinger blast with one of her gravity-defying sideways flips, then threw herself to the other side of the doorway to give Raptor and Hawk an open shot.

Rage notwithstanding, Hawk didn't like to shoot to kill. He did it when he had to, though. He took out the next two people as they stepped over the bodies of their associates, and Raptor shot the last one in the back when he turned to run. Hawk had to give Raptor credit for that. It was a shitty shot to have to make, and one that would burn a hole in him later. But he'd done it, just as he should.

"Full cleanse!" Fallon yelled, not waiting for her partners. She ran, stepping over the bodies.

Which meant they needed to split up and take out anyone left on the station, to avoid blowing their operation. Blackout couldn't afford for the slavers to know what they were up to. This was supposed to have been an easy op, no detection. Years of work might be wasted in the next minutes.

But there were no others to eliminate. Hawk was almost disappointed. Fallon called to Peregrine on their tiny fighter to get ready as the three of them made it to the docking bay.

As soon as they were on board, Per unleashed a volley of torpedoes specifically designed to make damage appear to have been caused by rapid depressurization. Containment was always a junk-station's biggest problem, and when one got slagged, it was almost always a pressurization issue. They might not fool the slavers, but hopefully Avian Unit could at least keep them uncertain for long enough to get their heads right into the noose.

Hawk wanted to be the one to kick the chair out from under them.

FALLON WATCHED the ice shift in her glass as it melted. She'd swallowed all the tea without even noticing, while Hawk talked. She hadn't realized so much anger ran beneath his skin. She knew he made plenty of bluster, but that stuff was mostly for show. What he'd shared with her was real, and it made her wonder about his life before the academy. Not that she'd ever ask him about it.

His story didn't seem more dire than Peregrine's story about the time pirates had followed Avian Unit away from dock, only for the team to find their propulsion drive had been tampered with. But this story seemed to really bother Hawk. She suspected he came from a rough background. He clearly had a need to protect the innocent.

"So you just threw me?" She decided to go with that angle, to lighten his mood a little. "Into a wall?"

His frown lessened. "You told me to. Made a terrible sound, though. Like a fresh steak hitting concrete. *Slap-thunk*."

"Yeah, remind me not to try that one in the future. It didn't even do any good, since those slavers showed up."

"They might not have been actual slavers, but they were a part of the operation, which made them just as guilty."

She nodded, in total agreement. There were no innocent bystanders when it came to people trafficking. Anyone aware of it became guilty by association.

"Did we take down the slavers, in the end?"

"Of course we did." He indulged in a grim smile. "Just took a little longer than we wanted."

"Good." She leaned forward and put a hand on his arm. "Thanks for telling me about this one. I can tell you don't like talking about it."

He shrugged. "No big deal."

Preparing to leave, she smoothed out her cargo pants and shirt. She felt a little odd in them after wearing her black jumpsuit for so long, but they were comfortable. "Want to meet for dinner later? Or drinks?" She wanted to be sure he had someone to talk to, in case old demons returned.

"Sorry. I have a date." At least that brightened his expression.

"Ah. Well, have fun." On impulse, she turned back and gave him a quick but tight hug before going. He returned it with the same vigor, though he took care to be gentle with her.

She went back to her own quarters. She wanted some time to think about the story he'd told her. She kept hoping that one of these stories might reveal a key either to her memory or the reason for her lack thereof. So far, just as she had with her other efforts to regain her memories, she'd come up with a big, fat zero.

SHE ENDED up taking her bottle of ale to Peregrine's quarters. Fallon wanted another story, and sharing some of the fine beverage seemed like a great way to make that happen. At least, she hoped so. Peregrine had just told her one the previous day, and Fallon didn't usually make her teammates revisit the past two days in a row.

"Let me guess," Peregrine said as soon as she saw Fallon. "You want me to tell you something we did that had a happy ending."

"Hello to you, too." Fallon handed the bottle to Per and walked in, uninvited. "But yes. How did you know?"

"Hawk told me he'd talked to you about Artelon Three. I figured the people trafficking would get you down as much as it does him."

Fallon leaned against the wall next to the porthole and gazed out. Nothing much to see, but still she looked. "Yeah."

"How about the time we saved Admiral Krazinski's daughter?"

"Was she kidnapped? Because that sounds like a good one."

"Not quite. But it *is* a good one." Peregrine perched on the arm of the couch and took a breath.

5

"Someone tell me again why we are invading a non-PAC planet, in the middle of a civil war, for the purpose of extracting people who chose to go there of their own free will?" Peregrine frowned down at Atalus. She knew perfectly well what they were doing and why, but the fact that an elite team of BlackOps was going into a war zone to retrieve one pampered princess didn't sit well with her.

"Because it's Admiral Krazinski's daughter and he's not only our superior officer, but one of the most important people in PAC intelligence. And he'd like to see his daughter again, with her head still attached." Fallon was obsessively double-checking all of her calculations. She didn't often get to fly directly into a planet's atmosphere, and Peregrine had no doubt she'd make the most of it.

"Nope. Still doesn't seem like a good enough reason, considering her big bleeding heart and delusions of making a difference brought her *voluntarily* to a place that people are climbing over one another to escape." Peregrine didn't feel good about this mission. Not because it was dangerous. They expected danger on their missions. She didn't like this job because the risk wasn't worth the reward. Blackout risked losing one of its best units. *The best*, in Peregrine's opinion, and she was hardly alone in thinking so.

Assuming everything went perfectly, all they'd get would be one spoiled brat, safe and sound, to reunite with her doting dad. What about all the Atalans who would gratefully give up their own lives to get their children off the planet? The effort seemed misplaced.

But then it wasn't her job to decide. Her job was to follow orders, and she'd do it to the death, if that was what it took. Because that was what she did. Dammit.

Fallon entered their trajectory and began the descent. The stealth fighter they'd been given for this mission took the rough ride well for such a small craft. By the time Fallon put them down behind a sand dune, Peregrine didn't feel as if all of her teeth had tried to rattle right out of her head. At least she had that.

Fallon stayed with the ship, keeping it primed for lift-off. The team might return hot, pursued by who knew what. They needed their pilot ready and waiting.

Which left Peregrine, Hawk, and Raptor to do the dirty work.

Atalus was a hot, sandy place, and they'd equipped accordingly. They had clothing that would help cool them and protect them from the suns, a lot of biogel to drink, and weapons. Big weapons. The kind of ordnance that made Peregrine glad to be alive.

They'd gotten a positive lock on Hollinare's transmitter. Not that Admiral Krazinski's daughter knew she had one. Peregrine supposed Hollinare would have to have a talk with her daddy about injecting her with the device, if she made it home. Peregrine was glad, for her own selfish reasons, that Krazinski had violated his daughter's bodily autonomy. It made her job a lot easier.

It had taken Krazinski three months to realize his daughter was even missing. Per had been an adult long enough to know that adult children don't always check in. Krazinski hadn't kept close tabs on his daughter, either, and when he realized she no longer worked at the hospital on Zerellus, he'd gone into a frenzy to find his only child.

Raptor had unraveled her plans in minutes, once he tapped into her personal voicecom records. Which had only made Krazinski more agitated.

Peregrine had found it fascinating, really, to watch a distinguished, top-of-the-hierarchy diplomat go from hard as nails to frantic parent. More or less. She still hadn't decided whether that made her respect him more or less. But Krazinski had stood up for Avian Unit more than once, such as after the disaster on Artelon Three. She and her team would back him up with whatever he needed, no questions asked. Well, no questions asked of *him*, anyway. Peregrine just might have a few things to say to Hollinare, when they found her.

In the distance, lights flickered and blazed, like a storm and a light show combined. A bombing. Peregrine hoped the action stayed far away, long enough for them to get off the surface of the planet. Atalus no longer had much working tech, so she didn't worry too much that their ship had been detected, but a firefight could break out anywhere, anytime on a planet like this. All she and the others needed was to stumble into the cross hairs of two of the four feuding factions, and that dumb bad luck could get them all killed.

Prelin, it was all so stupid. If the PAC had admitted Atalus into the cooperative, they could have stopped the war before it got off the ground. But the admission process was so long. The war had been raging for several years now and showed no signs of abating. The planet seemed doomed.

By the time she, Hawk, and Raptor hoofed it into the encampment, constantly on alert, waiting for gunfire to break out at any moment, they were all edgy and irritable. Not a single breeze broke the heat that poured over them like a suffocating blanket.

Peregrine felt like she was roasting, even inside her cooling clothes.

At least no one had shot at them. So far.

"Hollinare Krazinski!" Raptor yelled into the silent air from the center of the ragged tents and half-bombed-out buildings. It was as if there weren't a single soul within the camp, though Avian Unit knew better. The people were just hiding. "We're here to take you home." He spoke first in the standard PAC pidgin, then repeated the message in perfect Atalan.

A tent flap moved and their target stepped out with the grim look of someone too jaded to be scared. Clearly, she'd seen some action.

"I won't leave without my friends." She spoke Atalan, with a decent accent. She gestured and people spilled out behind her and kept coming. All told, Peregrine counted fifteen of them. Fifteen dirty, tired souls with haunted eyes.

"Who are they?" Raptor asked in standard.

"Friends." Hollinare crossed her arms over her chest.

"We don't have time for this," Peregrine muttered. "We're all exposed." Hawk grunted in agreement.

Raptor waved her off. He knew that. He kept his eyes on Hollinare and her friends. "Did they come with you, or are they native Atalans?"

"Some of both. They're all good people who need to get out of here." Hollinare's eyes dared him to tell her no. Grudgingly, Peregrine had to give her some respect for that. The admiral's daughter wasn't exactly the bleeding-heart lightweight she'd expected.

Raptor gave a sharp nod. "Fine. Bring enough water to keep you alive. Biogel if you have it. We don't have enough to share with that many. Anything you can't grab in two minutes is getting left here. That's all you get before we depart." He jerked a thumb over his shoulder.

True to his word, he herded up the group and pushed it

ahead of him, driving everyone hard. Hawk took point and Peregrine brought up the rear. She'd rather do that than babysit the civilians. She knew Hawk would feel the same. Of the three of them, Raptor was best equipped for that job, so he could have it.

She didn't relax until they were on board the ship with the hatch closed. They were exhausted and drenched in sweat, but Peregrine felt victorious. Only the heaviest-grade RPGs could pose a risk to them now, and Atalus probably didn't have any of those left. Still, she felt better once Fallon got the ship up into the atmosphere.

Peregrine's tension bled off, fading into a haze of success. Now that was a mission well done. Sure, they'd been lucky, not crossing paths with the feuding factions, but so what? Luck just as often went the other way for them. Today was simply their turn at having a good toss of the dice.

She sank into her chair and began tearing off her combat gear. Damned uncomfortable stuff. She needed a shower and fresh clothes. Raptor and Hawk followed suit, yanking off the heavy gear.

"Everything go okay down there?" Fallon asked.

"Yeah," Raptor answered, eyeing their passengers sardined into the rear of the ship's cockpit. Too small to even be called a bridge. He'd need to sort them into berths somehow. There wasn't nearly enough space, and Peregrine had a feeling she'd be sleeping on the deck plates. Whatever. She'd slept in worse places.

As intended, Fallon did feel better hearing Hollinare's story.

"What does she do now?"

Peregrine twisted the end of her ponytail absently. "She's still a nurse practitioner. Works on Barthon IV, a refugee haven. She's also a prominent fundraiser for charitable aid. A vocal lobbyist for streamlining the PAC membership process, as well."

"I'm sure Krazinski loves that," Fallon chuckled. "That must be uncomfortable for him."

"As far as I know, he's proud of her," Peregrine answered. "He supports her efforts, though his job is to keep the already-existing PAC worlds safe. I guess it's a matter of ideals versus reality."

Fallon thought of her Atalan friends, Kellis and Arin. "When you're starving and terrified of dying every minute of your life, you do what it takes to survive. Only those of us lucky enough to have a safe distance from the turmoil have the luxury of aspiring to ideals."

Per made a *hmph* sound of agreement.

"Thanks for telling me this one," Fallon said. She stood, stretching her arms. She checked the time. "I should get going. I have a knife lesson to get to."

"How's the doctor doing?"

"Well…he doesn't have a knack for it, but he sure tries hard."

"Gotcha," Per chuckled. "At least he's having fun, and sharing some good ale."

"My thoughts exactly." The door opened and Fallon stepped out, almost knocking into Raptor, who had raised his hand to ring the chime. The intense look on his face immediately put her on alert.

"I found something," he said without preamble.

FALLON RESCHEDULED her lesson with Dr. Yomalu, or Yom, as he'd asked to be called, though she endeavored to avoid doing so. Meanwhile, Hawk arrived at Per's quarters, sweaty and flushed.

"What've you got?"

Raptor gestured for him to take a seat next to Fallon on the couch. Peregrine leaned against the back of it. Raptor sat in the chair.

"The datastream we got from your guy didn't give me much. It had a lot on it, but mostly inconsequential stuff. It did have one classified message, but it had been blanked. Couldn't reconstruct it. I did, however, manage to extract the algorithm to decode it."

He paused, looking at each of them in turn to make sure they had no questions, then continued. "I got a ton of data from the hotel. Too much, really. Made it hard to sift through. But today I found another classified message. Blanked. But when I ran the algorithm on it, bam. I had it."

Fallon sat up straighter. "What?"

"A notification from Admiral Krazinski to all Blackout units and officials, saying that Avian Unit had gone deep undercover and was not to be approached, even if recognized. Highest priority."

Sudden silence filled the room as they considered what that meant. "That sounds like he's protecting us," Peregrine said slowly, thinking it through even as she talked. "He knows something's wrong and he's giving us cover."

"Maybe," agreed Raptor.

"Or…" Fallon said, hating to be the negative one. She much preferred Peregrine's theory. "He's making it look like he is. To make us trust him. He might even have planted messages just for us to find."

The light she'd seen in Per's eyes dimmed, and she felt bad for being the cause. But she didn't trust anyone in Blackout, other than the three people in the room with her.

"She's right," Raptor agreed. "So this might actually do us no good." He sighed with frustration.

"Keep digging," advised Fallon. "See what else you find. Let's see if the pieces look like they've been made to fit together, or if there's anything we can corroborate on our own." She injected a cheerier note into her voice. "Maybe Krazinski *is* on our side. We can't rule anything out." Until they had proof, Fallon wasn't willing to accept anything as fact.

"Yeah." Peregrine didn't perk up at the suggestion. Her typical frowning had degraded to a sustained grimace.

"Come on. We have almost three weeks left. Surely we can come up with some idea which way it is before we make it to Earth. And if not, then surely the data we get from the base will crack it." Fallon didn't like seeing her team so down.

Hawk started to leave but she caught his arm. "Want to have dinner tonight?"

That at least made him smile. "Nope. My time here is counting down, and I plan to make the most of it."

Fallon had somehow managed not to find out any details about his activities, and she preferred to keep it that way. "Happy hunting."

"No worries." He winked at her.

Raptor seemed disinclined to move after Hawk left. His distant gaze suggested he was mentally foraging through datastreams.

"Raptor?" she asked. "Dinner?"

That snapped him back to reality. "Uh, no. Thanks. Maybe tomorrow. I need to keep working." He gave them a distracted wave, then left.

"That leaves you and me," Fallon said to Peregrine.

Per's grimace eased a fraction. "Fine. You seem desperate, so I'll go to dinner with you."

Fallon laughed. "Very big of you."

"I do what I can for my team. Blood and bone."

BEFORE FALLON KNEW IT, she was touring the *Onari* to say her goodbyes. To Trin, whom she'd grown quite fond of. To Jorrid Yomalu, who assured her he'd keep practicing his knife throwing, though he'd never even attained the skills of a novice. To Corla and her cute little baby, who had begun to grow on Fallon. To Endra, who had looked conflicted, but genuinely wished her luck. And to Brak, who had become a deeply treasured friend. They stood at the entrance to the airlock before parting ways.

Brak clicked her teeth. "I wasn't going to say anything, because I'm not sure it will pan out, but I want you to know that I'm working on something to help you. An implant. Not like the kind I refused to make for the PAC—something reverse to that. I'll explain it all later if it works out, but this would serve as the intermediary between your memories and your recollection, bringing them back together."

Fallon stared at Brak. "So why are you telling me now?" She smelled anise, indicating Brak's worry for her.

Brak said, "So you don't take unnecessary risks. Whatever you find down there isn't your only possible link to regaining your past."

Fallon was touched. "You're an amazing friend."

Brak smiled. "Nonsense. I'm terribly opportunistic. I'm excited for you to be my...what's the phrase? Guinea pig?"

Fallon laughed. "Right. Well." She stepped in and gave her friend a hug, which was returned to her in kind.

Jerin arrived and Brak discreetly took her leave. Fallon glanced toward the airlock where Per, Raptor, and Hawk were all waiting for her.

Jerin took her hands. "I hardly know what to say, but I wish you luck." She pursed her lips, then added, "Don't get killed."

"I'll do my very best," Fallon promised.

"The *Onari* is always here for you to come back to."

"We've imposed on you enough." Fallon shook her head. "Hawk's already arranged the purchase of a high-speed, well-armed ship, now registered to an assumed name. No one's going to trace us to you, you can be sure. As long as your crew says nothing."

"Of course they won't." Jerin was about to say more when Kellis hurried in.

"Sorry I'm late." She sounded out of breath, as if she'd run through the corridor. "I...had a goodbye that took longer than expected."

Fallon wondered if it had been Trin. "It's fine. You're still on time."

"Take care of my engineer." Jerin's voice had gone dead serious. "I expect her to come back to me in perfect shape."

If things worked out the way Kellis seemed to be angling for, Fallon guessed that she might just end up in Blackout instead. Once they managed to cleanse it, of course. This mission would be a heck of a tryout for her.

"I'll keep her as safe as I possibly can." It was the best promise Fallon could make, under the circumstances. They were about to commit piracy and treason against the PAC, after all. She and her partners had explained to Kellis how dangerous this was, but she'd refused to reconsider. Fallon didn't share those thoughts with Jerin, though.

Instead, she bowed low, indicating deep respect. Jerin matched the gesture, returning the honor.

"Well, then," Fallon said to Kellis, gesturing to the airlock. "After you."

IT SHOULD SEEM ODD, Fallon thought, to travel with her team, along with an engineer asset, wearing disguises that made her team look like strangers. All so that they could infiltrate the security of the government that they backed, for the purpose of committing treason. But it didn't. It felt like being alive. Like taking her life back.

The five of them traveled across the docking station together, all but Kellis laden with their possessions.

Spirited debate among Avian Unit as to whether or not Kellis should be permitted to join them had continued up until that very morning. In the end, practicality won. They were better off with her than without her, and Kellis knew, more or less, what she was getting into. Peregrine had already begun singing Kellis' praises as a collaborator on Per's little tech devices. The two of them had gibbered a bunch of stuff that had started out sounding like real words and concepts, and quickly degenerated into technobabble that had gone right over Fallon's head. Whatever. They could handle their end of things and Fallon would handle hers.

Hawk led them to the docking bay that held their new ride. Fallon's breath caught when she got a good look at it. A sturdy little race car of a ship kitted out with all of the best technology. Fast engines, atmospheric landing capability, and long-range sensors. Fallon had to admit that Hawk's associate had really come through for them. She couldn't wait to get her hands on the controls. To that end, she pushed ahead of the others so she could dash to the cockpit and get to know her new darling. She paused only to drop her gear in the storage room. She'd take care of all that later.

The others filtered in while she familiarized herself with the ship. They stationed themselves here or there, waiting for her verdict.

"Gorgeous," she pronounced. "Everything we need, and a full complement of weapons, too." She looked to Hawk. "Your associate really nailed it."

He smiled. Very smugly.

Fallon had to laugh inwardly, though she kept her face blank. The Machine had come through for them. Of course he had.

She did a quick rundown of the plan and the expected timing, then nodded to Peregrine, who opened a pocket on her cargo pants and fished out a pair of pendants hanging from cords. She handed one to Raptor, then held the other up for him to see.

"Kellis helped me design this." She pulled on the pendant,

causing it to separate into two parts. The piece in her hand resembled a data chip. "Insert this into each voicecom terminal as you pass. It will lock it down and make it a dumb terminal. Security will only be able to access it by standing right in front of it. That means that if something goes wrong, it'll buy you some time in getting out."

Raptor arched an eyebrow. "And if I actually manage to *not* screw it all up?"

"Repeat the process on the way out. Those terminals will be restored, and we'll have a clean operation." Peregrine handed the pendant to Kellis, who curled her fingers around it tightly. Their new asset looked pale.

"You sure you're up for this?" Hawk asked her. "You can back out now, no harm done."

Kellis shook her head. "Raptor said I'd be the most useful to have inside. If we're detected, brute force won't get us out. We'll need a more...creative escape." She blinked under their combined scrutiny, her mouth tightening. "I can do this."

Could she? Infiltrating a PAC base was a far cry from anything the refugee-turned-engineer had done in her life. Then again, attacking the very thing Fallon had devoted her life to had to be even more diametrically opposed. So hey. Screw the past.

Fallon turned to the controls. "Then let's get it done."

———

GETTING to the PAC station wasn't hard. All PAC stations had public common areas. Only as a person went farther into the labyrinthine building did security get increasingly tight.

The team took their time getting onto the grounds. First Fallon and Hawk went in, politely submitting to the retina scans and fingerprints that kept track of visitors. Of course, they wore lenses on their eyes and synthetic skin fused to the pads of their fingers, applied by Peregrine and linked by Raptor to bogus citizen records. Tremendously illegal devices to have inside the PAC zone, to be sure, but standard issue for Masquerade's specialty. The trouble was, Blackout knew that, which meant the team had to be prepared for things to go bad, fast. A shame their weaponry was so limited, but security checkpoints ruled out anything conventional. Which left them with only the simple items designed to be undetectable. Between what they'd each brought with them and what Hawk had gotten from his unsavory associate, hopefully they had enough to get them out of a bad situation.

She and Hawk would wander along, enjoying the grounds. Nothing suspicious about that—many people did so every day. Tokyo had been the site of the very first PAC administrative building, and though it was no longer the headquarters, it retained a special place of honor. It remained a busy, high-profile facility, but also served as a global monument to the past. To progress. To a civility that Fallon knew was in danger of being annihilated.

Hawk carried a picnic basket over his arm as they strolled, pretending to delight in the architecture, the grounds, the fresh breeze. The long hair Peregrine had given him blew in his face every now and then, making Fallon want to laugh. For the moment, they had the easy job. They chose a spot and set up their picnic. Far too full of adrenaline to eat, Fallon did her best to pretend convincingly.

In a half hour, Peregrine would arrive and enter the building. Just the public area, low security. That would put two layers of backup nearby in case Kellis and Raptor ran into trouble. Those two would arrive fifteen minutes after Peregrine, then proceed immediately into the secured-access area, forcing their way right into the data core so that Raptor could rip records right out without having to wait for a system reset. He needed wide-open access for the extensive range of highly classified documents they were after.

If they were lucky, no one would notice the data breach. They shouldn't, since Raptor was the best at what he did—and since they were all incognito, because Peregrine was the best at what *she* did. But then Blackout would be on the lookout for something like this. They'd *know* that Raptor could do this. Which made everything a roll of the dice.

Kellis was Raptor's backup weapon, just in case everything went to shit. She'd studied the building and tech schematics Raptor had given her, and would be able to help him get out of the building in a number of unconventional ways. She also happened to be completely off the PAC's radar, since she wasn't a citizen. In the event of a forced interaction, she could do the talking while Raptor laid low. Hopefully, anyway. There was no telling whether luck would be their friend or their enemy today. Perhaps they'd waltz right in and out as planned, leaving them all feeling a little unsettled by how easy it had been. That was Fallon's hope.

The *Onari* should have broken orbit already, heading to the next outpost on its schedule. Even as Fallon made inconsequential small talk with Hawk for the sake of their cover, she felt relief at the crew's having gotten away before anything could throw suspicion on them. She would miss her friends, but better they stay safe. Besides, she'd have to rendezvous with the *Onari* to return Kellis to them, so she'd be seeing them again in the near future.

Hawk said something insipid about what a lovely day it was, and she agreed warmly. They packed up their picnic and began a slow walking tour of the tree- and flower-laden grounds. Peregrine would be in position now, and Raptor and Kellis would soon begin. The team had agreed on a communications blackout unless an emergency occurred. PAC intelligence knew everything they did about secured channels, and would likely hack into any communication Avian Unit attempted right there under the PAC's nose. Better to stay silent.

If they were lucky, Fallon would hear nothing until Raptor's check-in that he and Kellis had cleared the building on their way out. If the tiny earpiece Peregrine had inserted directly in her ear canal made noise before that, it would be bad news.

She and Hawk stopped to admire a huge maple tree with its branches lifted high to the sky. She made a comment about maple syrup and they talked about their preferences and what dishes they liked it on. Highly scintillating conversation.

Casually, they made it around the building, ending up near an emergency exit just about the time Raptor and Kellis should be breaching the data core. Hawk led her by the hand to a bench and they sat with his arm around her, slightly awkward in that new-relationship sort of way.

Her earpiece burst to life. "Bad news," Raptor's voice murmured, his words terse. "I got the data, but it had stickers on it. Alerts are going up now. We'll be coming out hot."

She and Hawk remained seated, but their eyes met. She pinched the pendant on her necklace, as if fidgeting with it, to activate the voice circuit. "We're ready."

Peregrine's voice echoed, "Ready," in her ear.

Two minutes. Three. Four. Fallon started to get worried. The longer Raptor and Kellis took, the less likely they'd get out. She didn't want to risk entering the building unless she knew they couldn't escape on their own.

She and Hawk continued to pose as lovers, even as her hands hovered within reach of her knives. Just as she was about to make the call to go in after Raptor and Kellis, she felt her bracelet vibrate, indicating that they were moving in her direction. Within seconds, Peregrine, Kellis, and Raptor flew out of the emergency exit.

Fallon felt her adrenaline spike as her teammates sprinted toward her. Action time. Normally that would be good. She liked action time. Just not when she and her friends were in such a vulnerable position.

Raptor slammed the door shut behind them as he ran, in an

attempt to buy them a little time. Fallon wished she had a stinger to fry the door, which would have afforded them a few extra seconds.

The door burst open, impacting the wall next to it with a heavy, metallic bang. One security guard came running out, followed by another. And three more. Prelin's ass, they'd been fast. They all had weapons on their hips, too. A distinct advantage over Avian Unit.

They didn't have time. Those guards would draw their weapons any second, as soon as they realized they were dealing with professionals. They'd have drawn them already if they'd known what Raptor had been up to when the alarms sounded. The exits from the base would already be locking down, with the perimeter closing in around them. Damn. She went to Plan B.

She grabbed the small, polymechrine knives that had been undetectable to the scanners and flung them into the wrists of the security team. It didn't matter if those stingers were set to lethal blasts or not. Getting caught would be as good as getting dead.

"Cover me," she said to Hawk, who nodded and took up position in front of her, shielding her with his body. They hadn't been able to wear armor or stinger dissipaters, since those devices would have been detected. So her only protection was her big meat brick of a partner. None of them could afford for Fallon to get hit before she'd brought in their transportation.

Raptor shoved Kellis behind Hawk before turning his attention to the security officers with a small dagger in his hand. But Fallon barely had time to notice the fierce fight that Peregrine, Raptor, and Hawk launched.

Fallon pulled a pair of goggles from the picnic basket, as well as a remote control. She pulled their ship out of sightseeing cruise mode at its low altitude, and set in a direct-route vector, at the maximum speed she could attain while being able to remote land the thing without smashing it into the dirt.

She engaged in an evasive flight plan, designed to avoid the anti-aircraft weapons that no doubt aimed right at her new flying darling. Like hell she'd let the PAC punch holes in their ride. In her favor was the knowledge that the base's personnel would be assuming an attack on the building. Her manipulation of PAC defensive protocols let her bring the ship toward the ground with only minor laser burns on the hull.

She adjusted the pitch and roll, and cut the propulsion way later than she normally would. Dangerously late. Their new ship hit the ground harder than spec, but it landed true and solid.

"Go!" she yelled. She felt Hawk's arm around her waist, practically carrying her to the ship she couldn't see with her own eyes because she was too busy operating the ship from the inside. She released the hatch and began reversing everything she'd just done to land the ship so that she could get it right off the ground again. Definitely not a spec-approved maneuver, even for a ship like this.

She heard Peregrine yell, "All in! Take off!"

Fallon didn't even have time to remove the VR gear. Pinging sounds indicated they were under fire, as did the flashing sensors in her peripheral vision. She plopped down on the deck plate just inside the hatch, flying the ship while jacked directly into its ops control.

No time for inertial stabilizers. She shut off several safety systems and launched the ship directly up into the air. She heard groans and scuffling around her even as her own stomach dropped. The ship stopped registering new damage.

"Up…up…*up*…" she muttered through gritted teeth. She had to get them out of the atmosphere before the PAC could scramble a ship to follow them. Or conscript one that was already out. She'd based their entire plan on the element of surprise and her intimate knowledge of PAC base security, and a firefight would significantly decrease their chances of success.

As soon as she had enough altitude to clear them from

weapons on the ground, she adjusted her pitch and aimed for the window to get out of Earth's atmosphere. Few ships had both interstellar and atmospheric capabilities, which was an edge she had over the PAC ships that would be available to pursue them.

It didn't make for a fun ride, though. G-forces shoved her down, pressing her head back too hard for her neck to overcome. She went limp, letting her body be pinned flat against the deck plate. No point in trying to fight that kind of pressure.

She got a read on the nearby ships. Two PAC vessels docked at the orbital elevator and in good order. They could be on her tail in ten minutes. She wished she could take the time to disable them, but they were far enough away that it was a bad risk.

Once she got out of Earth's atmosphere, she burned hard on a trajectory to take her behind the moon. The PAC would have a harder time finding her with a moon between them. She also started dumping clasiratate, which would eradicate their trail within seconds. Only direct satellite surveillance would see them, and she happened to know just where those satellites were.

Anxiously, she checked for enemy combatants, but she detected no close pursuit. Prelin's ass. They might have pulled it off.

She pulled off the goggles and rubbed her face, even as she took a look at her new ship. The outer hull might be pockmarked with burns, but she saw no signs of internal damage.

Flying VR was all well and good, but she'd do a better job the old-fashioned way. The others followed her up to the cockpit, and Hawk was the first to speak when they got there. He punched a fist in the air. "Whoo! Now that's an escape! Another one for the storybooks."

Peregrine smirked.

"We're not clear yet," Fallon reminded him.

Raptor turned to Kellis. The engineer looked pale and shell-shocked. "Are you okay?"

She licked her lips. "You tell me. Are we safe?" Her wide eyes sought Fallon.

Fallon squinted at the console's readout, ensuring there was still nothing to worry about. Well, there *were* those two ships closing in, and those were definitely going to become a problem. She could outrun them in the short term, but those large vessels would eventually overtake her when she had to stop to refuel. A definite logistics issue. But her team wasn't in danger at the moment, and she had other things to deal with in the meantime.

"Reasonably. For the moment." Fallon looked from Kellis to Raptor. "What happened in there?"

Raptor ran a hand over his cheek. "They were waiting for us. No doubt they knew we would come to one PAC base or another. They must have booby-trapped all of them. I got *in* just fine. But after I downloaded what I needed, I got hit with a bunch of stickers. They're the data equivalent of grappling hooks. Every one of them provided a tether from the PAC to my equipment."

"So, what, you're infected? Do we need to jettison anything?" Fallon didn't like the idea of the PAC having even a glimpse of where they might be. Well, sure, they'd just blown the last three months of anonymity all to hell, but as long as the PAC didn't have any hooks in them, they could get that back.

Raptor rubbed at his jaw. "No. I had to lose the gear. A shame. That was good stuff and will be hard to replace. But I'd prepared for that, and was able to strip and extract only the data chip. As of right now, I have no way of reading it, but once I get the right equipment, I'll be able to decrypt it. They'll know I got away with information, but they won't know what."

So good news and bad news, then. No, mostly good news. They'd gotten the data. Now she just needed to make sure she didn't let those big PAC ships overtake them. She checked them again, saw them closing at a slow and steady rate. Yep, that was the PAC method, all around. Not flashy, no unnecessary risks, but inexorable, like a spider eyeing the bug in its web.

"I wouldn't have gotten out of there if not for Kellis," Raptor said.

They all looked at the engineer, who only now seemed to be shaking off the experience, blinking and looking around at the ship as if she'd just noticed it.

"Oh?" Hawk asked.

"We got pinned down. No hope to get out. She knew exactly where the bulkhead was weak enough to slice through with a laser-cutter, while skillfully *not* frying us crispy on our way through. She was great." Raptor smiled at Kellis, who smiled weakly back.

"I didn't do much. You fought those people off." Kellis smoothed her hands over her forearms.

"You didn't panic though—you were completely calm and focused. That's a big deal." He moved closer to pat her shoulder. "We owe you a lot."

"I've always said we needed a mech," Hawk said with a wink. He swung his arms over his head and stretched. Fallon could sympathize with him. A sudden abatement to the excitement left them all with an overabundance of adrenaline. There was no way to just turn it off, and no way to spend the excess. She felt a little jumpy too.

"Where are we going now?" Kellis asked.

Fallon glanced at the controls and got a jolt of surprise. Now that was interesting. But she only said, "Away from here, as fast as we can manage. We need to get Blackout off our trail. But first we need to deal with what's on the other side of the moon."

She didn't mention what she'd seen because she wanted to be completely sure, but as they got closer she knew. She felt highly exasperated even as she experienced a rush of fondness. She fed the image onto a larger, wall-mounted panel for the others to see.

"Looks like someone wants to rescue us."

"The *Onari*!" Kellis exclaimed as they all stared at the ship hiding on the dark side of the moon. "It was supposed to be long gone by now."

Fallon felt a wry smile twisting her lips. "I'm guessing Jerin felt too protective of you, and maybe us as well, to leave as she was supposed to. That woman." She shook her head. She'd underestimated Jerin's gumption, and she wouldn't do so again.

The *Onari* was now in danger. If anyone suspected its association with Avian Unit, everyone on board could be in serious trouble.

Fallon opened a communications channel. "*Outlaw* to *Onari*."

Demitri Belinsky's crisp and certain voice replied immediately. "*Onari* here. Do you need assistance, *Outlaw*?"

"No, you need to get your asses out of here *now*. Ships are on their way. What do you think you're doing?"

"Jerin wanted to wait around a little while, just to be sure you all didn't need help. Said to tell you she expects to get her mech back in good shape. We parked here so the PAC wouldn't be able to see us on sensors."

"Which is exactly why I came here, and also why you're now in danger of being associated with us. There are plenty of satellites up here and if you crossed one, they'll know you were in the area." Fallon calculated the ETA of the PAC ships. Fifteen minutes at most. The *Onari* and the *Outlaw* needed to get out of there.

"I was ducking pirates and mercenaries years before I even started working on a hospi-ship, *Outlaw*. I know how to avoid a satellite." Demitri's voice was smug.

In spite of the situation, that made her smile. An idea occurred to Fallon and she tried to ignore it. But the opportunity was here, so why not take it?

"*Onari*, prepare for emergency quick-dock. Can your pilot do it?"

Belinsky's voice snapped back, "Affirmative. Establishing docking attitude."

Fallon ignored the surprised and irate sounds of the people behind her. They only had one shot at this. She positioned the *Outlaw*, as she'd named it on the fly, backward. She precisely matched the *Onari*'s drift and rotation. She cut the engines and coasted, using only auxiliary positioning thrusters to maintain alignment. She was moving too fast, and it would be a hard linkup, but it would be bang on, dammit. It would be perfect. They didn't have time to do it any slower if they wanted to stay out of those ships' visual range. She could fool sensors but she couldn't fool eyeballs.

"Brace for impact," she announced to both her crew and the *Onari*. "Linkup in five...four...three...two...*link*." The *Outlaw* slammed into the *Onari* with bruising force. But she'd held it true, without causing damage to either ship.

She executed the boarding sequence in record time. Before leaving her post, she announced, "Pressurizing. All *Outlaw* crew evacuating immediately." She grabbed her VR controls and took off at a run.

By now, her team had to know what she planned, and they followed on her heels. Raptor had taken charge of Kellis, which freed Fallon from worrying about the engineer's safety or state of mind. They flung themselves through the airlock and onto the *Onari*. Fallon dropped to the floor, putting on her VR goggles.

Hawk ushered everyone through, then closed the hatch.

"Depressurizing," she announced.

Her hands melded with the controller, her fingers moving faster than her brain. She undocked the ships and said, "Tell Demitri to get us out of here," as she moved the *Outlaw* to a safe distance.

She had no idea what happened around her body, except for the hardness of the deck plate digging into her tailbone. She saw only the *Outlaw*'s controls as she aligned everything she needed to do. Timing would be critical.

She hoped the *Onari* had escaped notice. She could see it

moving away from the *Outlaw*, which felt odd, considering her actual body was on the *Onari*. She had the bizarre sensation of being in two places at once. To fight it, she divorced herself from her body and focused hard on the *Outlaw*.

When she estimated the PAC ships to be only a minute out, she vented all of the *Outlaw*'s exhaust. To their pursuers, it would look like a compressor failure. Damage from their sudden takeoff from Earth's atmosphere. She set a course out of the solar system, not too fast for a damaged ship, but fast enough to keep the PAC pilots on their toes. She clipped past the sun just outside of tolerance for heat and radiation, watching her hull temperature rise and feeling glad she wasn't inside the ship. Then she vented all of the ship's irradiated oxygen and blasted it with superheated thruster exhaust—a highly nonregulation procedure that pleased her enormously—leaving a fireball in the *Outlaw*'s wake. If she were lucky, she'd have prompted a solar flare. She jumped the engines to maximum, followed the sun around to its other side, and cut the engines. Waiting.

She no longer had any awareness of her body or the *Onari*. Every exhale she made was into the *Outlaw*, never mind that it didn't have life support anymore. All she saw was what the *Outlaw* saw. Minutes ticked by. Lots of minutes. An hour. No pursuit. She checked the sensors, and no ships were in her immediate vicinity, unless they were playing possum like she was.

Either she'd toasted the other ships, or they were investigating the supposed destruction of her ship. If she'd managed a solar flare, it would have obliterated any physical evidence, making a more believable impression of a lost ship.

She set a course away from the solar system. She'd keep watching, but so far, she didn't see any sign of pursuit.

She needed to get the *Outlaw* someplace that they could retrieve it. Or at the very least hide it. No sense in mocking up a fiery death only to have the ship turn up later. She checked her charts, then checked in with her body.

"Hawk, you out there?"

"Right here." His voice came from just behind her ear.

"I'm headed toward Gamma Oridien. Who do you know who has a shipyard where our little darling can be hidden away? Someone you trust."

She heard him making some hard-thinking noises in his throat. "Nothing like that within range. You'd need to refuel and I'm guessing that's not an option."

"No. Raptor's signal masking program is good, but that much distance would put it out of range and if someone happened by the *Outlaw*, they might realize it was unpiloted. Besides, that would be too long for me to VR fly it. I need something closer."

More rumbling noises. "I do know a scrapyard where something like that would go unnoticed, with a little disguising."

"Where?"

He gave her the coordinates off the top of his head, so either he knew that scrapyard well or he just always had his contacts memorized. Either way, Fallon was impressed. She set a course.

"More than two days out," she said. "I'm going to need some help."

THE NEXT DAYS were a blur for Fallon. She didn't take off the VR goggles once. She chewed what others put in her mouth. She only let go of the controls long enough for someone to guide her to the necessary, where she did what she needed to do blindly.

She didn't sleep. The hours wore on, and she constantly monitored telemetry readouts and closed the distance between the ship and the scrapyard. The *Outlaw* had autopilot, but her plan depended on it not being detected.

The constant vigilance was exhausting. The two parts of herself pulled ever farther apart. The *Onari*, she knew, flew at a much slower rate back in the general direction of Dragonfire

Station, although on a much different path than it had taken on its way to Earth.

When Fallon finally docked her *Outlaw* at the scrapyard with automated messaging from Hawk to his contact, she sagged with relief. She pulled the goggles, which seemed to have melded with her face, over her head. And breathed.

Hawk watched her, all traces of his usual humor wiped clean. "You okay?" His blue eyes shone with worry, rather than their usual cherubic humor.

"I've been worse. I think. But I feel like all kinds of ass." She rubbed her hands over her face, blinking rapidly. Her eyes teared, adjusting to the brightness of her quarters. Her skin, where the goggles had been, felt raw.

"What can I do for you?" Hawk asked.

"A shower. I stink." She wished it could be a hot, steamy water shower, but the *Onari*'s sonic showers ought to do.

"You got it." He clamped an arm around her and guided her to the necessary. Efficiently, he stripped her out of her clothes so that she was bare of everything but the silver bracelet on her wrist and the tattoo on her stomach.

She considered telling him she could manage on her own, but it was so much easier to just exist as a passive lump of exhaustion and let him do all the work. So she did. He helped her shower with all the tender care of a parent. Then he wrapped her up in a robe and carried her to bed. A familiar-looking bed. The one from the quarters she'd previously used. Funny. She hadn't expected to see this place again. It felt like an odd step backward.

"Want some food?" he asked.

"Nah. Just sleep. Lots of sleep." She curled into the pillow.

"Want me to stay, or leave?"

She pried her eyes open. "Is it nighttime?"

"No."

She wasn't even sure it mattered. "Stay, please." After days of hypervigilance and VR burning into her brain, she felt both raw and isolated.

"You got it." He lay down on the bed, facing her.

She opened her eyes one last time. "Thanks."

"Don't worry about it. You've done the same thing for me."

She remembered the first time she'd met him, as far as her memory was concerned. He'd had a big slash in him and she'd sat up with him most of the night. There was no keeping The Machine down, though. He'd rallied in no time. She tried to answer him, but her tongue was too heavy, and the bed was pulling her in.

AFTER A SOLID FOURTEEN hours of sleep, Fallon dragged herself out of bed and dressed. It took some effort to correct her hair's straight-up-on-top-of-the-head attitude, but she managed to complete the maneuver successfully.

A good rest had cured her strain. Now she could use a good meal. Hawk had left at some point, but she'd expected that.

She felt strange, walking the decks of the *Onari* again. It was familiar, but in an odd way, as if she'd taken a step back in time. She'd assumed that once she stepped off the ship for Earth, she wouldn't see it again for a very long time.

The menuboard in the bar offered blistercakes and fried orritch eggs. So she ordered those, some lemon tea, and a cup of Bennite stew. Just in case. She didn't mind having both breakfast and dinner for lunch. She had some catching up to do.

WITH HER BELLY FULL and her energy returned, Fallon had a duty to attend to. When she called Kellis, she found that the engineer had taken the day off, but was happy to receive Fallon in her quarters. That suited Fallon just fine. She hadn't worked out exactly what to say to the woman who had been pivotal in getting Raptor out of the PAC base with all of his original parts intact. That was a big debt to owe.

Kellis wore a concerned expression when the door to her quarters swished open. As Fallon stepped in, Kellis asked, "How are you feeling?"

"Back to normal. No worries." She hesitated. "Actually, that's not a hundred percent true. The truth is, I feel awkward. I don't know how I've handled assets in the past, but I feel like I owe you something before I go, and I have no idea how to repay that debt."

Kellis looked as awkward as Fallon felt. "Oh. Well, I didn't actually volunteer to help you. I kind of demanded it. I was actually feeling like I owed you something for letting me tag along." An impish grin brightened her features. "It was a heck of an adventure. Not something most people ever see."

Fallon's discomfort eased. "I suppose that's true. When you put it that way, maybe we should charge some sort of admission price." She chuckled at the idea. "Really, though, I wanted to thank you for your help. Both for the devices you helped Peregrine make and the help on the base. You were remarkably courageous to take it all on."

Kellis shrugged away the compliment. "Not really. That was nothing compared to living on Atalus. I was in the pilot's chair, having chosen to be on that base. I mean, sure, I was terrified, but I wasn't just a helpless victim. I was glad to be able to do something useful."

"Even though you still have no idea what's going on?" Fallon asked, impressed.

"I have some theories. But yes, I was glad to score one for the good guys."

The good guys. *That depends on who you ask*, Fallon thought. Everyone always thought they were the good ones.

"Well," Fallon said, "if there's anything we can do for you, let us know."

"Whenever you're done doing what it is you need to do, will you look me up? I don't want to leave the *Onari*, at least not yet, but..." Kellis trailed off. "I just have this feeling that I should do more, you know?"

Well, that was something they could revisit in the future, assuming Fallon and her partners didn't get themselves killed. "Yeah. I do know, actually. And I think you could, too. So we'll talk. Another day."

Kellis nodded, satisfied. "Another day."

"For now, I think I'll go give Dr. Yomalu a surprise knife-throwing lesson. I overheard in the bar that he nearly brained himself."

Kellis laughed. "I hadn't heard that yet."

"I'd better intervene before he tries again and succeeds."

"Sounds like it. Thank you for stopping by. And for what you said." Kellis smiled. She was an odd mix of strength and vulnerability.

"Thank *you*." Fallon loaded as much sincerity as she could fit into two words. "I'll be in touch."

As she walked away from Kellis' quarters, Fallon felt paradoxically unburdened by her promise. She tried not to think too far ahead, but she couldn't help but feel a twinge of hope for the future.

FALLON CHECKED Kellis off her mental to-do list. Before she caught up with the clumsy Dr. Yomalu, she needed to check in with Raptor, to see if he had any updates for her. It was probably too early to hope that he'd have critical data already, but she at least wanted his initial impressions.

She found him in his quarters. When he saw her, he smiled, and she was reminded of how good-looking he was.

"You look way better than the warmed-over mess you were when I last saw you." He stepped back to let her in.

"Thanks," she said sourly. "Hello to you too."

He grinned. "Good job with that ship. Not many could have remote flown like our Fury did."

She was surprised to find she didn't mind the code name so much anymore. It wasn't really a code name. It was more of a pet name, assigned by family. "Thanks, but I'd just as soon not do it again," she admitted, settling herself on the floor in front of his couch. "Any updates? Anything I should know?"

He hesitated, which immediately put her on alert.

"What?"

He opened his mouth, then closed it. Picked at a fingernail. "Okay, I'm not sure exactly how to go about this. I had two data chips I was able to save. One, I can't look at until I get some more equipment. The other, I managed to put something together with a combination of my equipment, some *Onari* parts, and something I got from Peregrine."

"And?"

"I don't know how you're going to take this, so I'm just going to say it. I found some data on your past. Your first life."

The news struck her hard, like an invisible blow. She blinked twice. "Tell me."

"Your birth name was Kiyoko Kato. You grew up in a variety of places because your family moved around a lot. You have parents, Yumi and Hiro, and a brother, Kano."

"Have?" she asked.

"Yes. They're all on Earth. Alive and well."

That took the air out of her for a moment. She'd unknowingly been *so close* to a piece of her past. She'd been on Earth, with answers right under her nose. What a missed opportunity.

His face told her that there was more.

"What?" she demanded.

"Your parents are PAC officers. They actually work at the Tokyo base."

She stayed quiet for a long time thinking that through. She saw Raptor's sympathy, which she didn't want. She didn't need anyone's sympathy.

"Positions and titles?" she finally asked.

"Your mother is a commander, diplomatic corps. Your father is a captain. Intelligence."

She set her shoulders. "Do you think that means he knows where I am now? Where I've been?"

"I don't know. He doesn't seem to have any Blackout ties. He seems straight-up PAC intel. So he may very well not know."

"But he started teaching me to fight when I was a toddler, from the sound of it. That doesn't seem like something a desk-sitter would do."

"It doesn't," he agreed. "But it doesn't tell us anything, either. Not really."

"And my brother?"

He said, "A city planner. A stand-up citizen who does a lot of volunteer work."

"At least one of us is just a normal person."

She ran her fingers through her hair. So where did this leave her? She wanted to find out more about her parents. Ideally, she wanted to get back to Earth and see them. Talk to them. She'd been so very close, in the same city. Maybe her parents had even been inside the base when she'd been there. It was infuriatingly frustrating.

Her parents could hold the key to her getting her memories back. But then maybe they were complicit in what was happening to her. An unfortunate conundrum. She couldn't just approach them and risk being captured by Blackout.

She leaned back against the couch, thinking. "Even if the *Outlaw*'s destruction looked completely legit, you know they're still looking for us just in case. And they sure wouldn't expect us to go back to Earth, so there's a certain logic for doing the thing that they think we're not stupid enough to do."

"Maybe." Raptor didn't look entirely convinced.

She didn't let that faze her. "But we can't take the *Outlaw* back to Earth, and it would look highly suspicious for the *Onari* to go back there so soon. So if that's our destination, we'll need a new ride."

He nodded, but didn't say anything.

She found his silence suspicious. "Did you find out anything else?"

"Some pictures. Test scores. Vital statistics sort of stuff, the kind they used to decide whether or not to accept you into the academy."

"I'd like to see whatever you have." She didn't want anyone watching her while she did it though. "Maybe I could take it back to my quarters?"

"Sure. I can copy it onto a chip you can use on your voicecom. Just be sure to lock it down before you use it."

"Right."

"You okay?" He seemed unsure what kind of support to give her.

"Yeah." And she really was. "I just need some time to put that into perspective. Figure out how all that fits into the puzzle, you know? I thought that my family was dead. That maybe Blackout even had something to do with it. Now there's a possibility that they're *part* of Blackout." She shrugged, not wanting to think too hard about that detail right now. "Kiyoko Kato. It's a nice name. I wonder what she was like."

His mouth turned down. "You're still the same you, regardless. Don't let it mess with your head."

"I won't. I just need to figure it out." She sat forward. "Can you bring that chip by when it's ready?"

"Sure. Want to have dinner tonight?"

She wasn't sure she'd be hungry again so soon. "Maybe. I'll let you know."

"Okay."

She started to go, but he followed her to the door. "This is a good thing. We're closer to figuring all this out."

"I know." She'd make sure they did.

———

Looking at pictures of herself as a child felt like looking at another person. Fallon peered at the screen, seeing the familiar face, but not knowing anything about the girl who'd smiled and posed for the image. In several, she simply stared out with a hard look, far too tough and serious for a child her age. Was she just mugging for the camera, or did that say something about her upbringing? Maybe she'd been pushed into a life of intelligence. Or maybe she'd been proud to carry on a family tradition.

And maybe her parents had turned on her. But why would they?

Fallon abandoned the photos and studied her records instead. She'd gotten top marks in all her classes as a child. Not surprising for a future academy student. Also not surprising that she'd begun studying languages early in life. Earth dialects and the PAC standard, as well as languages from other planets. Had her parents encouraged that?

She turned off the screen, pushing away from it. Continuing to look at it would do her no good. She needed more information. More puzzle pieces. She needed to know the right questions to ask to find the answers that would help her unravel everything that had happened to her and her team. Could it all have been because of her? Because of her family? Did they have anything to do with the two moons?

6

Fallon knew she couldn't continue with the *Onari*. She was grateful for the cover it had given her, twice now, and she owed Jerin for that. She owed Kellis, too, of course, and she'd have to settle up with both of them later. But for now the time had come to part ways.

Her team had thought about selling the *Outlaw*, but it was too recognizable to the PAC. Besides, they weren't short on funds, and the ship might prove to be useful at some point. In the meantime, Fallon tasked Hawk with finding them another fast, high-end ship that they could buy on the quiet under a bogus name. Something big this time. Preferably also capable of atmospheric landings.

Instead of grousing about the difficulty of such a tall order, he seemed to appreciate the challenge. In four days, he conjured up a deal. The ship was much larger than the *Outlaw*, and more heavily armed. Both attributes suited Fallon just fine. The ludicrous price tag meant nothing to her, since funds were not a problem. Now they just had to meet up with Hawk's associate so they could collect the ship.

Avian Unit departed the *Onari* via a rusted slag heap of an outpost that Fallon wouldn't normally have set foot on. But Hawk had assured her it would be fine, and that their chartered transportation would arrive within hours. Their goodbyes with their friends on the *Onari* this time were briefer, since they'd so recently been through the process.

Fallon wished she could have taken Kellis with them as a member of their team. Her skills would be highly useful, but long-term protection of an untrained asset was too much of a liability. Maybe once Fallon had cleaned house in Blackout and settled herself at the helm, she could pull Kellis in and fast-track her through training. Kellis was clearly interested.

The transport arrived at the decrepit outpost just as Hawk had promised. Fallon had more than a few choice words for her partner, though, when she saw their ride. There were plenty of freighters, Rescan or not, she'd have no qualms about, but this particular Rescan freighter was of the creatively-attributed-maintenance-checks type.

Hawk promised the scow would deliver them to their new ship, anonymously and without trouble. Which was what they needed. Assuming they survived the voyage, they'd end up at the vessel that she intended to fly right into Blackout's eye. Figuratively speaking, of course.

"Insert maniacal laugh here," she muttered to herself. If she didn't have her sense of humor, then what did she have? She swung her backpack over her shoulder and prepared to step off the crappy little outpost for the even-crappier freighter.

"What?" Peregrine asked.

"Nothing." She stepped onto the Rescan ship, hoping it wasn't as bad on the inside as it looked on the outside.

IN FACT, the freighter's exterior had somehow hidden the acute crappiness of the interior. Hawk gave Fallon a rough pat on the shoulder blade.

"Don't look so glum. Arcy assured me that the engines on this boat are a late design, and properly maintained." Hawk seemed entirely confident about their new surroundings.

"Let's say that's true," Fallon answered. Over her shoulder, she saw that Raptor and Peregrine followed, listening. "What are the odds the hull can stand up to all that power, and won't rip right in two?" She eyed the filthy ship dubiously. She'd seen better-looking derelicts.

"Seriously. Don't worry. Arcy wouldn't risk the life of someone who's brought so many cubics his way." Hawk paused outside a door. "Ah. Here we are. Who's staying with who?"

They had two berths for the four of them. Fallon really didn't care who she roomed with. She shrugged and activated the door with the wall mechanism. Manually. Like a historical figure from Earth's neo-intergalactic period. When the door creaked open, she went in and set her backpack on the top bunk.

Peregrine stepped in behind her and set her gear on the lower bunk, then doubled back and closed the door behind her. "I figure you're the smallest of us, so I'd have the most space if I roomed with you."

"Good thinking." It was as valid a method of choosing a roommate as anything Fallon would have come up with.

Peregrine did a slow turn in place, taking in the small berth. "It's not as dirty as it could be."

True. The bed linens looked fairly clean, and had no apparent odor. She and Peregrine could be a lot worse off.

"We trust Hawk to know what ships we should and shouldn't risk our lives on, right?" Fallon had been going for a joking tone, because of course they did, but she sounded a little more serious than she'd intended.

Peregrine chewed on the inside of her lip, eyeing the plain-metal walls, the bed, and six storage drawers mounted into the interior wall. Which was all the room had to offer. She yanked the drawers open and slammed them closed again, all in quick succession. Pull, bang. Pull, bang. She sighed and sat. "Yeah, we can count on Hawk. On the other hand, the four of us are nothing but cargo on this bucket, and we'll just be whiling away the next two days in cramped quarters." She shrugged. "Whatever." She stretched out on the bed, staring up at the bottom of the top bunk. "We've had it worse."

"At least Raptor has something to do. Maybe he'll discover some more useful data," Fallon suggested.

A noncommittal grunt from Peregrine.

Fallon started looking through the storage compartments as well, though her perusal was slower than Peregrine's had been.

"There are some cards in here..." Fallon trailed off as Peregrine let out a soft snore. She closed the last drawer with a soft click.

Actually, some sleep sounded like a good idea. What else did she have to do? The crew wouldn't appreciate her wandering about.

She climbed up to her bunk and stretched out. As far as comfort went, it wasn't too bad. The hum of the ship's systems was a comforting lull. She closed her eyes.

TWO DAYS OF PLAYING CARDS, sleeping, and eating very subpar meals ended with Avian Unit's delivery from the Rescan slag heap to a comfortable passenger liner. Even better, a *fast* passenger liner. Fallon's heart leaped when she saw it docked to the trade outpost. Made for nothing but speed and comfort, that ride would get them to their destination in a quarter of the time it would have taken the *Onari*.

Thank goodness. Fallon was tired of the long-range travel game. She had questions, and she wanted answers.

After a perfectly pleasant trip, the passenger liner delivered her and her team to a lovely mercenary station. Or free-market station, as the tenants preferred to call it. Fallon had to admire its sleek angles and shiny fittings. Never mind that it was a non-PAC station in unregulated space, and likely to be at least partially funded by smuggling. She liked it, even the name. Dauntless Station. She appreciated the cheek of the entrepreneurs who had worked together to establish this hub of commerce, where the PAC had no authority.

Dauntless didn't have the size of a PAC station like Dragonfire or Blackthorn, but it wasn't too far off. As Fallon stepped out onto the concourse, she basked in the vibrant feel of commerce and life. Dauntless was a place where things happened. Cunning people made lucrative deals, while the less-savvy—or simply unlucky—lost fortunes. She saw people bustling about, much as they would have on the boardwalk of Dragonfire. But these people looked faster, more driven. Both smoother and sharper, with a certain alluring menace. Fallon liked it a lot.

Hawk had already arranged quarters for the team. They'd share again, but this time in a suite with separate sleeping rooms. It wasn't a good idea, he'd warned, not to have someone keeping tabs on you in a place like this.

Fallon didn't feel threatened, though. She'd have been one pathetic excuse for a former security chief if a little mercenary commerce made her nervous. She looked forward to checking out the station, if they ended up spending enough time there to do so. The passenger liner had provided excellent amenities and food, and the station had only slightly less to offer to those with the means to pay for it.

She appreciated the straightforwardness of such transactions. No contracts and no regulations. Just pay and receive. Simple and to the point. She wondered if mercenaries might be wiser than all the rest of them. In comparison, her backstabbing game of intrigue with Blackout seemed like a hopelessly messy endeavor.

Hawk had scheduled a meeting with his contact for the following morning, when the ship's controls would be released to him. Which left Fallon with an evening to explore the station.

Peregrine had no interest in going out. She'd holed herself up in her room with a holo-vid projector and a pile of room service. Hawk had some inquiries to make, he said, and then headed for the door.

"What about the buddy system, making sure you have backup?" Fallon demanded.

He made a dismissive gesture. "I know who's who here. You don't. Different thing." And off he went.

Which left Raptor. She doubted he'd want to go explore the station. He'd been buried in the stolen data ever since he'd gotten it. No harm in asking, though. He had to eat sometime, right?

"Sure," he surprised her by answering. "Didn't think you'd want to go with me."

"Why do you say that?"

He arched a knowing eyebrow at her. "I've had the feeling you've been avoiding being alone with me since we talked about our former relationship."

"That's not true."

He just kept looking at her.

"Okay, it's not true *exactly*. Yes, I'd prefer to avoid complicating things, but I'm not uncomfortable with you."

He grinned. "Good. I'm not uncomfortable with you, either." He indicated the door. "After you."

The more Fallon saw of Dauntless Station, the more she liked it. It was both rougher and sleeker than Dragonfire. Rougher in that it didn't have so many security precautions, so many redundant fail-safes, which the PAC required. But Dauntless was sleeker because it wasn't hemmed in by those requirements. Nonregulation stairways and lifts were designed in an open-air way that provided a bit of a thrill. Fallon felt downright exposed in a lift with walls that only rose to chest height—and she liked it.

They chose to eat at a restaurant with a dining area that spilled out into the commons. They sat next to a low wall, which allowed them to see the level below them as well as the foot traffic as it passed. Fallon greatly enjoyed the people-watching, and the conversation between her and Raptor lagged accordingly. In a comfortable way.

She caught him smiling at her. Looking, perhaps, a bit fond. "What?"

"I'd forgotten how much you like these places."

"Don't you like them?" How could he not?

"Sure," he agreed. "I do. But you light up like a kid who just saw her birthday cake."

"How many of these have we visited together? You never mentioned one before."

There were a lot of stories she still hadn't heard. He and the others had told her many anecdotes about their school and training days, as well as their missions. But she'd heard little of the smaller, more personal stuff.

"Oh, I don't know. A few. Not many are as nice as this one though." He cut a slice of his roasted fowl and put it in his mouth.

"For work?"

"Yeah." He paused to swallow. "Except once, when we were looking for a promotion gift for Hawk."

"What did we end up with?"

Raptor looked abashed. "Well, Hawk doesn't need or want much in terms of possessions. So we ended up setting him up with a couple of—"

She followed his line of thought and cut him off. She already knew Hawk's favorite non-work-related pastime. "Yeah, I gotcha. Anyway."

Raptor smiled. "Anyway." His eyes hitched to the right and she felt him become more vigilant.

She leaned in. "What?"

He angled himself closer to her over the table, speaking in a low voice. "There's a Rescan and a human, both male. They've come by here three times now. Maybe it's paranoia, but there's no reason for them to do that. They're not carrying anything and they're just walking from one part of the boardwalk to another."

She kept her eyes on him instead of turning to look. "What are you thinking?"

"Nothing. Nothing really. Just, we should keep an eye out. And maybe finish eating so we can move on."

"Right." She'd nearly finished, anyway. She scarfed the rest of her sandwich and pasta salad. She'd hoped to order dessert, but she could always have that delivered to the room later. She enjoyed the spoils of living on stolen Blackout money. Spending Blackout's cubics felt pretty good.

"Let's take a walk along the shops, see if they follow us," Raptor murmured, putting his arm around her waist as if whispering sweet things in her ear.

She gave him a moderately dippy look, as if swept away by his romance. "All right."

She liked the shops. An all-out arms merchant had some hardcore artillery displayed right there on the boardwalk. He didn't exhibit anything that would be illegal in the PAC zone, but Fallon was pretty sure that such things existed out of sight. She'd have liked the chance to peruse the items for sale, but there was no reason to let their possible pursuers know that they were the kind of people who had an interest in heavy weaponry.

She leaned into Raptor. "They're three shops down, behind a clothing rack. You think they're just tagging us because we're human?" Humans tended to be softer targets than other species, given their dependence on the PAC. That made them more prone to random attacks in neutral territory.

"Maybe." He kissed the top of her head and they strolled onward.

"Hey, spender." A Trallian smiled up at Raptor. Clearly he

meant to flatter Raptor, calling him a spender—a person of influence and means. "Buy a necklace for your lady?"

The merchant stepped aside, revealing a display of exquisite carved-bead necklaces.

"Those are gorgeous." Fallon moved closer to examine them.

The Trallian beamed at her. At a dozen or so centimeters shorter than her, he was an example of a tall member of his species. His thick mottled-brown skin reminded her somewhat of tree bark. His eyes and smile were big, and she found the fellow quite adorable. Which probably meant that someone nearby was about to bash her on the back of the head and pick her carcass clean. Fallon was no fool. But Raptor had her covered, so she wasn't worried. And perhaps the Trallian really was just a genuine craftsperson. Sometimes they were.

"I like this one." She plucked a necklace from a display and ran her finger over it. Smooth, polished blue and black beads alternated around the strand. At the front of the necklace, a half dozen bird charms dangled with tiny articulated wings that made them look as if they were in flight. How he managed to do that with stone, she had no idea.

"You have excellent taste," the merchant murmured approvingly. "That's the best of them all. Put it on, see what you think." He angled a mirror toward her.

She was supposed to play tourist, so she would. She fastened the necklace and admired it in the mirror, giving herself a slight shake to make the wings quiver. "It's amazing." She glanced toward Raptor. "What do you think?"

Raptor's game smile faltered when he examined the jewelry, but only for a second. It came right back. "Incredible artistry. How much?"

They engaged in a hearty battle of haggling, and ended up with a fair price for both sides. Fallon transferred the funds via the infoboard the merchant provided, and after a touch more praise for his skill, they moved on.

They stopped to admire some clothing, and then some hand-etched saucers and cups, but it was only a pretense for watching their pursuers. And they were definitely pursuers. Not terrible at doing so, but still easily recognizable to Fallon and Raptor.

"That's enough," Raptor finally said. "I don't like this. Let's get back to our room."

Once they arrived, they sent a message to Hawk, warning him. Peregrine had already retired to her bedroom, which left Raptor and Fallon alone in the living area.

She settled on a low settee and ran her fingers over her new jewelry. "Tell me about the necklace."

He stiffened, pacing to the minibar and filling a glass with water. Fallon had found it amusingly apropos, in a decadent sort of way, that the suite had a minibar and not a proper kitchenette.

Raptor took a long drink of water, and she got the feeling he was stalling. Finally he put the glass down and leaned back against the bar. "I bought you a necklace on a mission once. It looked nothing like the one you're wearing. But it reminded me."

Questions jumped to her lips, but she fought them back. She stayed silent, letting him tell the story his way.

He grabbed a straight-backed chair and dragged it over, planting it backward and straddling it to face her. "I probably should have told you about this sooner. Or maybe not. It just seemed like it would complicate things, and you seemed… complicated already." He took a breath. "So it was a Blackout job, a job gone wrong. Our intel turned out to be way off base. We lost assets, as well as a member from another unit. Some local kids got in the way and we lost them too. Then you got hit with shrapnel. The big, jagged, flay-you-wide-open kind. I got you to our hideout, pieced you back together, and Hawk and Peregrine hadn't returned. It was one of the worst missions we ever went on."

She toyed absently with the necklace, wondering what the other one had looked like. She also wondered why she hadn't heard this story before. They'd been going chronologically, so maybe they just hadn't gotten to it yet. Or maybe there was a reason Raptor hadn't wanted to share this one.

"That necklace was made of shells. A local design. I bought it because the kid was cute, and obviously hungry. You really liked it. It was around your neck when the shrapnel hit you, and got so caked with blood I couldn't even tell it was shell by the time I got you stabilized."

Dead, starving children, a split unit, and the near death of a partner. Yep, sounded awfully bad.

"I couldn't get your heart in rhythm, see. It kept going out. I'd think I had it, and then no. Eventually I started to think I was going to lose you. When I finally got you out of danger, and you woke up, we were both riding the adrenaline. Since it felt like it might be the end, and all." He studied her, watching for her reaction.

"I see. So what you're saying is that we reacted in a pretty human way to being thrown together into a desperate situation?"

"That's a fair assessment." He rested his chin on the backs of his hands, and leaned forward against the chair.

Should she even care about this? Or did it indeed complicate things, like he seemed to be worried about? *She* didn't feel like it did. Some things are just to be expected in extreme circumstances. But if it had meant something to him, then she didn't want to completely brush it aside. The necklace had seemed to ignite some deep feelings.

"Did I used to be all hysterical about sex, or something? Like it had to mean something?" Yeah, not what she'd meant to say. She'd been aiming for something more noncommittal.

He smirked. "No."

"So, are you? All hysterical about it?"

"Not particularly."

"Fine. Then it happened. I'm not worried about it."

He didn't seem relieved. "Even if it was more than once?"

"What, you mean like regularly?" That ran counter to what she'd been led to believe. "I thought that kind of thing was a bad idea, part of the same unit, special bond of four, blah blah blah."

He winced. "Not regularly. Just, you know, every now and again. During the worst times. Not an ongoing thing, or something that would compromise our unit."

She tried really, really hard to think of why she might give a damn. But she didn't remember it, so this more recent intimate relationship with Raptor wasn't more relevant than the older one. She even understood why he'd think it might complicate things for her, but it didn't. Maybe it would have, before, but she'd since been married to a woman whose culture considered monogamy an unnatural thing. So maybe she was more open-minded now?

She quirked a shoulder. "Okay, so fine. Thanks for telling me, I guess?"

"You're welcome, I guess?" He looked as perplexed as she felt.

She barked out a laugh and he relaxed, laughing with her.

She shook her head, smiling. "I'm going to bed. You'll wait up for Hawk?"

"Yep. Was planning on it." He moved to take her place on the settee, arranging a holo-vid projector.

"What, no data while you wait?" she asked.

"My eyes need a break. I've been making myself blind."

Guilt flooded her. She should have realized he'd been pushing himself too hard. She remembered remote piloting the *Outlaw* and how Hawk had taken care of her. She determined to take better care of Raptor.

"Good night," she said softly.

"Night." He fiddled with the projector, not watching her go.

FALLON, Peregrine, and Raptor ordered breakfast into their room. As scheduled, Hawk went to seal the deal with his pal "Arcy."

Fallon had half a mind to meet this fellow for herself, but that was Hawk's territory.

Before going, he instructed them to be waiting for him at the docking bay. Shortly afterward, Fallon, Raptor, and Peregrine gathered their things and left the suite. Almost immediately, Fallon had a bad feeling. Like a weight on the back of her mind. A shadow that wouldn't move off.

A glance told her that her teammates felt it too. A certain awareness wafted off them, even though their posture and gait didn't change. It was just something Fallon could sense. The three of them spread out slightly as they walked down the corridor, Peregrine taking the front position and Raptor and Fallon following, forming a roughly triangular shape.

Fallon went into hypervigilant mode, scanning for anything out of place, any threats, anything suspicious. There weren't enough people out for that time of day, that was for sure. The corridors were just too quiet.

A shame they were so loaded with gear. Each of them carried a heavy backpack, along with a bag or two. At least Hawk had taken several bags with him, so they weren't as encumbered as they could have been. Perhaps someone was just after their gear. Looking for a grab-and-dash.

But the four figures that leaped around a junction at them obviously didn't intend to just snatch what they could and run away. They clearly meant to take it all. Peregrine was at a disadvantage, standing at the front and weighed down by two large bags. Fallon tried to get to her, but a hooded figure blocked her, moving in to attack.

Fallon ducked the first punch, pivoting around the guy so that her front was against his back, with her knees pressed into the backs of his so that he was off-balance. She wrapped her arms around him and forced him to the ground. He struggled hard, and was stronger than her, but she had leverage and balance. She whipped a zip-cuff out of her pocket and bound his hands, then his ankles.

She turned to find Raptor standing over one guy as another advanced on him. Peregrine landed a hit to her opponent's face, staggering him. She pushed her advantage, taking him to the ground. Fallon flanked the guy about to mix up with Raptor, but the dude broke and ran back the way she and her team had come.

She shrugged at Raptor, not caring if he got away. They'd been after the gear, most likely. Perhaps they'd been hoping Fallon and the others had physical currency on them to keep it untraceable. Their objective didn't matter, though. They weren't pros and had posed no real threat. Only a major inconvenience.

Fallon zip-cuffed the other two, making sure they couldn't get very far.

"We need to get Hawk to the dock so we can depart immediately. Station security will arrive before long, and we don't want to be here to answer questions." Fallon frowned at the three would-be thieves on the floor. Hopefully security would ban them from the station, ensuring that other, less prepared travelers wouldn't have to deal with them. But a mercenary station might not work that way.

Fallon activated her comport. It wasn't polite to use it out in public like this, but no one else was around. "Hawk. We'll be at the meet point in two minutes. We need to leave without delay."

They'd just arrived at the docking bay when Hawk replied. "Just finished up and got the control codes for the ship. I'll be there in three minutes."

Time ticked by excruciatingly slowly as they waited for Hawk to arrive. Station security might already have responded, if the scuffle had occurred on a security feed. Or if someone had reported the zip-cuffed people.

Finally Hawk rounded the corner, carrying several bags but somehow managing not to look overburdened. He punched in the code, which released the airlock door, and then gestured the others through.

Fallon felt better as soon as she stepped off Dauntless Station. Her mood improved further when the airlock door closed and pressurized behind her, even as she ran for the pilot's chair. The others took up posts on the bridge, but she barely noticed them.

She executed a textbook departure, complete with all the proper permissions and responses. Finally, she maneuvered the ship away. Only then did she take the time to admire her new ride's burly design and powerful propulsion. Skimming her hand over the weapons array, she hummed pleasantly as she locked in their coordinates and fired the main engines.

She sighed as Dauntless Station fell farther and farther behind them.

"So what happened to you three?" Hawk asked.

"We got jumped," Peregrine said. "Amateurs. But they seemed to know we'd be coming out this morning. Guessing they got some tip about our departure."

Hawk frowned, rubbing his beard, which made a rough, scritchy sort of sound. "I'll tell Arcy about that. He'll handle it from his side. That kind of thing's bad for his business."

"How do you know he didn't have some part of it?" Raptor asked.

Hawk made a snorty, scoffing sound. "Not something amateur like that. If Arcy wanted to put us down, he'd get the money for the ship, then do his best to make us dead, quietly and cleanly. Then he'd get to keep the ship, whatever gear we had, and the cubics too."

"That might have sounded reassuring in your head," Raptor told him, "but it doesn't make me feel better about your pal Arcy."

Hawk gave him a wry look. "We don't have anything to worry about. Arcy and I have an understanding. We each know things about the other. Things that would end us, fast. Mutually assured destruction is the ideal means of ensuring peace. It's just good business."

"Right." Peregrine frowned at Hawk.

He glared right back at her. "It's light-years better than relying on a person's sense of loyalty. Or worse, their *morality*." He spat out the word like it was filthy, and Fallon got another glimpse into what must be a rough personal history.

He was probably right, too, but Fallon didn't want to think too hard about that just then. "I've laid in a course for Earth. Unless there's somewhere we should go first."

She looked from one face to another, giving them an opportunity to suggest that finding her parents wasn't their highest priority. She wasn't entirely sure that it should be. But it was possible she might get some answers that would help in their current situation, especially considering that her father was a PAC intelligence officer, and she hadn't come up with any better ideas.

She settled her gaze on Raptor. "Have you uncovered any new data? Anything that would supersede tracking down my parents?"

Raptor shook his head. "Nothing useful yet. I'll keep at it, but while I'm working through it, we can either go to Earth, or hijack more data nodes. That would give us more data to put into the pile."

Which he was already overburdened with. The rest of them needed something to do in the meantime.

"Okay," Fallon decided. "Back to Earth."

She was glad to confront her past sooner rather than later. She really wasn't much of a procrastinator. A thought occurred to her. "Oh, and Hawk?"

He raised an eyebrow at her.

"Thanks for buying me such a pretty ship. I'm going to have fun with this one."

Fallon named her new ship the *Nefarious*. The others expressed skepticism about the name, but the way she figured it, she'd spent her whole life do-gooding. Well, sometimes maybe bad-doing in the name of do-gooding, but at the time, those had been value judgments she'd been willing to let others make. Apparently.

Now she intended to make those decisions personally. Which, perhaps, pushed her into nefarious territory. She kind of hoped so, anyway.

She fell for the *Nefarious* in a big way. She'd liked the *Outlaw*, but she'd barely had a chance to get to know it in person. The *Nefarious* was something else altogether. She ran her fingers over every console, every panel. She crawled through the maintenance conduits. She studied every schematic. She knew the *Nefarious* in the way that only a pilot could, a relationship that formed a near symbiosis. This was *her* ship.

She'd loved keeping Dragonfire Station secure, and knowing that the people there had confidence in their safety. She'd been good at that. She liked going on missions, too, engaging in a fight-or-flight scenario of life and death. That made her blood sing, made her feel more alive than she'd known she could feel. But piloting a ship like this woke something up inside her. Something that she'd only just rediscovered.

The ship had autopilot, and each of her teammates could handle basic operations. Over the following days, she had time to eat, sleep, and find time for some recreation. Which usually involved either physical activity or looking after the ship. Even better if it was both at the same time.

Aware that she might otherwise be deemed boring by her teammates, she occasionally engaged in a match of Two-ten-jack or some other card game. Her heart wasn't in it though. She felt better when the white noise of physical activity gave her a break from thinking. Sitting still and playing cards did not have the same effect.

Raptor had gotten an address for her parents. Yumi and Hiro

Kato. Their daughter Kiyoko, aka Emiko, aka Emé, aka Fallon, aka Fury, was coming home. They didn't know that yet, and Fallon could only hope it would be a pleasant reunion.

That depended entirely on what they knew of her life now, and how they felt about it. And, of course, whether or not they were involved with Blackout's attempt to ice Avian Unit. Either way, she and her team would learn more about what they were dealing with. Fallon hoped her parents would prove to be allies, but she had to prepare for the possibility that they could be anything but. Most of all, she hoped they could provide a key to her memory.

She wondered if Brak had made any progress with the implant she'd described. Fallon found it impressively loyal that Brak would even attempt such a thing. She knew how Brak felt about developing implants related to memory. Sure, Brak was trying to address the issue of lost memory rather than augmenting existing memory, but technology, once invented, had a way of gaining a life of its own and finding new applications. Even Fallon knew that.

She'd have to leave the morality and risk of such a technology to Brak, though. That was Brak's realm of expertise. Which left Fallon to focus on her own. As she docked at the orbital station above Earth, she felt like she was finally on the verge of getting some real answers. Not only about the state of Blackout, but about who she really was.

Peregrine had given all of them elaborate disguises this time, complete with synthetic skin to alter their facial structures. Fallon had become blonde, green eyed, and just a little chubby. Even her own parents wouldn't recognize her like this.

She'd be able to identify them, though. She'd studied their active files in the PAC database. Pleasant-looking people. Fit, and fairly unremarkable in appearance. Except for the fact that she'd recognized the shape of her own eyes on her mother's face, and her father's chin looked just like her own.

Family ties. But what did they tie her to?

She and her team had discussed numerous ways of approaching her parents, but they always ended up with a containment issue in the event that the Katos didn't turn out to be allies. That left Avian Unit only the option of an in-person visit, with Fallon and Raptor going in and Peregrine and Hawk watching their backs, prepared for an extraction.

"We're sure that coming back to Earth so soon is a good idea, right?" Hawk asked as they waited for the airlock to pressurize so they could board the docking station.

Fallon had no doubts. "Yep. So soon after our last quick escape, they definitely won't be expecting to see us back here again. It's far too stupid a move for us to make."

"Which makes it exactly what we want to do," Raptor agreed, grinning.

The airlock opened.

Hawk's eyes sparkled with humor. "Just checking. Let's go. Blood and bone."

FALLON'S PARENTS lived in a small, freestanding home in a village just outside Tokyo. Easy traveling distance to the PAC base, she noted. But far enough out that they could escape high-rise living.

Which was good and bad, strategically. She and Raptor would have to approach the home from out in the open, but anyone arriving at the house after them would be forced to do the same. If the message they'd intercepted had been legit, then officially Avian Unit was on deep-cover duty and not to be messed with. But combatants would have to recognize them before realizing that. Besides, there might well be private orders countermanding the official ones. There was no reason at all to think they'd encounter any friendlies out in the field.

Fallon was sick to death of what-ifs. She just wanted to get shit done.

She rapped on the door to the modest home. A little too hard, but she wanted to be sure to be heard. She didn't want to stand on their doorstep for longer than necessary.

Her father answered. "Yes?" he asked in Japanese.

She gave him a deep bow, as was proper to give an elder, which he returned politely but briefly, in accordance with her unknown status and identity. "Greetings, Mr. Kato. I hope we can ask the favor of entering your home. We are friends of your daughter."

His polite, open expression dissolved into something far more grim. "Of course." His words became clipped. He moved aside and waved them in.

Inside, her mother glared at them with fury. When the door closed behind them and they all had moved into the tidy, tastefully sparse living space, her mother took a step forward.

"How dare you come to our home. What do you want?" She spoke as if she had fire on her tongue.

"Mother," Fallon said. "It's me." She removed the wig and began pulling the prosthetic skin from her face, careful not to tear it. She'd need to put it back on before leaving.

Her parents' expressions didn't soften. Well, scrap. This didn't bode well.

"How would we know it was you?" her mother asked, still speaking in Japanese. "We haven't seen you in three years. Our daughter might well be dead."

Her father spoke. Unlike her mother's hard anger edged with fear, his eyes flickered with both wariness and hope. "What did I call you when you were a little girl? When I'd tuck you in at night."

Without knowledge of her childhood, this meeting could go south really fast.

"I don't know." She held her hands up, staying her mother's

anger. "Something happened to me and I've lost my memory. These others with me, they're my unit, but my memory is about six months old at this point."

Her parents exchanged a look, then her father stepped forward, studying her face. Was he looking for a birthmark or a scar? She didn't have either of those. Only a tattoo, and that surely wouldn't help identify her to her parents.

Her father struck hard and fast. His hands came down like lightning and she barely had time to throw up a block and shift sideways to deflect the force. She stepped back, getting more room between them, and dropped into a low fighting stance. Without waiting for him to strike again, she did a combination. Light hit to the face, palm strike to the sternum, kick to the knee. Not to injure him, but to throw him off-balance. His attack had put her on the defensive, and she needed to gain the upper hand.

He wasn't going to give it to her. He anticipated her combo: block, block-repel, hit. He caught her in the chest, pushing her another step back.

Of course. He knew how she fought. He'd taught her. That meant he'd fight the same way. She grinned suddenly and dropped to the ground, trapping his leg and flipping him over. He was not much taller than her, which meant she could effectively grapple with him. But she quickly found that the cosmetic weight Peregrine had put on her hindered her too much.

A light strike to his stomach gave her time to jump to her feet, leap back, and launch herself into the air. She tucked her knees into her body hard, one straight into her chest and the other twisted in toward her body, giving her a sideways trajectory. Not too shabby, she thought, with ten pounds of fake jiggle on her. She landed more than a meter away, bouncing on her heels and ready for him to come after her.

But he didn't. His face brightened like a sunrise. "My daughter." He stepped forward and folded her into a fierce embrace.

Apparently, flipping around the living room and trying to kick her father's ass was proof positive of Kato blood. Well, fine then. She didn't mind the hug, although this man was a stranger to her. He obviously knew her, and loved her, and damn if that didn't mean a lot to Fallon. She'd take whatever she could get at this point, and she returned the hug. "Hello, Father."

She lifted her head only to find that her mother had crossed the distance like an assassin, standing nearby to sweep her into a death grip of a hug, scented with lily of the valley.

"Kiyoko-chan." Her mother held her shoulders, moving back just enough to study her face. Then she went all in and cupped Fallon's face, squishing it gently, as a mother would do to a baby's chubby cheeks. "We thought you were dead."

Hawk and Peregrine joined from outside, then removed their disguises, along with Raptor. Fallon removed her extra weight, as well, so that her parents could see what she really looked like. They deserved that after not having seen her in three years.

They all settled on their knees around the low dining table. Her mother had insisted on serving tea. Fallon took a polite sip, as did her teammates, but no one really wanted a hot beverage.

"Why did you think I was dead?" Fallon asked.

"Not just you," her father said. "Your whole unit. We saw the no-interference order. Given how long it had been since we'd seen you, and how strange things have been at intelligence, we thought you might have been eliminated, with your employers not wanting anyone to know about that."

She noted his way of referring to Blackout. "So you're not… employed by the same people?"

He shook his head. "No. I do purely on-the-books classified work. I'm aware of your employers, but that's it. I actively try to avoid any deeper knowledge."

"Why?"

Hiro sighed, looking tired. "It's not like it used to be. In recent years, there's been a closing of ranks. A leadership has emerged. A hard leadership. One that a nine-to-fiver like me doesn't want to get involved with."

"The kind that will either pull you in or take you down, if you're useful," she supplied.

He agreed with a small nod.

Yumi set her teacup down gently. She hadn't been drinking the tea, either. "In my line of work I tend to get wind of things, in an unofficial capacity. When I stopped hearing anything about you a year and a half ago, I knew something was wrong. But we couldn't turn up any information."

At least they would understand why she couldn't explain anything in great detail. They'd know that it was for their own good, as well as her own.

Her father spoke again. "There was a data breach at the base recently. If you were involved, I need to not know about that. But if you were, I hope you got something good. You won't be getting in there again."

"Yeah." Fallon liked the way her father phrased things. "I imagine that would be the case."

"So what can we do for you?" her mother asked. "How can we help?"

Fallon thought about it. Keeping them unaware of things that could get them killed was not conducive to describing her situation. Nor could she ask them to steal information that would surely be traced back to them.

"In these shakeups in the intel division, have you heard any names? Any whispers of who might be responsible? Or of someone who might be an ally?"

Hiro's mouth pursed as he thought. "Admiral Colb is clean, I'm sure of that."

Admiral Colb had sponsored her application to the academy. She'd seen that on the real records Raptor had extracted.

"He might be useful. If we can manage to contact him without endangering him." Fallon liked the idea of Colb being an asset.

Her father nodded. "He and I went to the academy together, and you grew up with him as something of an honorary uncle. He's always been a good friend. You can count on him."

She'd had no idea about Colb. That was certainly useful information. "Anyone else?"

"Whelkin," Yumi said decisively. "I'm sure of him."

"Ross Whelkin?" Raptor hadn't said anything since the introductions, but spoke up now in surprise. "The combat instructor at the academy?"

Her parents both smiled, as adults do to naïve children. "He's not *just* an instructor."

Fallon didn't remember the man, other than what her team had told her, so she didn't experience the surprise that her teammates showed.

"How do you think intelligence knows who their ideal candidates are? We recruit from the inside." Her father cupped his hands around his teacup, but didn't lift it.

Fallon liked the tiny smile on his face. It wasn't smug or anything like that. He simply seemed amused to provide a detail that a team of BlackOps had missed.

She thought she might grow to appreciate her father's sense of humor. If she got the chance. She tried to think of more questions, but there was little more she could ask or say without pushing them into the quicksand of her life.

"I guess we should be going," she said, feeling a deep reluctance. She hadn't learned much personal information, and so far, she hadn't found anything that felt familiar. But the longer she stayed, the more of a risk she posed to her parents. That now eclipsed her desire to know about her past. At least if she protected them, they'd still be around later for her to talk to.

Hiro and Yumi exchanged the look of a couple married so

many years that they can have entire conversations with their eyes.

"Stay the night," Yumi entreated, her eyes anxious. "Please."

Fallon started to refuse, then stopped. This might very well be the last time she spoke to her parents. If she got herself killed, they'd never see their daughter again. Besides that, she'd been gone for three years. They understood the risk, and they deserved one evening with their child.

"How's your security?" she asked.

"Excellent," her father answered, confident.

She smiled at him. "I can make it better."

Fallon studied the picture on the image display of her as a toddler, standing next to her father, mimicking his pose.

"That's how you started," he told her. He sat to her left at the low dining table. The others had retreated to the nearby sitting area, making small talk.

Her father continued, "I'd be practicing, and you'd toddle over and start doing the same things. Surprisingly well, too. So it seemed natural to teach you. You always asked for more."

He flicked through several more images and her age advanced to her early teens. She noted her hairstyles and every article of clothing, but nothing looked familiar. Only the faces of the two people did. Her own face, growing and maturing with age, and her father's, always watching her with pride.

"Whose idea was it for me to go to the academy?" she asked.

"Yours. Always yours. In fact, your mother threatened me too many times to count. She wanted you doing something nice and safe, right nearby." He chuckled.

"At least she succeeded in that with my brother." Her father had told her how Kano had become a successful city planner. So much so that he often traveled to other cities to help them expand to accommodate a growing populace."

Hiro sighed. "He will be incredibly disappointed to have missed you. All things considered, though, I think it's better. We'll tell him sometime in the future."

To keep him safe. "Of course."

He squeezed her hand. "I knew you'd understand." He craned his neck to look down the hallway. "Do you think your friends will be okay with one spare bedroom and the parlor? I'm afraid we don't have much space. Living in a freestanding home is very costly."

"They'll be fine. You should have seen the scow we stayed on a few weeks ago." She laughed when she thought of the Rescan ship. Her parents' house was a paradise in comparison. Especially since her mother kept trying to push food and tea on them.

"What can I do for you, Kiyoko-chan? I know you want your memories back. How can I help you do that?" He reached for her hands.

She looked at their hands together. They were the same warm, tan hue. They had the same-shaped fingernails, and they both wore them clipped short. They were remarkably similar hands, and it felt nice to stop and share something with her father, who represented a large piece of her past. Her origins.

But it didn't bring her past roaring back into her brain. Didn't let loose a tsunami of recollections. Didn't get her any closer to figuring out what her future looked like.

Damn. She'd hoped it would be that easy. "I don't know. Is there anything that meant something to me? Something really significant? Images, or something I owned, or something I used to do?"

He frowned thoughtfully. "Training. But we already did a little sparring session and you've seen pictures. Other than that, I'd say your bedroom. Sit in there awhile. See how it feels. You were always a very deep, thoughtful girl who spent much time alone in her room." He sighed. "Otherwise, I don't know. To be honest, I'm struggling with my own feelings about your memory loss. Knowing that you don't remember me or your mother doesn't feel great."

"I know. It must suck, and I'm sorry."

He smiled. Fallon liked his smile. She could imagine him looking at her like that when she struggled to master some new skill as a kid.

"Don't worry about me," he assured her. "I know you'll figure it out. You always have."

"Thanks." She appreciated his faith. She didn't remember him, but he knew her—and he believed in her. It meant something.

"I like your team," he added. "They're going to be there for you."

"They are." If nothing else, she was entirely certain of that.

He rose to his feet with the smooth grace of a dancer. Or a highly trained fighter. "Shall I walk you to your room, then?"

"Are you sure Mother won't be upset if I disappear?"

He chuckled. "She's in her element, entertaining. To tell you the truth, I think she's completely fascinated with your team. No doubt she's trying to pull them apart to figure out how they tick, right now."

They walked down a narrow hallway and he gestured at a closed door. "I hope there are some answers in there. Either way, your mother will be looking forward to making your favorite breakfast for you in the morning."

"I wish we could stay longer."

"You'll be back." His eyes lit with determination, and he suddenly reminded her of herself.

Impetuously, she gave him a hug before entering the room and closing the door behind her. She'd learned to trust her instincts, and the smile that lit Hiro's face made her glad that she had.

7

Fallon entered the room slowly, cataloguing its contents in a methodical way. That was how she approached any new situation. Log the facts first. Fill in the gaps as she went along.

Light-blue walls, a narrow but comfortable-looking bed with a simple frame. A small desk in the corner with a voicecom display on it. A dresser. A lack of knickknacks and clutter. An altogether tidy space.

Her father had told her that she'd begun living in this room at the age of ten, when he and her mother had bought the house. Even while attending the academy, she'd stayed in this room during visits home. They'd changed little about it, though it no longer held many of her personal belongings. She'd have either gotten rid of them or taken them with her, she supposed.

Which left her with very little to look at. She opened the closet and found only a hooded sweatshirt with the academy's insignia. She pushed her arms into it and settled the hood over her head. Pressing her nose to a sleeve, she took a deep inhale. It didn't smell of anything in particular.

She seated herself in the slim chair facing the desk. The voicecom awaited her command, but she had none to give it.

What, then? Photos? Her father had shown her a number of images and they'd prompted nothing. Neither did this room. It could be any room, though she had to admit that the sweatshirt felt particularly comfortable.

Fine, the voicecom, then. She tapped through the local files and saw images of herself through the years. Mostly with friends, posing for the camera, or stern-faced and holding herself rigid, in the midst of martial-arts training. She paused at the knife-throwing images, clicking through them much more slowly than the others. But she didn't recognize the people or places. No voices rang in her ears, and nothing made her feel connected to the scenes in front of her. Not even the image of her with a good-looking boy, who looked at her with eyes that expressed more than friendship. A boyfriend? If so, she appeared to have done well. He was remarkably good-looking. Of course that didn't mean he wasn't a jerk, but she hoped she'd have been smart enough to steer clear of that kind of guy.

She started looking at the documents. School projects, mostly. Thermodynamics. Art history. Nuclear chemistry. Her nose wrinkled. Scrap, that sounded positively awful. Whatever she was, she was not a scientist. But she supposed she'd needed a working knowledge of all the major disciplines. Must have been hell to get through. Ugh.

She found her application to the academy. It showed high marks and a stellar IQ, along with making quite a show of her memory. The irony forced a laugh out of her. Her spectacular memory, now completely hobbled by her inability to access it.

She sobered. But maybe it wasn't ironic at all. What if... She let her mind expand, taking her new idea through the quagmire of what-ifs.

Even the most secure system could be breached. She knew that. Raptor proved it. He was the best, and he could design the highest-quality security database in the universe. But no system could be better than the best designer, which meant that anything that could be created could also be destroyed, or at least broken into, by that *very same best designer*.

Feeling like she was on to something, she followed the train of thought with a growing sense of excitement. What was an under-the-radar intelligence outfit to do, if it *really* needed to keep a secret? It couldn't store that information in a computer, or in any storage device that could be accessed from the outside.

So what about something that could only be accessed from the inside? By one single user? Like a brain?

Like *her* brain.

She double-checked the logic, but it made sense. Blackout could have given her an implant. Something she would safeguard as well as she would her own brain, because it was *in* her brain. She might or might not have been aware of its presence there. And if Blackout decided they wanted it back...they would have taken it.

Possibly damaging her long-term memory in the process. From what Brak had told her about neural implants and brain surgery, as well as what Fallon had researched on her own, it made sense. Might fit. Could be an answer.

If it was true, she'd need to find out if her memory loss was intentional or accidental. Her initial assumption would be accidental, because why spend years training an agent to be one of the best, only to waste her for no purpose? But there could be factors she didn't know about. There might be things that Blackout had not wanted her to remember. Maybe they'd hoped to remove what they didn't want her to know, leave her none the wiser, and maintain her as a BlackOp. But then what would have changed to make them decide to send an assassin for her?

She wished she could talk to Brak about it all, but Brak was on a slow course back toward the heart of PAC space. She definitely couldn't discuss these matters over the voicecom. Even a secure channel was not secure enough for a conversation like that.

She pulled the hood off her head and ran her fingers through her hair. First the short side, then she unnecessarily smoothed the side that hung down to her jaw. She pressed her fingers against her skull, cradling the brain that seemed to be the center of everything. Somewhere in her gray matter, she became increasingly convinced, the answers either still existed or had once existed. All right there in her head.

The room felt too small all of a sudden. Its tidy simplicity irritated her. She wanted something loud, something messy, something she could focus her agitation on. What the hell was she doing? Overnighting with her parents? No.

She'd conclusively proven that no amount of nostalgia was going to restore her memories. She was wasting time, and putting her team at risk for nothing. Her parents, too.

Purpose filled her. Glorious, motivating purpose. She strode to the other bedroom and tapped briefly before opening the door. Inside, Peregrine sat on the edge of the bed.

"Time to go," Fallon said.

"Finally." Peregrine leaped to her feet, grabbed her bag, and walked down the hall.

Hawk and Raptor sprawled in the living room's chairs, but were already straightening to stand when they arrived.

"Moving out?" Raptor asked.

"Yes. I just need to say goodbye to my parents." She held herself still, letting Peregrine efficiently reapply her disguise.

Her parents appeared. Her father placed his hand on her mother's shoulder. Comforting, maybe. Or cautioning.

"I didn't think you'd make it until morning." Her mother's smile was sad, but knowing. "Probably for the best. You have work to do." She approached and put her hands on Fallon's cheeks, forcing Peregrine to pause her work on Fallon's forehead.

"Figure it all out, my daughter," her mother intoned, as if

saying a prayer. "Whatever your father and I can do, you let us do it. Understand?"

She clearly expected to be obeyed. Fallon nodded. She might indeed need her parents' help before all this was done.

Yumi moved aside and Hiro took her place. He kissed each of her cheeks. "Take them down. I always knew you'd make the universe a better place."

That made Fallon smile. "Thank you, Father."

He hugged her tightly, then stepped back. "Anything you need."

She nodded. "I understand. I'll be in touch, as soon as I can."

Her father's eyes showed humor. "You'd better. We haven't nearly caught up yet."

She bowed, a deep, reverential bow. He returned it, in a way not customary for a parent to do for a child.

"Thank you both. You've been a big help to us." She gave her parents a last smile before turning to the door and walking out of her childhood home.

———

FALLON HAD to give Hawk points for the inventiveness and longevity of his swearing. She lounged in the pilot's chair of the *Nefarious* while he paced around its small bridge.

He was spitting a little as he talked, too. "So you're saying that you think Blackout used your *brain* like a safe? Like they put something in there to keep it secure, until they wanted it back?"

"Or until they decided they wanted me to access it," she added. "It's entirely likely that it was wired right into my memory. Accessible, if I knew what to look for. Like a computer program. Install it and run."

"That's a bloody cold way of treating a person's brain. Prelin's ass!" He added a few more curses for good measure while Fallon waited for him to get back on track. "It's one thing that we expect to get shot, skewered, or blown up. It's another to have our own agency hiding things in our brains like a little kid hiding peas in the mashed potatoes."

"Your objection is noted." She found his anger somewhat amusing and even endearing, because she knew it stemmed from his protectiveness of her and his outrage at the idea of their own department not operating within ethical norms.

Blackout could burn an operative at any time. That was part of the job. You got shot, you got blown up, you disappeared never to be seen again. But getting burned shouldn't be the result of some conspiracy. A double cross involving a person's own brain. It turned her stomach. She kept thinking of some parasite laying eggs in her brain and waiting for them to hatch. That was what Blackout had done to her. And then, when something went wrong, they decided to assassinate her and her entire team, just like that. Their lives wiped out for nothing. She was prepared to die for a purpose. But not for *nothing*.

It made her angry, and there was no doubt that her teammates felt the same way.

"So what I need you to do, Raptor, is dig through the data you got for any mentions of neural implants, brain surgery, any of that. Anything remotely similar. I think that's what this is all about." Fallon sensed that whatever had happened to her memory was the key to the entire mess.

"What's the priority? You looking for who in the hierarchy was involved, or the technology itself?" Raptor rubbed his chin, clearly thinking about his strategy. "The more I know about what I'm looking for, the quicker I'll find it. I'll do much better with that than just sifting through the huge mass like I have been, looking for a needle in a haystack."

"I want the technology. Memory augmentation. Neural implant. Anything along those lines, as well as the people responsible for creating it. If we get that info, we can take it to Brak, and we'll finally have something real to work with. We can track the tech back to the source."

Raptor nodded. "I'll get to it then. I'll let you know as soon as I find something." She watched him stride out with purpose in his steps. It always felt so much better to have a defined goal.

Which left her, Hawk, and Peregrine on the bridge. They'd already left Earth behind, which had been a relief to all of them. As of yet, Fallon had no particular destination, so she pointed them in the general direction of Blackthorn Station and held their speed to a moderate, energy-conserving pace. The vastness of space practically guaranteed their anonymity, far better than any moored location could.

"What can we do?" Hawk asked.

"Sleep," Fallon answered. "I'll need you two to take shifts at ops control, so that I can sleep later. Or stab my brain with pointy things, or whatever."

Her attempt at humor fell flat, gaining a sour smirk from Hawk and nothing at all from Peregrine. But they both went off to sleep, which was what mattered.

Four hours later, Peregrine arrived to relieve her, and Fallon was glad. She was worn out. The emotional toll of meeting her parents and the late hour combined to have her crawling into bed with her clothes on. At least on the *Nefarious*, they each got a moderately sized berth of their own. Fallon appreciated the privacy, and let her thoughts wander to her parents as she drifted to sleep.

FALLON OPENED her eyes to find herself standing in a tunnel. The odd thing was, she knew it was a dream. She felt the hazy bendiness of the not-universe surrounding her and had no doubt that she was traveling the recesses of her own brain.

Well, hell, she thought. *This is exactly where I've been wanting to be. It's about damn time.*

If only she had a map to take her where she wanted to go. Raptor stepped out of a door that hadn't been there a second ago, wearing nothing but a towel wrapped around his waist. Droplets of water ran down his arm but didn't land anywhere. They just rolled and then disappeared.

"Cheese is important," he said meaningfully. "Always the cheese."

"What?"

But he'd gone through another door. She tried to follow him, but the seam of the exit had melded back into the tunnel.

"Ookay…" Apparently, her brain was strange.

She struck off down the passage, watching for any turns, doorways, or additional underdressed people. But nothing. Just more tunnel. She walked on for what felt like forever.

"I'm not getting anywhere." She cast a look behind her, where the corridor yawned backward. It reminded her of time, somehow. Time, stretching out both ahead and behind, with no other ways out. The past, and the future.

But the future wasn't a straight path. It had choices. Twists. Unexpected obstacles. So where were they?

Something tickled the top of her head and she reeled back, ready to fight. But it was only a rope. It dangled down a long shaft above her.

She sighed. Nothing could just be easy, could it? "Fine."

She backtracked several paces, then ran, leaped, and managed to catch the end of the rope. Pulling herself up hand over hand, she got far enough to finally wind it around her leg and foot, taking the pressure off her arms.

She worked her way up the long length of rope. Sweat dripped down her face and her hands stung, but her muscles felt perfectly at ease.

A light flickered up above, then grew more distinct. She

heaved her feet up through a hole in a floor, inelegantly scooting herself in enough to let go of the rope and crawl into the space. This room seemed cartoonish, with different colors of doors everywhere, some the size of an apple, others massively wide and low.

Doors. Portals? Pathways? She opened one of the small ones and peeked in. She saw nothing. She tried a tall, skinny door.

Fallon stared through it at her office on Dragonfire. Every detail was precise. Her desk, the couches, everything. Should she go in?

She debated for a moment, then closed the door and opened another. Empty. Just darkness, like an abyss of space, stretching across a galaxy.

A round, purple door drew her attention. She had to bend to peer in. She saw an image of her and her father. Her looking resolved and him looking proud. Not the actual memory, though. Just the static image she'd seen.

Were these memories? Some she couldn't recall, as blank spots, and some that she could? What if she chose to enter a blank one?

She opened a gray door, big enough for her to fit through. The darkness within worried her. She didn't want to walk into the darkness. Without a weapon or a light source, she'd have no means of defending herself.

But this was her brain, wasn't it? Her mind? Did she need to defend herself?

She stepped through the gray door and the passageway behind her disappeared. Darkness became absolute, making it hard to keep her balance. She flung her arms out, feeling for a wall or something to guide herself with, but she found nothing. She wobbled and fell, coming down hard on her hands and knees. She scooted her palms over the floor. No, the ground. The first texture she felt was grass. Cold and damp, like she might find on a dark night. Her fingers curled around the damp blades, feeling them feather against her palms. As if they were real.

Faint white light began to filter in, bringing shadows with it. The motion of a branch shaking in the breeze made her realize that a tree ahead of her stood nearly concealed in the haze. It drew her attention upward, where she saw two moons.

Those bloody moons again. They were like the ones from her nightmare. Maybe not exactly, but close enough. One larger, one smaller, with a similar glow. These didn't press down on her though. They remained high in the sky.

Fallon heard a voice but couldn't make out what it said. She turned toward it, only to find no one there.

Only an idiot would call out, advertising her position. Fallon was no idiot. She stalked forward, looking for the source of the voice, but there was nothing but grass, shadows, and moons.

So why was she here? And how could she leave? If this was nothing, she'd try something else. Another door. Another rope.

Something wet landed on her cheek, and she brushed it away. Looking at her fingers, she saw a smudge of blood. Hers. Somehow she knew it for a fact.

The moons had moved closer. They no longer hung so high in the sky. They seemed to want to come to see her. They kept advancing. Fallon backed up, but how can a person run away from a moon? She tripped and fell backward, with the moons continuing to come for her. She held her hands up, trying to ward them off. Then they stopped. They seemed to be asking a question.

She tried to speak, but her voice was rough. She cleared her throat and tried again. "I think I understand."

Only then did the moons recede back into the sky where they belonged, apparently satisfied.

———

FALLON DIDN'T RUSH to tell her teammates about her experience. She wanted a little while to try to process it first. To figure out how she'd even explain it to her partners.

In the mess, she worked at generating enough leave-me-alone energy to keep the others at bay. So far it was working. Hawk and Raptor played cards, while Peregrine finished her shift on the bridge.

Fallon rested her arm on the table with a full glass of Zerellian ale resting against the crook of her elbow. The chill of it against her skin served her far better than the actual beverage, at the moment. She wanted to be rooted in the physical world, not drifting up into her own head again. She needed to hear the hum of people around her, even though she didn't want to interact with them just now. Fortunately, her teammates understood her well enough to know when she wasn't in the mood for conversation.

She pretended to study the ship's inventory on an infoboard as she tried to characterize the experience she'd had. She couldn't call it a dream. Though it had had a surreal, dreamlike quality, she'd been entirely lucid, and she felt certain that those tunnels had represented the neural pathways of her mind. She'd been poking among things she knew she remembered and memories that remained missing. Disconnected from her, but still nestled in her brain. So definitely not a dream. Some sort of post-hypnotic manifestation of recovered memories, then?

Brain stuff really wasn't her area of expertise. She'd leave it to the doctors to explain the medical things. What mattered to her was being sure of what she took away from her experience. Tactics. Planning. That was her thing.

But what should she do next? For the first time, the burden of leading her team bore down on her. Not because she lacked the desire to be everything her team needed, but because she suddenly had a doubt as to whether she was up to the task.

A bead of condensation welled up and began to roll down her

glass. Fallon touched it, breaking its surface tension and causing it to burst against her fingertip. She drew an idle trail of moisture in a straight line across the faux-wood tabletop, then smeared it with her palm and watched the edges evaporate.

Tactics. *Identify the objective.* What she really needed was to fill in the gaps inside her head, then go storm the castle. The "castle" being Blackout, of course. Not just a base or an outpost, but headquarters itself. The big target. The place where Raptor could yank out every bit of data they could possibly need, telling them exactly who had subverted Blackout, when, and how. Where she and the rest of her team could look into the eyes of the person, or people, who had caused all this. Once they could do that, it was all downhill. A simple matter of raining all manner of hell down on the traitors. The fun stuff.

Identify the means. Both Brak and Raptor were working on finding tethers to her memories that she could yank on to pull them into place, but that left Fallon oddly disconnected from the process. She needed *them* to help her connect with her own memories. Her own thoughts, even, as they pertained to her past and how the past affected their present.

Oh, it was twisty. But she had to forget that. She had to stay on task. That was her job, what Avian Unit depended on her for. *Identify the means.*

Fine. The means. What could *she* do to bring back those memories? Once Raptor had finished looking for the technology behind the implant she suspected Blackout had buried in her brain, she'd ask him to search through the slush of data for mentions of Blackout missions on planets with two moons. She was certain now that the two-mooned planet from her dreams had been the point where everything had started going wrong. A real thing, not just some interpretive nightmare.

And if none of that brought back her stubborn memories? Should she just keep trying to sleep, to see if her mind would offer up its own help? She was too keyed up at the moment. She couldn't sleep now if she tried, and she wasn't about to drug herself into slumber.

Her patience for head games had worn thin. She couldn't sit around forever while whoever was at Blackout's controls continued with their plans.

Time was running out. If she didn't get those memories very soon, then they'd just have to storm the castle without them and let the debris land where it would.

———

"Yes, I know it sounds like some sort of psychosis. But it's not." Fallon studied her teammates. After getting a handle on her objectives, she'd called Peregrine down for a team meeting.

Her partners wore expressions of doubt. Raptor seemed mostly puzzled, while Peregrine frowned deeply. Hawk leaned against the bulkhead of the small mess room, picking at his index finger.

"It's just hard to know how seriously to take this dream, or memory, or whatever it was." Raptor spoke carefully, clearly not wanting to insult her.

"It was a memory, but framed within a dream. I'm not certain which parts were literal and which weren't, but I'm certain it's all based on a real event. Something that marked the point in time everything started going wrong for us. Whatever happened under those moons led to us being split up, and to someone at Blackout eventually deciding they were better off having us killed."

Peregrine perched on a blocky stool, nibbling on the pad of her thumb. "We need more to go on. A planet name or something."

"I'm hoping Raptor can glean that from the data we stole from the base in Tokyo."

Raptor asked, "Should that be the priority now? I'd have to

stop searching for the implant tech, and I think the tech is the better bet. That's a much bigger target with more pieces. I'm more likely to find something there than searching for some probably undocumented occurrence on a two-mooned planet."

She wished they could look for both, but Raptor was only one person and he had to sleep sometime. "No, you're right. The tech has to come first."

Too bad she couldn't get her father's input. Maybe he could have turned up something for her about that mysterious planet. But even if she could get a secure message to him, if he started looking around, he might trigger some alarms that would get him in deep, deep trouble. She'd be helpless to protect him from so far away.

"All right. I'll get to work then, since everything seems to be resting on me." Raptor didn't look happy about the fact as he pushed back from the table and started to stand.

A hard impact made him lose his balance, landing back on the stool and almost toppling off. He made a grab for the tabletop to keep himself upright.

The rest of them managed to keep their balance. No one bothered with inane questions like "What was that?" They just ran for the bridge.

"Pirates," Fallon announced as soon as she threw herself into the pilot's chair. Hawk took the other seat at ops while Raptor and Peregrine glued themselves to the auxiliary panels.

"Attacking a ship like this? They must be nuts," Hawk muttered.

"Maybe not," Fallon countered. "There's only one right now, but I see three more coming in fast." Her suspicious nature made her wonder if the ships might have a connection to Blackout, but if they did, she'd be looking at something with bigger engines and more firepower. No. Just ridiculously damn stupid luck.

Hawk cursed. Something to the effect of what those ships could do to one another, as well as what he'd do with the people inside them if he got his hands on them. Mostly anatomically impossible things, though Fallon had no doubt that Hawk would make a dedicated effort, if given the opportunity.

She ignored his inventive threats, focusing on the data readouts. "They hit us with a shaker charge. Apparently they want to know if they have a good chance of taking us before they get serious." A shaker wouldn't cause damage, but it would pull a lot of data. They were designed to attach to the hull, then bore into a ship's systems to sift out details about defenses.

She located the shaker and tried to cut off power to that portion of the hull, but no luck. The shaker had prevented that, and now she had no way of getting it off her ship.

"All right, in about a minute they're going to know exactly how valuable this ship is. Hawk, heat up the cannons. Peregrine, open the torpedo bay. Raptor, you're on energy charges."

They wordlessly set to work.

Fallon didn't have shaker charges, but she had something better. An extensive memory of ship schematics and specs. She could tell by examining close-ups of the pirate ship that it didn't have the speed or the firepower of the *Nefarious*, although it was remarkably well kitted for a pirate vessel in unregulated space. Normally the ships out here were rough jobs, looking to pick off cargo ships or personal cruisers traveling through established routes. The *Nefarious* must have stumbled across one of those.

Her team needed to wipe this ship off the playing field before the other three arrived. She wouldn't have a chance of defending against all four at once.

"Peregrine?"

"Ready."

Fallon readied for a quick acceleration. "On my mark." She lit the engines, causing g-forces to slam them before the ship's systems could compensate. Definitely not standard operating procedure. It would have been fun, if she hadn't been concerned with the little things, such as survival.

The pirates, anticipating her attempt to flee, kept close.

"Three." Fallon prepared a quick deceleration, which would bring the ship right on top of them.

"Two." She entered another sequence of commands, which would accelerate them again as soon as she hit the program.

"One."

The engines of the *Nefarious* screamed and the ship shuddered as they instantly lost just enough acceleration to put the nose of the pirate ship right up their aft. Peregrine loosed the torpedo, far too close for the other ship to avoid. Fallon had aimed it right for the least reinforced part of the ship's hull structure. Every ship had a weak point.

One second before the torpedo impacted, Fallon initiated the re-acceleration, holding her breath against the g-force to keep the air in her lungs and hoping she could outrun the explosion.

She couldn't, completely, but it was brief and the hull of the *Nefarious* handled the heat, and all four members of Avian Unit gasped when the pressure eased enough to allow them to breathe again.

On the panel, Fallon watched the destruction of the pirate ship. It hovered momentarily, as if it didn't know it was already dead. The front end yawned open into space. Then the entire thing shuddered. Some sections imploded under loss of containment while others exploded, only to almost instantaneously be extinguished by cold, empty space.

The other three ships were moving in fast, each from a different direction. There'd be no avoiding all of them. The first to catch up to them would pin them down until the other pirates arrived, so that the three of them would be able to work in concert. None of those ships could begin to measure up to the *Nefarious*, but working together they'd be more than a match. Especially if they were good at their job.

So she picked the closest ship and set an intercept course. Her advantage was that those ships wanted hers intact, but she had the completely opposite viewpoint on their vessels.

A laser cannon blasted under their belly, rocking the *Nefarious* hard. It was a nice hit, she had to admit, aimed for the ship's life support systems. That was the best course of action, for pirates. Kill the people inside, keep the ship mostly intact.

She rotated the ship, angling its belly up and away. She had to fight to maneuver in that unwieldy attitude. Her acceleration reduced dramatically, but she held steady, hurtling the *Nefarious* toward the other ship backward and at a forty-five degree angle.

"Quit smiling. It freaks me out," Hawk muttered.

Fallon didn't look over at him, keeping her focus on her screens. "I'm not."

"Yes, you are."

Whatever. All of them had thrill issues. If they didn't, they wouldn't be on this ship to begin with.

"Shut up," she answered instead. Not brilliant, but succinct. "All hands, target critical systems. Lay in everything we've got and obliterate that slag."

She brought them into range, flying full bore right toward the ship. If they didn't blast it out of their way, they'd crash straight into it. The trajectory would put her in an excellent position to face the remaining two ships at once, since they were just beginning to warm up the ass end of the *Nefarious* with a few potshots.

"*Now!*" As soon as they were in range, Peregrine loosed a volley of torpedoes at the engines. Hawk had to wait a moment for his shot, then opened up the laser cannons, while Raptor joined in last, shooting precise energy charges directly into volatile areas filled with compressed gases, where he'd get the biggest *boom* factor.

And boom it did. The hull of the ship cracked open like a crustacean she'd once eaten. Once the breach in the center opened, the rest of the ship fell away in smaller, imploding pieces.

But they didn't drift away fast enough. At this speed, any of those pieces would take out the *Nefarious*. Hawk and Raptor kept firing, breaking up the pieces and giving them additional propulsion to push them out of the way.

They scraped through the center of the wreck. With all of the volatile gases vented, the remaining pieces of the ship went cold and dark, demonstrating how thin the margin between life and death was in space.

"Two hostiles closing in," Peregrine intoned.

Fallon rolled the *Nefarious*, taking a position below the other ships and angling the bow downward to protect its belly. The pirates no doubt still had hopes of taking the ship, or they'd have fled instead of advancing. But they'd be much more wary now, and more likely to shoot to destroy.

Which made the fight a little trickier for Fallon. Plus she still had two ships to contend with, instead of one. Fortunately, her *Nefarious* outmatched them in both design and power.

Ship B threw an energy discharge at them but she dodged it, only to get hit with one from Ship A. The blast knocked her off her trajectory and she had to abort her attempt to get past them. She looped around and launched her ship up, giving them an enticing shot at her belly.

"Peregrine, torpedoes."

The *Nefarious* shook under two energy charges and Fallon began getting readouts of impending systems failures. But she'd provided enough of a distraction to drop those bombs on them, which neither ship managed to dodge.

Ship A lost its attitude control, but not navigation. It kept coming after her, listing to one side and blasting out wild energy shots, along with cannon fire.

Ship A was in desperate condition, which was good because that meant it was hurt, but bad because a desperate foe is an unpredictable one.

Ship B did nothing. She suspected the crew had been distracted with saving containment, or possibly life support.

Fallon decided to ignore Ship B. She'd have liked to finish it off while it was vulnerable, but she didn't have the time. She'd lost a little maneuvering precision due to some damage to the auxiliary thrusters, but her engines were at full power.

She moved back, putting Ship B between her and Ship A. Hopefully it would choose not to take out its own ally.

"They're venting dry plasma," Peregrine reported. "Off their port nacelle."

Definite containment problems, then. Perfect. "Raptor, target it. On my mark."

She threw them into an acceleration, pointing the belly of the *Nefarious* away from the ships and fighting the protesting engines into a tight arc. Engine two kept trying to shut down but she boosted it with emergency releases of coolant to keep it alive long enough to finish their business here.

As soon as she got them into range, she barked, "Now!"

One beautiful, glowing energy charge streaked out between them and the enemy ship. Lit the dry plasma. Crackled for a moment, like fireworks. Then turned the ship into a fireball, ever so briefly. But quite satisfyingly.

Fallon turned her attention to the remaining ship. She couldn't just leave it. Crippled or not, it could point others toward them, or make repairs and follow on its own. She didn't relish firing on a crippled ship, but when mercy came at the price of risking her team, no mercy was possible.

"Peregrine. Take it out."

Three torpedoes and the last ship fell away in glittery bits, which went dark within seconds.

Fallon allowed herself a moment to appreciate the victory, then began taking stock of their most critical systems.

"We've lost engine two. Engine one will burn out fast on its own." She pulled up another screen. "Containment is stable, life support should hold." Another screen. "Weapons nominal. We won't make it through another fight."

She switched her attention to Hawk. "Who's the closest person you know who can do repairs for us?"

From the way he rubbed at his beard, she suspected she wouldn't like his answer.

8

"This is one of those times that really makes me wish we had a mech on the team." Fallon wasn't happy about their repair options, but they were lucky to be only a few days out from a place that Hawk assured her could fix them up.

Engine one could get them to his proposed destination, if she was careful. But Hawk's suggestion of landing on a planet entrenched in a civil war rubbed her all kinds of the wrong ways. All of them, in fact. *All* the wrong ways.

"Atalus is not someplace a person goes on purpose, unless you're a humanitarian worker or a price-gouging trader. Or maybe a smuggler. The planet's own people are literally dying to get off the planet." Beyond Fallon's doubts about their safety, she had deep ethical concerns about contracting the services of someone who perpetuated the war by dealing arms to the opposing factions.

"I know what you're going to say." Hawk faced off with her in the mess room. Up on the bridge, Raptor and Peregrine stayed on alert, making sure they couldn't get hit again by pirate ships equipped with devices to thwart their sensors. Which had been a completely bogus tactic, and the kind of PAC-outlawed tech only a real piece of scrap would use.

She really needed to get some of those.

"Let's hear it then." Fallon crossed her arms and leaned against the bulkhead.

Hawk held his palms up in a beseeching gesture. "I get it. We're trained to measure up the greater good, to help the needy, to protect the weak. It's what the PAC is about. But here's the thing."

He rapped on his skull with his knuckles. "You don't remember the things we learned from firsthand experience *after* training. Right and wrong aren't two different roads. They're just different addresses on the same road, and sometimes, those numbers get swapped without warning. Reality is messier than ideals, and I work in those in-between places. And you know what I've learned there?"

"I'm sure you're going to tell me."

Hawk pushed a stool out of his way with his foot and slid down the wall into a knees-up position. "Here's the thing, Fallon. I've met weapons merchants I trust more than some captains and admirals. A person's means of making a living doesn't tell the whole story."

"Criminals with hearts of gold, you mean?" She wasn't buying it. The universe was full of opportunities. Legit opportunities.

"Come on, don't be so closed-minded. Take your friend Kellis. She was born on Atalus, right? Didn't have a choice."

Fallon nodded, and Hawk continued. "So imagine the only way she had to protect her family was to sell illegal goods. Would you blame her for that?"

Fallon rolled her eyes. "Lame. You're going to do the old, 'Is it wrong to steal bread for your family if they're starving' thing. But we're not talking about helpless victims. That's something else entirely. Your associates have enough money to get out but they choose to stay in the game. If they were upstanding people, they'd leave as soon as they had enough cubics to buy their way off the planet."

Hawk shook his head. "Says someone who grew up viewing the PAC as a benevolent parent entity. Someone who never saw her world get sold off as a bargaining chip in a treaty. Someone who was never at risk of becoming a casualty of peace just because she grew up on the wrong planet. Open your eyes, Fallon."

"I'm listening. You just haven't convinced me."

He laughed. A helpless, humorless laugh. "Okay, I'll put it this way. My friend Arcy grew up on Davidia Three. Deals in weapons, illegal services, counterfeit papers. You know why he does that?"

"No."

"Because on Davidia Three, nearly everyone's born into slavery. They don't call it that, but if you aren't the right kind of person, from the right place, you're expected to stay in your neighborhood and toil away until you die way too young. Effective slavery. So Arcy decided to help others like him. He keeps people alive, gets them off planet if they want. Helps them carve out a future that doesn't involve slavery."

She dropped her arms to her sides and shifted so that her back was against the bulkhead. "Dirty deeds for a good cause."

"Not always. I won't pretend he's a saint or an altruist. He's a realist. He'll shoot you in the face if he thinks you're a threat. But he also makes sure all the kids in his old neighborhood get enough to eat and have shoes on their feet. And when those kids are old enough to make choices, he can help them. He helps to counteract unfortunate circumstances. He didn't plan those circumstances. The people at the top did."

"So it's the fault of his government that he's forced to do what he does." Hawk was right, to a degree. She just wasn't sure what degree.

"Not exactly. But people just want to survive, you know? Don't they have the right to try?"

Of course they did. For every one of her personally held ideals, there were a billion people in the universe. People with family and love and hope for a future. Her ideals might feel more immediate or more important to her because they were *hers*, but a person's life was worth far more than any one of her beliefs.

She slid down the wall to sit next to him. "Okay. I understand that. But how do we justify giving money to an arms dealer?"

He shrugged. "It's not up to me to figure that out. I just know that my guy on Atalus is not evil. Yes, he profits off the war. He started out as a teacher, and would still rather be doing that, so long as he could do it on his own planet, which he can't. He doesn't fight the war. He's just living in the world he was born into."

"But he has the money to get out. Why doesn't he?"

Hawk shrugged again. "That's his business. Maybe he has family that won't or can't leave. Maybe he can't bear to abandon his world. Maybe he just doesn't know how to live any other life. It's not our business. You're putting your own values on him, and that doesn't work."

"Fine. I get it." She sighed. "Besides, it's not like we have other options."

He slapped her knee lightly. "There you go. That's it exactly. When the universe hands you nothing but garbage, you make a big garbage sandwich and take a bite. Anyone looks at it and cringes away can screw off. They have no right to judge."

"Yeah. I guess so."

So they were headed to Atalus, then. To get their ship repaired amidst a civil war, by an arms dealer. Yay.

———

OTHER THAN BEING MELTINGLY HOT, their stay on Atalus didn't

prove to be too terrible. Hawk's associate Tee, as he preferred to be called, housed them in his compound, far from any fighting or civilization. Buried in the middle of a burning-hot desert.

Shade, fans run via small generators, and large amounts of water helped, but the days passed in a blur of wavy heat lines that made the ground look psychedelic. Two days in, Fallon wondered if she was hallucinating just a bit. What she wouldn't do for hard-wired electricity and climate control.

She had something to look forward to, though, and she focused on that like a lifeline. Hawk had arranged to have someone load the *Outlaw* onto their ship and haul it out to them. Fallon would tuck the *Outlaw* inside the *Nefarious*, giving her both ships. Which made her almost giddy. She kind of wanted to rub her hands together and make *mwa-ha-ha* sounds when she thought about it.

Repairs went slowly, though, which served to tamp down her enthusiasm. Tee's team could only work so many hours in such hot conditions each day. There were also some parts that he had to track down and negotiate for. Atalus no longer had its own ships. The vessels and the facilities that made them had all been bombed out, which left Tee searching among scrap to find what they needed for the *Nefarious*, or waiting for a freighter to arrive. Once again, Fallon wished she had her own mech to certify the repairs. She'd have felt a lot better if she had Kellis to approve the ship before she attempted an in-atmosphere takeoff. Since there was no getting around the situation, she tried not to think about it.

At least in that respect, the heat was a good thing, as her intense discomfort made it hard to think about anything at all, besides escaping the planet. She had literally nothing to do but while away sweltering minutes that dissolved into hours. She didn't know how people lived like this. She wasn't the only one melting with boredom, either. She wished they could stay on board the *Nefarious*, but that idea had been nixed almost immediately. Though the ship would maintain a temperature that would protect their tech and gear, life support would not be operating during repairs. Which left the four members of Avian Unit sprawled out on cool stone floors, breathing what felt like fire.

Slightly after the point where she felt she'd dissolved into an unrecognizable pile of goo, the *Nefarious* was given the green light. Avian Unit wasted no time in thanking their host and getting the hell out of there.

She led her team onto the ship. The first cool lungful of reprocessed air came like a revelation, and she greedily tried to suck up all of it she could.

Conditioned air clung to her like a second skin, coating her in a layer of comfort even though the rest of her still felt gelatinous. She collapsed into the pilot's chair once she got to the bridge, willing her innards to solidify enough that she could fly this rig.

Finally, the cool relief sank all the way through her and she felt human again. She opened her eyes and found none of the others had followed her all the way to the bridge. They must have gone to their berths. Which would have been smarter, actually. But she'd been focused on the pilot's chair for a week, and had no patience for further delay.

A shower really was in order though. Even though it was only a sonic unit. Ah, well.

IT FELT good to be clean again, without the salt and sweat hanging heavy on her skin. Add a fresh jumpsuit and she felt almost normal. She just needed some food. Something cold.

When she made it back to the bridge, Raptor awaited. He smiled when he saw her. He also wore a fresh uniform.

"Ready?" she asked him.

"Way beyond ready."

"I sent Hawk and Peregrine to rest. We'll be on six-hour shifts until we arrive at our destination. Should take us about two weeks."

"Nice." Raptor studied the panel in front of him, checking out the flight path as she laid it in.

"Yep. Glad we bought this baby." She patted the panel affectionately.

"And when we get to Zerellus?" he asked.

"I'm hoping by then you've come up with something on the implant technology. Then it's all up to Brak to make sense of the memory soup in my brain."

He grimaced. "No pressure, right?"

She thought of Brak and smiled. "She's up to the challenge."

AVIAN UNIT quickly fell into a comfortable routine of meals, duty shifts, and recreation. It felt good to be back on a schedule. Productive.

Rec consisted of card games, Go, and workouts in an ad hoc gym they set up in the cargo bay alongside the *Outlaw*. Far from ideal, but Fallon's body thanked her. She got achy when she didn't work out regularly, as if her muscles became angry at her inattention.

Each night, she drifted to sleep, determined to map out more memories behind the doors in her mind. Her sleep on Atalus had been so restless and fitful that she'd come up with nothing, but on the *Nefarious*, her mind cooperated. To a point. She saw things, but often didn't know what to make of them.

She didn't understand the significance of the tired mechanic who had given her an apple. She couldn't see herself in the memory, so she had no idea at what point in her life it had happened. The same for a struggle in a back alley where a pair of local toughs had tried to steal from her. Without context, the memories meant little. But she kept spelunking through the corridors of her sleeping mind, finding a pleasant meal with her parents and brother behind a big yellow door and a soft blanket patterned with cherry blossoms behind a blue one.

Of these minor memories, seeing her brother interested her most. He looked a great deal like her, and had an easy laugh she could now pick out of a crowd. He'd been warm, affectionate, and teasing. All the things she'd have hoped for in a brother. Now, she only hoped she'd get the chance to meet him in real life. Back on Earth, he still didn't know she'd visited their parents. Probably wasn't even sure she was alive. But she *was* alive, and thinking of him. Somehow that made her feel good.

The scrapyard parts that had gotten the *Nefarious* back in shape had been far from ideal. She'd need to have some of them replaced almost immediately. But if they could just make it to Zerellus, that would be no problem. It was a delightful planet—similar to Earth but with a different and much younger culture, and plum with all of the amenities a person could want.

After months of tight quarters, scows, and one boiling planet, Fallon had every intention of indulging in a few pleasant pursuits. She knew that Hawk and Peregrine were planning the same thing, in their own particular ways. Fallon most looked forward to steamy showers and some decadent, gooey desserts—preferably ones that contained chocolate. Oh, and a real workout in a fully equipped gym.

She made arrangements for the four of them to share a suite in a fancy Zerellian hotel. She elected to remain within the transportation hub to keep the team ready for a quick departure, but there were plenty of hospitality options right there. She counted down the days until they arrived.

When Zerellus came into view, Fallon felt mildly surprised that they'd managed to arrive without experiencing pirate attacks or brain aneurysms or massive malfunctions. She'd almost started to expect things to go wrong.

By the law of averages, she felt like the universe owed her some good luck any time now.

"I FEEL a little odd about docking the *Nefarious*," Fallon admitted to Hawk. "Are you sure it'll be in good hands?"

He gave her a quit-being-stupid squint as he stood and hefted a duffel bag onto his shoulder. "Of course it will. Now quit your fussing and get your ass through the airlock. If you miss the elevator, I'm not waiting on you."

"Do you have a date already lined up, or something?" she teased.

"More or less." He negotiated himself and the bag through the doorway and was gone.

She'd double-checked all of her security protocols, just for good measure. Hawk was right, no doubt. Her baby would be fine.

She patted the pilot's seat as she left, making her way to her berth to grab her gear. Once she got through the airlock and onto the docking station, she found that she had a half-hour wait for an orbital elevator. She gave Hawk a dirty look for needlessly rushing her. But the bustling station wasn't unpleasant, and the time passed quickly enough.

None of them said much on the ride down. Her partners were probably thinking ahead to the things they were looking forward to, just as she was.

Upon arriving at their suite, they performed a thorough security sweep. Then Fallon closed herself in her bedroom and fell onto the huge, overstuffed bed covered in fluffy white bedding and big puffy pillows. She stretched out, trying to touch all four corners as she breathed the cool, quiet air. The unrelenting whiteness wasn't usually her thing, but it seemed like the perfect antidote to months of space travel's murky blackness.

After several heartbeats, she leaped up and ran for the shower. She stripped off her clothes as she went, leaving them in a trail behind her. When she wore only her silver bracelet, which she never took off, she stepped into the water.

Her possibly record-breaking shower left her feeling clean and refreshed. Finally, she toweled off and wrapped herself in a fleecy pale-yellow robe. She strode into the parlor, running her fingers through her hair, then stopped dead. Raptor sat on the white couch, a dark blot on a pristine field.

"The Ghost strikes again." She was surprised to feel no annoyance.

"We need to talk," he said. The look on his face suggested that she wouldn't like what he had to say.

———

Fallon leaned back into the couch cushions and propped her feet on the sleek, clear table.

"How old was the message? Do you think Whelkin is legit?"

One side of Raptor's mouth twisted up. "At this point, I won't vouch for anyone who isn't Avian Unit. But everything does add up. Your father said he trusts him, and if he's on our side, it would make sense for him to be hiding from Blackout." His half smile smoothed out. "As for the message, it had been there for a while. Once we got back to PAC space, I did a sweep of all my channels. He sent the message eight weeks ago."

"And what would make him think you'd ever monitor that channel? Doesn't it seem convenient that he'd reach out to you? Assuming it's him and he's legit, might someone else have intercepted the message?"

Raptor shrugged. "First two questions, I don't know. But I saw no evidence that anyone else had seen it, and I wiped it out of existence."

Fallon wasn't eager to trust anyone involved with Blackout, or with the PAC in general. Unless she had a real reason to. By all accounts, she'd liked Whelkin a great deal, and had kept in touch with him over the years. But liking him didn't mean he wouldn't put a lethal stinger shot through her brain.

She had to consider the possibility that he was on their side, though. "If he *is* for real, he must be in the same situation we're in. Which means he'll be staying underground, if he's even still alive. We might not be able to find him." She didn't like Whelkin's odds, on his own.

Raptor picked at a thread on the couch's arm. "If we decide it's the right move, I can leave a message on the same channel. If he's still breathing, I guarantee he'll be monitoring it." He pulled the thread loose and worried it between his fingers. "If he's for real, we could use him. We need all the allies we can get."

"Why would Blackout turn on him, too?" Whelkin was a trainer and a recruiter. A mentor. He had nothing to do with Avian Unit's ops, or the implant in Fallon's head. As far as she knew, anyway.

"I don't know. But then I don't know why they've turned on *us*, either. I think it's worth the risk."

She agreed, although reluctantly and with many reservations. As much as she hated the idea of making them vulnerable, they needed more assets. She also hated the idea of leaving someone out in the cold. And her father *had* vouched for Whelkin.

"We'd have to run it by Hawk and Per. I'd want a unanimous decision on this one." If it turned out to be a double cross, she wouldn't bear the fault alone.

"Of course."

Silence stretched out between them. There were too many possibilities for Fallon to map out contingency plans. She'd have to wait for more information. She hated waiting.

She frowned at him, still lounging on her white couch like he owned it. "You said there were two things. What's the second?"

He smiled. "I saved the best for last. I got a message from Brak."

She straightened, instantly interested. "Oh?"

"She said she was on to it, and would have it soon."

"That's it?" Fallon slouched back against the cushions.

"Yeah. She used the algorithm and channel I gave her, but I warned her to be brief and as vague as possible."

Fallon had hoped the message meant that Brak had already cracked it. Progress was good, but what she really needed was results. If she could recover her memory, maybe she'd have exactly what she needed to infiltrate Blackout and end all this.

Fallon had continued, each night, to shop amongst the doors in her mind and pick out random scenes and images from her life. Some of them were nothing more than a feeling, or a scene frozen in time. Often, she saw an object she didn't recognize. Her mind held innumerable bits of minutiae, apparently.

Seeing these things didn't make any memories come blazing back to life. She remembered what she saw in the dreams, but they were images apart from her, nothing like remembering.

"I was kind of expecting more," Raptor mused.

"More?" She blinked at him, trying to recall whether she'd missed part of the conversation. She'd disappeared into her own thoughts and lost track.

"I tell you Brak just about has a method to recover your memories and you just sit there."

"Was I supposed to jump around and squeal?"

"Sure. That would be entertaining." He flicked away the white thread he'd been fiddling with and smiled.

"Not happening. I'm sure there's somewhere you could go if you want to be entertained, though. This place has just about everything."

He stretched expansively, making himself at home on her couch. "Yeah, I could get used to this."

"It would be a shame if you did. Our frequently deplorable conditions would seem all the worse for you, by comparison."

He sighed. "You have to ruin everything, don't you?"

She gave him a cheeky grin. "Not everything. But some things."

He surprised her by scooting closer so he could loop an arm around her shoulders. "We've been through a lot together. This could be our last mission, you know."

"Every mission is potentially our last. We didn't exactly go into a career known for longevity."

"Some of us do make it into old age, though. Krazinski and Colb started out in ops."

"And how many other field agents can you name who made it to middle age?" She waited, but he didn't answer. "It's surprising that all four of us have made it this far."

"Just shows you how good we are." He gave her a little jiggle with his arm.

"I'm serious."

"So am I." He let his arm drop so he could turn sideways to face her. "Sure, we've had a lot of close calls, but we're still here."

"I don't think I ever objected to dying in the line of duty." She raised her eyebrows at him and he shook his head in confirmation. "But it scares me to think we might not get this one right. That we might not be able to fix Blackout." She felt like a tiny piece of flotsam, trying to take on a supernova.

Raptor patted her knee. "Now you've gone all glum. But when have we ever failed to get the job done?"

"I'm not really the person to ask about that," she reminded him.

"Exactly. As far as you know, we're paragons of success."

"Not true. Per and Hawk told me about some missions that went south."

"Because of anything we'd done wrong?" His eyebrows rose high on his forehead.

"No. Bad intel. Or bad luck."

"Right. And even on those missions where things went sideways, we still all got out in one piece. We're going to do that this time too." He tapped her knee with his index finger. "We'll fix Blackout."

"Right." She tried to sound convinced.

"We will. Blackout can't exist as a corrupt entity. Simple as that. We'll either clean it up or wipe it out. There can't be any other outcome."

His certainty reassured her, but she still felt daunted by the enormity of the task. She really needed to not focus on odds of success. She had to maintain a massively abundant ego to make all this work. A minor god complex definitely would help.

She had just started to say something to that effect when Raptor leaned forward and gave her a chaste little kiss. She leaned away from him. "What was that for?" She waffled between patiently awaiting an answer and being annoyed.

He smiled. "No good reason, really. Just that I've rarely seen you sad or worried, and it reminded me of something."

She hated guessing games. She raised her eyebrows at him, waiting for more.

"Graduating the academy," he said. "When you realized Hawk would take top honors in combat for our graduating class. You'd been determined to have that spot for yourself, to make your dad proud."

"I told you that?" Her mind flashed back to the images she'd seen of her father teaching her to fight. Telling Raptor about wanting to please Hiro seemed like an awfully personal thing to do.

"It was clear to me that you had some reason to be so driven. When you told me that making your father proud was part of it, I felt like I'd really connected with you. We hadn't shared a lot of deeply personal information. Anyway, when you told me, I kissed you."

"So you thought you'd do it again, for old times' sake?" She fixed him with a dubious look.

"Yup."

It didn't justify his presumption, but what the hell. If it had been Hawk or Peregrine, she wouldn't have thought a thing about a little peck. Her past with Raptor made her more sensitive about that sort of thing with him.

The door chime sounded. Fallon didn't mind the opportunity to end the conversation. Hawk stepped into her cozy white parlor. A few minutes later, Peregrine joined them.

Together again, as four, Fallon felt reassured. There was just something about them as a team that made her feel like they could actually do all the crap they had planned.

She and Raptor filled them in on the message from Whelkin and asked what they thought.

Peregrine didn't hesitate. "We make contact with him. No question about it." She looked to Hawk, who nodded agreement.

"He could be the perfect way for Blackout to get us to stick our necks out," Raptor reminded them.

"Yes," agreed Hawk. "But if that's the case, then every rope has two ends. We can yank on Whelkin and see what's on the other side."

Fallon smiled. She liked that imagery. "Then let's start planning."

FALLON DIDN'T MIND SPENDING two weeks lazing about on Zerellus. She used the time to exercise like a fiend and brush up on her language skills, just to be sure she could speak all thirteen languages her records said she could. Her records proved correct. After putting in a good day's work, she stretched out on the cushy white furniture and stuffed her face with delicacies and sweets. And did it gloriously.

Repairs to the *Nefarious* proceeded right along, and Fallon was pleased to get their weapons restocked as well. She added twenty-five percent to the weapon stores, exceeding normal protocol and pushing weight capacity. With the *Outlaw* on board, they didn't have a great deal of variance left, but as far as she was concerned, the munitions were non-negotiable.

Thanks to Hawk's network of friends, sensor blockers like the ones the pirate ships had used to sneak up on them would now be put into use on the *Nefarious*. If the PAC caught them with tech like that there'd be major penalties, but since Blackout had already tried to kill them, there seemed no particular downside. The PAC couldn't execute them *and* imprison them for owning contraband.

Raptor sent out a vague coded message for Whelkin, but did not receive a response from their former instructor. If he'd been on the run for eight weeks, there was a high likelihood of him being dead. Fallon and her team couldn't afford to wait on a message that might never come. Instead, she'd have to forge ahead with the possibility of Brak helping to regain her memories.

Which meant meeting up with the *Onari* again.

As they departed Zerellus, Fallon had to admire Peregrine's almost-smile. The woman looked practically chipper. Fallon didn't mention it, but she knew that Peregrine had scored some supplies that made her very, very happy. Fallon didn't yet know what they were, but she hoped she would at some point.

As Fallon set their course and destination coordinates, excitement shot down her spine. They'd arranged to meet up with the *Onari* at Dragonfire Station. That would be a very interesting homecoming for her.

Given the *Onari*'s current position, Fallon knew Jerin and

Demitri had to be pushing the engines to tolerance in order to make the rendezvous. Probably beyond. Fallon would make sure she took care of any ship repairs they might need, and would handle the vastly increased fuel cost.

Fallon sat back in her seat, watching the atmospheric data roll across the screen. She'd charted a slow, roundabout path to Dragonfire. The *Onari* wouldn't make it for two weeks yet, which left Fallon with time to kill. Flush with supplies, weapons, and a freshly refurbished ship, she and her team needed only to bide their time.

In the meantime, perhaps they'd hear from Whelkin. She also wanted to find a way to make contact with Admiral Colb. While she couldn't remember him as the kindly uncle-type her father had described, Hiro trusted Colb, and had vouched for him. That didn't mean she was ready to trust him, but it gave Colb the greatest likelihood of trustworthiness of anyone within Blackout. Besides the possibly dead Whelkin, of course.

Fallon had argued for remaining longer on Zerellus. She'd enjoyed the five-star accommodations and the genuine sunlight and fresh air tremendously. Security wasn't much of an issue either, so long as they laid low.

But Raptor had argued—correctly, damn him— that he'd be more likely to pick up rogue message streams outside of a planetary atmosphere.

Which left her with plenty of time to plan her return to Dragonfire. The station provided the perfect opportunity to gather all her allies in one place she knew she could defend. She also liked the irony of fighting Blackout from a PAC station. Not that she planned to stay there long.

Defensible location, check. Allies, check. Now they just needed a plan of action. If she wasn't going to be pampered in Zerellian style, she might as well be stabbing the bad guys through the heart. And the eye. And the crotch.

"Doing okay?" Peregrine had come up to the bridge to give Fallon a meal break.

"Sure. Why wouldn't I be?"

Peregrine sat in the co-pilot's seat. "Returning to Dragonfire might bother me, if I were you. And waiting for Raptor to find info we can use is frustrating for us all."

"Nothing I can do about it." Sure, Fallon was impatient, but she'd become accustomed to these drawn-out periods of inactivity, which seemed to exist only to be shattered by sudden action. "At least Raptor found some info that might mean Whelkin is legit."

The academy had reported him missing eight weeks ago, which corresponded with his message. The PAC had almost immediately removed that classification and listed him as on special assignment. Which seemed awfully similar to Avian Unit's own official status.

Peregrine didn't look directly at her, instead focusing on readouts from the external scanners. "He always seemed like a really good guy."

"It'd be nice for that to actually be true, wouldn't it?"

"Always nice when people don't surprise you by being an asshole," Peregrine agreed. "And having him as an ally would be good too."

After Fallon's meal break, she slept for a few hours, then returned to the bridge to relieve Hawk. He, she, and Peregrine handled the bridge duty shifts so that Raptor could devote himself to shoveling through the data he'd collected. Fallon wished that she could be helpful with that, but then again, the idea of charting, cross-checking, and generally going blind nearly made her suicidal. And that was if she could even decipher all the lines of code, which she couldn't. So, yeah, better Raptor handled that while she took care of the ship.

The days rolled by. Nothing noteworthy happened, which was good. But in the darkness of space, time curled out in infinite swirls of ambiguity. Fallon had nothing to do but wait, and wonder about all the things she didn't yet know.

Fallon felt her energy build the closer they got to Dragonfire. Finally, they quietly docked, with the *Onari* doing the same shortly after. The *Onari*'s return would be met with great fanfare, while Fallon and her team would go all but unnoticed.

Avian Unit had moved into two executive suites, side by side on Deck Four. One accommodation for Fallon and Peregrine, and one for Hawk and Raptor. Each small suite had room for both an official and an assistant. Though "small" was a relative concept. After several months of living on ships, Fallon found Dragonfire's accommodations perfectly comfortable, albeit nothing like the luxury on Zerellus.

Captain Nevitt paid them a visit soon after they arrived. Or more specifically, she paid Fallon a visit while her teammates made themselves scarce.

"Captain." As Nevitt entered the suite, Fallon gave the proper bow of respect for a superior PAC officer.

"Chief." Nevitt returned the bow, slightly shallower, befitting a captain to her second officer. Which was, in itself, a show of respect. Nevitt hadn't replaced Fallon as chief of security. She should have, of course, but Fallon understood that the captain was playing a very long game.

"I trust your operations are progressing?" Captain Nevitt asked. "It's been quite some time." She remained statuesque and mildly intimidating in a fine-edged way. Her dark brown skin and eyes complemented her hair, arranged around her head in short, textured twists.

Nevitt lifted a demanding eyebrow. Damn, Fallon admired her nerve.

"Yes. We have goals, we have targets. We just need some...collaboration."

"I see." Nevitt folded her hands behind her back and paced the suite's parlor. "And when do you expect to complete your goals?"

"Uncertain. Too many factors in the mix to pin things down. Could be weeks. Could be months."

Nevitt paused, narrowed her eyes slightly, then resumed her pacing. "Is there anything you can tell me at this point?"

Not about Blackout, to be certain. But she could give Nevitt some personal information.

"I've had some limited success with reacquainting myself with my memories. Some vicariously, as told to me by people who experienced the same things with me. Others from my own mind, but in a one-dimensional way. Brak's going to be helping me with that."

"I see. I trust you'll keep me apprised." Nevitt dipped her chin, then locked her eyes on Fallon's. "In the meantime, I have a matter for you to attend to."

"Security?"

"No. Morale. My lead mechanic has been depressed for, oh, six or seven months now. I want you to see her before you leave again. Un-depress her."

Fallon froze. "I don't think—"

Nevitt cut her off. "I'm not interested in what you think. You left some fallout in your wake—fallout that is affecting the function of my station. I expect you to fix it."

The idea of seeing Wren made the backs of Fallon's thighs feel like bugs were crawling on them. But she owed Nevitt. Owed her big. And Nevitt knew it.

"I'll go see her. I can't promise she won't feel worse afterward," Fallon warned.

Nevitt smiled. A self-satisfied smile that Fallon would have to practice in the mirror for her own future use, because *Prelin's ass* was it ever annoying. "I trust you to make her feel better. Not worse."

Fallon gritted her teeth. "I'll do what I can."

"I know you will." Nevitt's tone remained brisk. "If there's anything I can do to assist you, let me know. Otherwise, I'm leaving it to you to keep my station safe. If your activities here bring any harm—"

Fallon held her hands up in a staying gesture. "I know. I'm on it."

"Very well then. Call me if you need anything, keep me posted, and..." Nevitt paused on her way out the door. "Good luck."

She hadn't even bothered with a bow. That captain of hers proved to be more and more interesting all the time.

"So you see doors in your mind, and the memories stay behind them?" Brak asked. She sat in a straight-backed chair near the porthole in Fallon's suite. The rest of Avian Unit looked on while Jerin sat quietly on the couch, hands folded in her lap as she listened.

"Yes. Why? Is that not right?"

Brak tilted her head. "There is no 'right' and 'not right.' There's just whatever you're experiencing. I've never heard of such an organized dichotomy between memory storage and conscious thought. It's fascinating."

"But is that good? Or am I just some test specimen that has shown unusual properties? I'm looking for value judgments here." She smiled wryly to make sure Brak knew she was kidding. Sort of.

Brak chose her words carefully. "I'd say it's good, in that such organization bodes well for what I've designed for you."

"Oh, good. I was hoping you had something awesome planned."

Brak ignored her pseudo-humor. "I've devised an implant. Nothing like what must have been in your head previously. This is almost the reverse of that. Instead of holding information and pushing it out through your brain tissue, what I've devised will induct the memories. Serve as a synapse between them and your awareness."

"If it works, will I be able to experience memories as actual memories? Or will they still be like objects that I look at?"

"My hope is to restore your normal cognitive function. So ideally, this would return you to your normal self. The same as you were before all of this happened."

The way Fallon had been when she first went undercover to investigate Wren.

"You need to know that there are risks." Jerin's lovely voice belied the seriousness of her statement.

"Okay. Tell me."

"First, this might not work at all. You might endure surgery for no benefit. The expected side effects of the surgery are similar to the procedure that Brak performed on you before. Headache, nausea, balance problems. If things go wrong, those problems could be permanent. Worse, we might end up damaging the memories that you already have. You need to think about this very carefully."

She saw her teammates exchanging glances with one another, but she ignored them.

"So you're saying that I could end up waking up with no memory of myself all over again? And have to start from scratch?" Fallon looked from Jerin to Brak.

"Yes," Brak answered. "It's a possibility."

Fallon then looked at Peregrine, Hawk, and Raptor in turn. They all returned her gaze, saying nothing.

At least if things went wrong, she'd have her team to get her on track right from the beginning.

"When can we get started?"

9

Brak began with tests. Fallon spent the morning submitting to those, then went to handle the matter Nevitt had foisted upon her. If she had to deal with Wren, she might as well do it while she still had all of her current memories intact.

Raptor might be the Ghost, but Fallon was not without skills of her own. After ensuring that Wren had left work, she made her way up to Wren's quarters. Which happened to be the ones they had shared, back in their married days. Well, that ought to make this extra fun.

She touched the chime and let time tick by as she waited. When the doors whisked open and they saw each other face-to-face, Wren sucked in a loud breath. A momentary silence fell as they stared at one another.

Wren looked the same. Lovely, with her icy blue eyes and pale pink hair up in a messy bun. She hadn't yet pulled it down after her day of work.

"Can I come in?" Fallon asked.

Wren stepped back wordlessly, then gestured toward the sitting area of the living room. The doors closed behind them.

"Mind if I…" Fallon gestured vaguely at the quarters, asking permission to give it a security once-over to ensure no listening devices had been planted.

Wren made an impatient gesture, then crossed her arms and leaned against the wall.

Fallon made a quick physical check, but primarily used the small device she kept on her belt for just this purpose. Standard Blackout issue, with a few Peregrine modifications. It took up very little space alongside her comport and stinger.

When Fallon had finished, Wren just eyed her, still leaning against the wall. Okay, fine. Clearly she didn't want to make this easy. Fallon sat on the edge of the couch, folding her hands over her knees.

"This wasn't my idea. Nevitt insisted." She decided to get straight to the point. Making pithy remarks about how she hoped Wren had been well would only piss off her former wife.

"Why?" The single word came out sharp.

"She says your work performance has been less than satisfactory." That wiped the wary, vaguely hostile look off Wren's face. Fallon wasn't sure indignation was an improvement, but at least it was a change.

"I've gotten all my work done on time. That's ridiculous." Wren pushed away from the wall and flopped down into the chair alongside the couch.

"Nonetheless. I've been sent to straighten you out." Fallon lifted her chin slightly. A challenge. Wren had once been able to read her. She was willing to bet she still could.

Wren's eyes narrowed. "You're just about the last person who could help." At least she'd moved on to open anger. That was more productive.

"Since it's my fault to begin with, right?"

"Exactly." Wren took a breath and straightened, sitting up taller.

Fallon leaned forward, her hands still on her knees. "I'm very sorry for any unhappiness I've caused you, Wren. I really am."

Wren gave her a hard look, then deflated, her shoulders sagging. "I know. It just feels better to be mad at you." She ran her hands over her head, then wrenched the pins out of her hair, letting it fall down her back. She raked impatient fingers through it. Fallon's gaze lingered on the long tresses of pink.

"Yeah. I get that." Blame and anger were always easier than hurt and disappointment. Fallon could relate to that all too well.

"I thought I had this awesome life, then all of a sudden, I found out it wasn't real."

"At least some parts were," Fallon countered. "I don't have answers yet for my time here with you, but I'm certain I wouldn't have married you if I didn't care about you. You weren't just an assignment."

"How do I know that?" Wren seemed stuck between vulnerability and a desire to fight.

"Couldn't you tell if I were lying?"

"I used to think I could." Wren's gaze didn't waver. When Fallon didn't respond, she asked, "You still don't have your memories, then?"

"I've learned some things. As far as memories, though, no. I don't have those yet."

"Do you expect to?" Wren didn't quite manage to hide her hope.

"It's my plan."

Wren's chin lifted. "Well, let me know if you succeed."

"I will. In the meantime, is there anything I can do for you? I came here because of Nevitt, but I don't want you to be unhappy. I mean, we were married. I care about you being okay."

Wren sighed. "I'll be fine, but I want you to be okay, too. It doesn't thrill me that you're out there, doing who knows what."

"So you're worried?" She risked a gently teasing look.

Wren relented with a small smile. "Of course I am."

Fallon grinned at her and rose to casually perch on the arm of the couch. "Well, let me tell you, then." She leaned in closer. "I mean, I can't give you actual details, but it turns out I'm totally badass. And I have these partners, who are more than totally badass. You should see the things we can do." She raised an eyebrow and nodded in a mock-confidential way.

Wren rolled her eyes, then reluctantly laughed. "That's only somewhat reassuring. Also mildly alarming. Besides, I've already seen some of the things you can do." She raised an eyebrow and Fallon caught a hint of double entendre. She felt a catch—a pull toward Wren and the connection between them.

Awkwardness almost immediately elbowed in. Wren stepped toward the kitchenette, away from her. "Can I get you anything? A drink?"

"I probably shouldn't stay." Except she kind of wanted to. Instead, she moved toward the door. "I just wanted to make sure you'd be okay."

Wren closed the space between them and put her hand on Fallon's arm. "Do you have to go right away?"

Fallon wasn't sure how to answer that. "I'm not leaving the station right now, but I don't think I should be here. I don't want to complicate things."

"Things are already complicated." Wren stepped into her personal space, her eyes locked on Fallon's.

Yeah, about as complicated as they got, relationship-wise. Married and never married, attracted and repelled, comforted and agitated. Whatever Wren's problems with Fallon were, Fallon had her own objections. Wren had ditched her at the first sign of trouble, after all. Sure, that sign had been less an inkling and more an exploding nova, but whatever. Fallon had deserved better from someone who'd made marriage vows to her.

But there Wren was, edging closer until Fallon could feel the warmth of her skin and smell the oddly enticing hint of grease solvent. Wren's eyes held her in place, and Fallon could only stare at all of her textures. The soft wave of her hair, the curve of her bottom lip, the fringe of her eyelashes.

She felt Wren's breath on her neck and knew that if she didn't step back now, things would only get more complicated.

She didn't step back. She didn't seem to have a knack for retreating.

FALLON OPENED her eyes inside the confines of her mind. She'd grown accustomed to finding herself pacing the labyrinth of doors. She'd become more picky about selecting them, too.

A pattern had recently emerged. Round doors tended to be small things. Objects, like a book or a jacket. Without context, they meant next to nothing. She avoided the round doors.

Red ones, though. Red ones meant something fraught with emotion. Perhaps a combat scene or a verbal fight. Fallon liked the red doors. They seemed the most likely to show her something useful.

They were tougher to find, though. Her memory seemed to be chock full of spoons, hats, flowers, and other useless things. Perhaps a function of her ability to retain so many memories. But it made it hard to wade through all the doors to find a red one.

She turned a shadowy corner and finally found one. Small, though. Its little square frame wasn't big enough to get her head through. She lowered herself to her knees and grasped the small protrusion on the front. More of a handle than a knob. The door popped open with a small tug and she stuck her hand in, all the way to the shoulder. Usually, if she kept pushing inward...

Ah, yes. She was in a small room. She twisted into a cross-legged position and waited. These memories showed up whenever they damn well pleased.

She didn't mind the wait. It wasn't like she was in a real room, with a real floor under her ass. She sat in a shadowy figment, wrapped in layers of sleep. Not at all unpleasant.

The room lightened gradually, and Fallon watched a beach

scene take shape around her. Golden sand pressed into her legs as waves of heat drifted down to her from the sun. Trees swayed in a gentle breeze, and partygoers milled about. Wait. She'd seen this before. What was it?

Right. Her wedding. Wren had shown her images. Fallon saw herself in a gauzy pink-and-white dress with flowers in her hair, which hung much longer than she now wore it.

The image zoomed, so that Fallon could see only her face, with a periphery of other people just at the edges. Memory-Fallon smiled and nodded, then fell back, letting Wren and the others proceed past her. Her eyes tracked Wren, though, and her lips curved in a contented smile. Then her eyes snapped to the left and the right quickly, and Memory-Fallon's face became alert. Hard. Worried. For just a microsecond. But in the time-variance of the memory, she replayed that instant over and over.

Fallon knew perfectly well that if she woke herself up, she'd find Wren sleeping next to her. This was the first time she'd accessed a memory relevant to the current events of her life. It could be entirely coincidental, sure, but she didn't believe that. She'd made a mental connection between Wren and this memory. A moment of worry at their wedding. Why? Worry that Wren would find out about her? Or worry for Wren? Or maybe just worry about all the reception details going smoothly.

The memory started to turn fuzzy, pixelating into gray haze. It always happened this way. After a certain amount of time, her memories kicked her out. Made her sleep. As her thoughts grew blurry, she tried to remind herself to...something. Later.

FALLON WOKE UP ALONE, which suited her fine. She took a long shower to give her jumpsuit enough time to get clean in the processor. As soon as the unit stopped, she dressed and braced herself.

She stepped out of the bedroom cautiously. Wren leaned down with one hand on the couch, putting on her shoes. She turned her head to look at Fallon. "You can let yourself out, right? I need to get to work."

Fallon's fears of an emotional scene eased, though she stayed wary of an ambush. "Sure."

"Are you going to be around long?" Wren straightened, smoothing out her mechanic's coveralls instead of looking directly at Fallon.

"Not sure. I'm not leaving right away, that I know of." Fallon sidled into the room, slowly drifting toward the door.

"Relax," Wren said with a laugh. "I'm not going to be throwing myself at you, begging you not to leave. I'm still pissed at you, and just so you know, this does *not* make us a couple."

Actually, that did reassure Fallon. "That's a relief. I'm not that thrilled with you, either."

A smile lit Wren's face. "Good."

Wren strode to the door, pausing only to say, "I'll see you later. Or not. Try not to die," before walking right out.

Fallon lingered for a moment in Wren's wake. Sometimes Wren made Fallon work really hard to avoid remembering how easy it was to love her.

FALLON HAD HOPED to find a message from Brak regarding the procedure when she returned to her quarters. But when she entered, she discovered her partners waiting in her suite. Their expressions put her on instant alert.

"We were just about to call you. Whelkin made contact ten minutes ago." Peregrine's frown cut deeper than usual.

Fallon jumped right into fight mode. "Where is he?"

"In trouble. Hiding behind an asteroid. Life support failing.

We need to go get him." Hawk leaped to his feet and flipped his backpack onto his back.

"Immediate departure?"

Hawk slanted a look at her. "Unless you think he can somehow survive without pressurization."

"And if this is a ploy to draw us out?"

"Then we take *him* out," Raptor answered, eyes dark.

"Right. I'll grab my bag." She didn't need to pack it. She kept it ready. A moment later she returned. "Let's go."

As soon as Fallon got the *Nefarious* free of the station, she entered the coordinates Raptor gave her.

"Did he give any additional information?" she asked. She needed details. His reappearance in their lives would either be a boon or a disaster. It would be nice if she had a clue as to which.

"No time," Peregrine said. "He said he was diverting all power to emergency containment."

"What's our ETA?" asked Hawk.

Fallon studied her readout. "Four hours at maximum velocity. Can't do it any faster."

"Let's hope he has that long," muttered Hawk.

"On the bright side," Peregrine mused, "if we show up and find him dead, we know he was legit."

They all stared at her. She shrugged. "It's true."

Since a dead Whelkin wouldn't be any use to them, they had to hope he'd be alive, whether friend or foe.

His ship turned out to have been a poor one to start with. Amazing he'd gone on the run with the patched-up little starrunner. Not much more than a joyride ship for hopping between close-set planets. It definitely had a plasma leak, which Fallon saw reading hot on the sensors.

"Hawk and Raptor, you're up. Save and subdue. Make sure he's under wraps."

They nodded and made for the airlock. Fallon's problem was docking with a ship in crisis. If the damn thing blew, it would take her and her crew with it. She matched the ship's attitude and rotation, then gingerly made the connection. She didn't want to create any more friction or vibration than she had to, for fear of setting off a chain reaction. Hawk and Raptor boarded the little cruiser while she stayed glued to the sensors.

Waiting was not her strong suit. Minutes ticked by, and then more minutes. Fallon kept a constant watch for any temperature peaks or buildups in energy. When she finally heard Raptor give the all clear, she threw herself into getting them away from the time bomb of a ship as fast as she could make it happen.

With it safely behind them, she felt relief for one danger averted. Then Hawk and Raptor marched Whelkin up to the bridge and she faced another.

Ross Whelkin looked good, other than a bruised cheekbone, a bloodied chin, and a layer of grime. He'd grown his hair out, and the shaggy blond mane made him look younger than middle-aged. A human who'd transplanted to Zerellus early in life, he had the tanned good looks of someone accustomed to sun and fresh air.

"Fallon," he said. "Good to see you again. I was afraid I wouldn't."

"I bet." She gave him a hard look. "I'm sure you can appreciate the situation we're in. We have no way of knowing if we can trust you."

He nodded, then shifted his weight. He seemed to be favoring his left leg. Probably an injury. Raptor could check that out later.

"That's why I brought you this." He held out a data chip to her, but she indicated he should hand it to Raptor instead.

"What is it?" Raptor asked.

"Hopefully, everything you need to bring Blackout down. But

while you look at it, would you mind if I get a little first aid and some food? I haven't eaten in days."

Piloting could be the best job, and sometimes also the worst. Fallon sat at the controls while Raptor worked on the data chip and Peregrine and Hawk saw to Whelkin. She wanted to know what was going on, but wasn't about to leave the pilot's chair. Not with who-knows-what out there searching for Whelkin.

Raptor returned first. She tried to glean something from his expression, but he gave nothing away. "He might be for real. If he's not, then the entirety of Blackout has been subverted, and I don't think that's the case."

"Why not?" Fallon asked.

"It would take too many people. Nothing we've encountered has indicated that all of Blackout has gone bad. We've always assumed a few rogue individuals quietly manipulating it to benefit their own agenda. That's much more the style of those people. Who wants to be in control of something that everyone knows is corrupt? It's too big to keep quiet."

It was a reductive, roundabout sort of logic, but it rang true to her.

"So you think Whelkin's for real, then." She'd hoped for that, but suspicion and caution always outweighed optimism.

"I think he most likely is."

She'd opt for cautiously optimistic, then. For now. "So what's on the chip he gave us?"

"Strategic positions. Pass codes. Contingency plans. And Krazinski's name is all over it."

"Krazinski." It was almost too predictable, really. Krazinski had been the one to blackmail Brak, trying to get her to engineer memory implants. He'd always been the most likely suspect, and every time they got close to the problem with Blackout, Krazinski's name bubbled to the top.

Fallon wondered if she should feel personally betrayed, given how close Avian Unit's relationship with Krazinski had apparently been. They'd even rescued his daughter, for Prelin's sake. She searched Raptor's face, but found only drive and determination.

"Fingerprints?" She didn't mean actual fingerprints, but data authenticity. No one could identify signs of tampering like Raptor.

"Not a thing. They're as clean as it gets."

She let out a long, slow breath. "So do we trust Whelkin, then?"

"Of course not." He grinned at her. "But we can give him enough rope to hang himself. And if he turns out to be clean, then all the better."

So they'd given Whelkin the appearance of their trust, all the while monitoring him closely. Raptor saw to the man's healthcare needs, and Whelkin saw to his own makeover. When he returned to the bridge in a clean jumpsuit, he made Fallon pause.

He still looked like the dashing young instructor that a great many academy students, by all accounts, had fallen for. He'd washed his hair, but it remained a dirty blond that seemed to suggest debauchery somehow. He was just good-looking enough to be attractive, but not so much as to suggest vanity. He seemed rough, loose, and a little wild.

Raptor caught her checking him out and raised a sardonic eyebrow. She smirked at him. No, she had no designs on their former instructor. She made a mental note to warn Hawk off, though. Just in case. He'd been eyeing Whelkin like he was birthday cake.

"Decided to trust me?" Whelkin asked.

"To a point," she hedged. "You know how we work."

"That's why I wanted to get this to you. See if we could figure it out together. Things have smelled wrong for over a year now. When it all started to reek, I couldn't keep ignoring it, assuming there was a good reason. I had to start digging."

"What took you so long to bring it to us?" Hawk asked.

"Lack of proof to incriminate anyone, and the fact that I didn't want to tip anyone off that I was sniffing around. I also needed to be sure that you weren't part of it. Then, when I was ready to talk to you, you all just disappeared. Off the grid. 'Special assignment' was the official line. But I started digging there, too, and found you'd been separated. That's when the reek became a stench."

"We weren't too excited about it either," Peregrine remarked dryly.

"So what have you learned?" Whelkin paused, then rephrased. "Is there any intel you're willing to share with me?"

Good question. They hadn't figured that out just yet. They sure couldn't risk letting him know anything that involved Dragonfire. Just his knowing about the *Nefarious* made Fallon uncomfortable.

"Fine." Whelkin didn't seem perturbed. "I get it." He turned to Raptor. "Look in the pocket of the uniform I had on before. You'll find a splitter. I want you to use it on me."

Everyone stared at him. Splitters had been outlawed by every government on record a hundred years ago.

"Come on, we don't have time to waste," Whelkin said. "I need you all to trust me, and that's the only way it's going to happen."

"Would the thing even work?" Peregrine looked doubtful.

"Given what I had to do to get it, it had better." Whelkin's voice had an impatient edge.

"You know there's no way back from that," Raptor said.

"Like I said, it's the only way you're going to trust me. We don't have time to waste."

Fallon exchanged a long look with Raptor. She got the impression he had the same thought she did. She nodded. "Fine. Do it." She looked at Hawk. "Watch over them."

When the three men had disappeared to the ship's tiny infirmary, Peregrine spoke up.

"Will Raptor really do it?"

Would Raptor implant Whelkin's brain with a device that would allow them to monitor any data he saw, hear every word he said, and tell whether or not he told the truth? Splitters were classified as an illegal torture mechanism. They were invariably fatal, giving only a lifespan of about a week past implantation. Raptor would do what he needed to. "I trust him."

Peregrine nodded.

Of course they had complete trust in Raptor. But the idea of putting a splitter in the brain of someone they'd once cared about rubbed Fallon, and no doubt the others, the wrong way. The fact that Whelkin had suggested it, even planned for it, indicated that he was for real. Which would mean that he was one of the good guys.

A half hour later, the men returned. Whelkin looked tired and stressed, but Raptor and Hawk had relaxed. Fallon peered at Raptor questioningly.

"He's with us. I injected him with a subdermal vitamin pack and he didn't even flinch."

Fallon's jaw unclenched. Raptor had made Whelkin think he was going to install the splitter, using Whelkin's willingness as a litmus for his trustworthiness. He'd passed the test, and kept his brain intact. A big win for Whelkin. Not too shabby for Avian Unit, either.

She stood and gave her former instructor a proper bow. "Welcome aboard, Captain Whelkin."

THE THING about hot information was that if you didn't act quickly, it would evaporate into nothing. And Whelkin definitely had hot information, even if some of it was a few months old.

He'd gotten his ass—and ship—royally kicked in trying to follow up on that information. He'd been on communications blackout during that period, which explained why they hadn't heard from him sooner. All the while, he'd been orbiting a little lab located on the dark side of the minor moon of an uninhabited planet.

But Whelkin's scrapheap of a ship had started leaking neutrinos, causing him to be detected. He'd only escaped by luck, and if Avian Unit hadn't arrived when they had, he still would have died.

"So what's in the lab?" Fallon asked after she punched in the coordinates he'd given her. If she didn't like his answers, she'd veer off long before they got close. The planet was of no consequence, so far as she could tell. It didn't even have a name recognized by the PAC, just a numerical designation.

"Biotech. Advanced stuff. Endocrine boosters, neurotransmitter enhancers. Garbage that doesn't make a person less killable, but makes them much slower to die." Whelkin's face showed his disgust.

Fallon's lungs stalled, as if she'd walked into an unpressurized airlock. Her body heated and she felt light-headed. She'd known they were chasing down something big, but these things…they were crucial items that all PAC treaties hung on. Just like neural implants for augmentation. The only reason to have such things would be for espionage or war. Some sort of plan for galactic domination?

Regardless of intentions, if the PAC was in possession of such things, it could mean a breakdown of the entire cooperative. Full-scale warfare would be inevitable.

Why would someone deep inside intelligence want to risk tearing this sector of the universe apart? And what kind of scientist would even agree to work on that kind of tech? Fallon's shock transitioned into fury, and she channeled that feeling into cold professionalism.

"And neural implants, right?" Fallon kept her voice even.

"Yeah." Whelkin seemed surprised. "How did you know?"

She smiled humorlessly at him. "Meet one of the first test cases."

Understanding and pity dawned in his eyes. "Taravok."

She knew that name. Had come across a vague reference recently during her digging for planets with two moons. "Tell me."

"I saw the mission notes. You were scheduled to be there. But there was no mention of why, and then you went off the grid. I assumed you recognized our destination."

"Why would I?"

His forehead crinkled in confusion. "The coordinates I gave you are for Taravok."

"According to the PAC, we're headed for 942864-B." She felt cold all over.

"Taravok isn't its official designation."

That explained why she hadn't been able to discover more about it. But now Whelkin had put them on the path to the place that had been plaguing her for months. "Apparently I did go there. And thanks to Blackout's experimentation on me, I've lost every memory I had prior to the past six months." She corrected herself. "Almost seven now."

He grimaced, but ultimately only said, "I'm sorry."

She understood. There weren't any words for losing your whole past. She'd been used for something, it seemed. Then they'd wiped her memories and tried to kill her. But she'd retained fragments of herself. Instincts and slivers of memories, combined with things that others had described to her. She'd never lost who she truly was and now, she'd take the things they hadn't managed to steal from her, and she'd ram it all right down their throats. Then she'd get her ass back to Dragonfire and take back her memory.

"Increasing speed to Taravok."

―――

"You okay?" Peregrine had stayed behind when Raptor and Hawk took Whelkin to the mess to get some food.

"Better than okay. I'm ready." Fallon didn't have any doubts.

Peregrine sighed. "I'm not good with the emotions stuff, but it seems like you might have a lot going on in your head right now. Are you sure you don't need to, like, talk about it or some shit?"

"Oh. Well, when you put it *that* way." Fallon snorted out a laugh.

Peregrine snickered.

"Now that you mention it—" Fallon smirked, "—I was hoping we could talk about my inferiority complex."

Peregrine chortled. "Okay, but after that, let's get into my fear of abandonment."

They both hooted with laughter, only to have Hawk charge in, looking ready to tear apart a planet with his bare hands. When he saw them, red-faced from hilarity, he pulled up short.

"Uh. What?" He looked from Fallon to Peregrine.

Fallon tried to answer, but didn't manage anything coherent. His perplexed look added fuel to the fire.

Peregrine choked out, "Overcompensating for something," and they both howled.

―――

Fallon didn't think she could feel any better. She was in command of the pilot's chair on one entirely badass ship, wearing a bandolier of knives, with stingers strapped to her arms and thighs—all set to kill. Best of all, she had a sword holstered on her back. She felt like the embodiment of vengeance, a tool of righteousness. And she didn't give a damn if that was egomaniacal or delusional. Scrap that. If she needed to search her feelings after they stormed the lab, then she could sit down with Per for some more girl talk.

The idea made her snort, and Hawk sent her a dirty look. He hadn't quite forgiven them for their bout of stress relief earlier. She hardened her features back into their warrior mask, and he looked satisfied.

She'd never seen Avian Unit looking so fine, with all of their weapons and equipment. Well, not that she remembered anyway. Hopefully soon, she'd know for sure.

She enjoyed the aggressive approach vector, which exceeded PAC safety regulations. Fallon was more concerned with speed, to prevent the lab from calling help. Fortunately, the target had no air support at all. Probably because there was no point in hiding a lab only to draw attention to it with defenses.

She pulled off a rough-and-fast landing on the moon, and then their boots hit the ground. Hawk and Whelkin took the front. Per and Fallon followed, with Raptor covering the rear. Getting in was easier than anticipated. They had the pass codes, thanks to Whelkin, and there were no DNA checks. Sloppy work, in Fallon's opinion, but she wasn't going to complain.

Just before they breached the building, Fallon had a moment of clarity. As far as her memory was concerned, this was her first frontal assault with Avian Unit. Was she ready?

She absolutely was.

Her team walked right in, surprising the hell out of the dozen fully armed guards stationed just inside the lobby. Her adversaries had put some effort into keeping this place secure, after all.

Raptor had hacked the proximity sensors beforehand, which allowed them to catch the guards completely unaware. Hawk and Whelkin pressed forward, taking most of the targets out before the others could do much. Fallon flung her knives whenever she had a clear shot past her team, but with so many bodies in the room she had to be careful not to knife a friend in the neck. Peregrine pushed forward and engaged hand to hand.

Finally they made it into the lab itself. First priority: neutralize the scientists. They'd intended to stun and zip-cuff them, in order to question them, but damn if all the people in the lab didn't have weapons.

Change of plan.

The lab workers wielded their weapons poorly, like the inadequately trained scientists they were. Fallon's team neutralized them in moments, but she regretted the need to do so.

She and Whelkin went to see if any scientists still breathed while Raptor and Hawk took on the database.

"Rip the whole thing out. I want it all," Fallon ordered as she pressed her fingers into necks in search of a pulse. So far, nothing.

"It'll take a few minutes," Raptor called, engrossed in the process of removing the emergency data core. "I have to make sure everything has copied."

Meanwhile, Peregrine crammed equipment into bags. Every now and then she whooped something unintelligible. Fallon had no idea what Peregrine was finding, but clearly it was good stuff.

"Got it!" Raptor eased the self-contained core into a polymechrine case and snapped it closed.

"Help Peregrine finish."

Hawk, Per, and Raptor made short work of grabbing any other equipment that looked important.

Fallon touched the final scientist, a human woman, and was surprised to find a faint pulse. She turned the woman on her back and checked for breath. Breathing, but barely.

Fallon went to the drug locker Peregrine had almost emptied and located a powerful stimulant. She injected it into the scientist's neck. Within seconds, the woman's eyes opened.

"We're clearing this place out. Is there anything important not contained in this room? A separate storage area?" They'd check either way, but if the woman had details, Fallon could use them. She was well aware that she didn't have much time left. A distress signal had been sent out as soon as the people at the lab realized they were under attack.

The woman's pale face moved from side to side. "That's everything," she wheezed. Her eyes were wide. "Who are you? Blackout?"

"We're the ones who are going to keep the PAC intact."

The woman's eyes clouded again. The stimulant was strong, but it couldn't stave off death. "That's…good." The woman went still, and her eyes fixed on some unseen point, unfocused.

After confirming that there was nothing else of note in the small building, Avian Unit hustled their stolen goods out of there. Then they threw themselves into the *Nefarious* and launched. Which was fairly easy, since the moon had no atmosphere.

As the distance between them and Taravok grew, Fallon felt a rising tide of triumph. They'd turned the tables. Blackout now needed to be very afraid of *them*, and what they could do with everything they'd discovered.

The reversal almost seemed too easy. Everything always turned on a pin the width of a hair. One tiny change, or one fact falling into place. She lived a life of serendipity, long jags of waiting, and sudden surges of activity. Meanwhile, always waiting for that other shoe to drop. It was a strange existence.

She took a last look at Taravok and its two moons before clearing the solar system. They weren't identical to the ones in her dreams, but no matter. They were pieces of the puzzle, and the puzzle was starting to come together.

10

When Fallon saw a ship coming in fast, she knew it wasn't a coincidence. She hadn't expected to get away with looting Krazinski's lab of war crimes without consequence, and here came the consequence. Game on.

She flipped through her sensors, gleaning as much as she could about the incoming ship's specs and armament. "That's a beauty right there, Ravager class, stripped down and modified with two extra engines. No way to outrun it."

She had to admire the sleek lines of the ship and its hulking engines. So much power. Faster than her *Nefarious* without a doubt, but without the maneuverability.

"When you're done drooling, think you could get to work on our tactics?" Peregrine's tone was halfway between exasperated and amused.

"Already on it. I can plan and admire at the same time." She'd launched into calculating armament and maneuvers, while taking nearby stations and planets into consideration. Cascades of information flowed through her brain as she mentally simulated the battle over and over before it even began. She increased speed just short of maximum to keep them out of reach for as long as possible while she thought.

She pronounced, "They've got us overpowered and outgunned. But we've got more maneuverability and the best pilot in Blackout. It'll be a good contest."

Whelkin gave her a sidelong look. "As far as I know, there's no Best Secret Intelligence Pilot Award."

"Sure there is. You win it when you don't die." She began programming sequences for maneuvers into the voicecom. She had a plan, and without a second pilot of equal skill to back her up, she'd need to prepare meticulously.

"How's your piloting, Ross?" Fallon decided that the current situation warranted a switch to his first name, though it felt a little odd for her to say to a senior officer. "Hawk's the best of these three, but he's more of a gunner than a flyer."

"Better than average. I guess I'm your guy."

"Guess you are. I need you in the copilot seat, so I can show you what you'll need to do."

She timed it all out in her head, trying to compensate for any surprises. She pulled back on the throttle, allowing the other ship to close in on them gradually. She explained her plan.

If Ross had doubts, he didn't show it. He might turn out to be a decent teammate.

THE *NEFARIOUS* TURNED to take the enemy ship head on. Ross went in at an angle, nose down, looking for a shot at the enemy ship's belly.

No luck there. The ship twisted away, circling around the *Nefarious* and letting loose with two torpedoes. The *Nefarious* rolled and went into a steep dive, avoiding one torpedo while the other grazed the stern of the ship, causing the *Nefarious* to shudder and alarms to start shrieking.

It wasn't enough to endanger them. Poised to do her part, Fallon reminded herself to wait. Be patient. Find the right moment to unleash her surprise. Until then, Ross would have to keep dodging and taking hits.

The ships continued to circle one another. Dry plasma began to vent after laser-cannon blasts glanced the port side of the *Nefarious*. Fallon eyed the misty streams from her front-row view as they dissolved into space.

The *Nefarious* did well at dodging the blasts of the stronger ship, but the constant potshots began to concern Fallon. If her opening didn't come soon, they'd all end up as vapor. At least at such close proximity, the other ship's speed didn't give it any advantage.

The *Nefarious* dove away, spinning, then pitched right back up directly toward the enemy ship. A hail of laser-cannon fire singed across the upper bulkhead. Fallon could imagine the streaks of black marring her lovely ship, and felt a surge of fury. She was sick of this shit.

"Attack plan delta," she announced over the voicecom, silently wishing Ross and Hawk luck. Time to go for broke. The *Nefarious* bore down on the ship with Hawk firing a barrage of torpedoes and cannon fire. Everything they had, basically, thrown all at once. If this didn't work, they'd be done for.

Then she saw it. A decompression from a side hatch knocked the ship off course. That was her moment.

Fallon detached the *Outlaw* from the belly of the *Nefarious*, where she'd waited for the entirety of the fight. Ross' maneuvers had cleverly concealed her position.

From this distance, she couldn't miss. She aimed the *Outlaw*'s laser cannons point-blank at the hatch that had decompressed.

The damaged section of the enemy ship blew up in her face, as planned. With less time to pull away than she'd hoped for, pieces of the other ship slammed into the *Outlaw*. Shrill alarms alerted her to microfractures in the hull. Force fields struggled to maintain the ship's containment, which put a strain on the life support systems. She tried to hold her breath but her chest felt heavy and she ended up choking and gasping.

The back of the cockpit had emergency containment suits, but she couldn't spare a second away from the controls. Having air to breathe wouldn't help her if she exploded.

Finally the haze cleared as she maneuvered away from the enemy ship, which blazed bright with multiple explosions. No doubt the *Nefarious* had done that, but she was too busy trying to get out of there to pay attention to the battle.

Too late. She felt a blaze of heat light up her back the same instant her sensors started shrieking. Her skin felt raw, as if she'd been charred over an open flame like a kabob.

Her eyes and hands still worked just fine, though, and with gritted teeth she circled twice to get the correct position to return to the cargo bay of the *Nefarious*. Her starboard thruster was blown to hell, and she could only adjust attitude by spinning all the way around.

Finally she eased the *Outlaw* into the *Nefarious* and shut down its complaining power systems before it could do something unfortunate, like blow up the bay. While the *Outlaw* cooled, she pressurized the bay. She hoped the *Nefarious* had fared better than her little race car, which might be nothing more than scrap at this point.

She heaved herself to her feet, only for burning pain to take her down to her knees. She coughed hard, unable to draw enough air. Were the life support systems compromised? She hadn't thought so. She crawled toward the exit hatch, which fortunately opened when she slapped it.

She dragged herself out onto the cool deck plate of the cargo bay. She'd thought it would make her feel better but it didn't. Her lungs were on fire. Breach gas, then. Her lungs had been scorched from the inside by the very thing designed to keep her ship from bursting into flames and exploding.

She appreciated the irony as she sank into darkness.

A TINY DOOR appeared in the gloom. The tall rectangle of orange seemed lit from within as it hovered in the haze.

She reached out for it, only to find she had no hands. No, wait, she did. She could feel the fingers of one of them on the opposite arm. But she couldn't see them because they were as dark and hazy as the shadows around her.

She emerged in a room, though she hadn't taken any steps. She'd simply materialized there, standing in what looked like a dorm. Or an efficiency apartment, maybe.

"That's stupid." She heard her own voice and turned toward the sound. She saw a young version of herself perched on the edge of a bed, hands curled into fists in her lap. "Why would we settle for less? I want to be the best."

A teenage Raptor sat next to her, taking her hand and prying it open, then pressing his palm to hers and entwining their fingers. "It wouldn't be less if we were *together*," he argued. "And we might even live to see old age. Does that not sound at all good to you?"

She started to pull away, then sighed and leaned into him instead. He wrapped his arm around her.

Fallon was struck by the tortured expression on his face as he held the earlier version of her. Realization dropped into her stomach like a ton of hot slag. He loved her. *Really* loved her.

Judging by the conflict on her own younger face, she loved him too. Prelin's ass. That certainly complicated things. Why had he lied? No, she knew why. To keep things between them less complicated. Because complication sucked.

She stepped closer, studying the young couple. They looked strong and healthy, though he was much more attractive than her.

Even this young, Raptor had a rakish charm, along with an appealing earnestness.

"I've aimed my whole life at being the best," she watched herself say. "As much as I care about you, I can't forget about that. If I missed my opportunity, I might grow to resent you. Maybe even hate you."

He rubbed her hand between both of his, hope morphing into grim acceptance. "I guess that's it, then."

"I'm sorry. This is just the way I'm made." Her eyes pleaded with him to understand. To not be hurt by her refusal. But Fallon could see the loss already taking the glow from him.

"I know. I always knew that." He nudged her and smiled. "I just thought it was worth a try. To be sure. Now we know."

"Yeah. I guess."

"After graduation, we'll have to find a way to be just partners."

Even then, they'd known the parameters of the job they'd be taking on. Maintaining a deep tie would compromise both of them in too many ways.

"I know." Young Fallon raised her hands to cup his face. She leaned in and kissed him tenderly. "That's three weeks away though. For now, we can just..." She trailed off, sliding into his lap and running her hands under his shirt. Raptor didn't argue with her plan.

Fallon felt torn about remaining. The memory rightfully belonged to her, and Raptor had the same images in his head. But watching it from the outside still gave her a creepy feeling of voyeurism, and that was so not her thing. So she turned away, leaving the past to be swallowed again by the shadows.

SHE WOKE up to agony slicing its way across her back. She groaned, only to find her lungs sore. She coughed on the roughness of her own breath.

"Easy." The dim illumination increased and she saw Raptor next to her. She lay in the tiny infirmary, on a basic version of a techbed. Enough to get the job done, but without the comfort of a full-sized one.

"How's my ship?" she croaked, trying to sit up.

Raptor laughed as he adjusted the techbed controls, bringing the bed to a moderate incline. "In about the same shape as you. Shitty, but surviving." He handed her a cup of biogel.

Drinking it didn't quench the soreness in her lungs, but it eased her throat. "And the rest of you?" She looked him over, but other than fatigue, he looked okay.

"A little banged up, but fine."

"My diagnosis?" Each word hurt, so she opted for brevity.

"Third-degree burns down your back. Chemical burns in your lungs. But you're on the mend, and you'll feel much better in a day or two."

"Repairs?" She had no idea how much damage the *Nefarious* had taken.

"We'll make it to Dragonfire, as long as we don't get any more company. By the time we arrive, you'll be feeling better. I wish we could deliver you to their infirmary sooner, but if we try to push the engines harder, we might lose them."

Yeah, no one wanted to sit in a fireball. She'd given that a whirl, and it wasn't that great.

She handed the empty cup back to him. "Thanks." Not just for the biogel, but for taking care of her, and updating her on the ship. Everything. She knew that he understood.

"Sure. Now settle down and rest. I want to keep you here for the rest of the day, and if you remain stable, I'll release you to your berth. I'll continue to monitor you there."

She nodded and lay back. She was tired. As long as no more ships showed up, she wouldn't mind just resting for a while.

She re-evaluated her priorities when nestled in a tight little berth with Raptor hovering over her, probably counting her respirations. The pain in her lungs had eased, though her back still felt completely raw. That was to be expected, after all of the flesh had been regenerated from the muscles up. She'd been lucky it hadn't been worse. Though when every movement brought a new wave of pain, she didn't feel so lucky.

"Hungry?" Raptor asked once she'd settled onto a stool in her berth. A backless seat felt far more comfortable than the techbed had. She'd tried to insist on going to the bridge but he'd shut her down cold. When it came to medical decisions, Raptor had the final say.

"No." The idea of food made her stomach go sideways.

"Maybe a smoothie? Would get some nutrition into you and should feel good on your throat."

That sounded nice, actually. "All right."

He smiled. "I'll be right back."

She felt relieved when he left. Her memory of them together replayed itself in her head. Whether or not he still harbored any such feelings for her, he once had, and it made her feel squicky about him sharing her quarters. She knew the only way to exorcise it all would be to talk to him about it, but that seemed like a really crappy conversation that she didn't want to have.

So when he returned and handed her the smoothie, she took a sip and delved right in. "You lied."

His face creased with puzzlement. "About what?"

"Us. You said we mutually agreed that our jobs precluded a relationship."

"No. That's true."

She took another sip of the smoothie, which was creamy, laden with tart tango fruit, and actually quite tasty. She shook her head at him. "Yeah, it's *true*, but it's not the whole story. I *saw* us talking about it. In a dorm room."

His face went still. "Oh."

She sipped her smoothie, feeling a little ridiculous about doing so during this particular conversation—but darn if the thing wasn't delicious, and she found she'd actually been quite hungry after all.

"So...what do you want me to say?" he asked.

She felt horribly tired, suddenly. She was tired of not knowing her past, not knowing her future, not knowing anything at all. She wanted at least to know where she stood with him.

"Are you in love with me?"

Raptor grimaced. "It isn't that easy. You and I are like emergency ballistics foam. Nonreactive most of the time, but in a crisis situation, we go straight to basic chemistry. An explosive reaction that fills in all the gaps and makes everything solid."

She pressed on. "You said before that we've hooked up. After our breakup at the academy."

He rubbed his chin. "Yeah. On rare occasion. When things have been dicey and we're jumping out of our skin with adrenaline and the fact that we're still breathing. It's not like we have romantic dinners and take long walks while holding hands."

"But are you in love with me?"

He sighed. "Fallon..."

"It's a yes or no question."

His expression tightened, angry. "It really isn't. You're reducing something complicated into a toggle switch, and life doesn't work that way. You used to know that."

It was an unkind thing to say, but she refused to be sidetracked. "Fine. Were you *ever* in love with me?" She'd seen it in the memory and already knew the answer, but she wanted to hear it from him.

His anger drained away and his shoulders slumped. "Before we joined Blackout, I'd have said yes. But this life we lead, it's not like other people's lives. It changed things. Changed how we are."

"So you're over it, then."

He shifted restlessly, trying to pace but coming up short in the tight space. "Dammit, Fallon. I'm not someone who buys a house and comes home from work every day. I don't expect to live to see old age, much less to have someone to grow old with. I intend to keep going out into the abyss, doing my job, until one day I don't come back. There's no future there. We decided that, years ago."

She could just let it go. Just sidestep the situation. Tiptoe around it. But that wasn't her thing. She wanted all the truth about her past, not assumptions and innuendos. "That's a lot of words that aren't a straight answer."

And the anger returned. His face flushed. "What do you want? You want me to say that you're the love of my life, whatever that means? That when I die, I hope it's your arms I bleed out into?" His voice had been rising steadily, and at this point he was shouting at her. "Fine! But it doesn't mean anything! It's just... sentimentality. The stuff that sneaks up on you in the dark when you see the time on your counter about to reach zero. That's it."

His voice softened, returning to a normal volume. "You used to understand all that."

She still did. She understood it perfectly, and that might make him the perfect match for her, in all their broken ways. If she wanted a match. Which she didn't.

"Life's more complicated than it seems," she admitted. Her smoothie had lost its appeal and she set it on the tiny side table.

He leaned against the bulkhead. "Avian Unit is all we need. The four of us have nearly died for one another a bunch of times. That's what we do."

"What's wrong with us that made us choose this life?" She felt almost philosophical about it, wondering what made her so different from all of her friends back at Dragonfire Station. Whatever it was, Raptor had it too.

He lifted a careless shoulder. "There's nothing wrong with being what we are. We use it for the benefit of other people. If we did it the other way...yeah, we'd be monsters."

"A fine line, then."

He ignored her amusement. "I don't need to soul search to justify my place in the universe."

Her amusement disappeared. "Because you already did that, and came to your conclusion. But I'm doing my reckoning right now."

He blinked, suddenly looking contrite. "Damn. You're right. I'm sorry. You're just figuring it out again and I'm yelling at you." He sighed, sinking onto the bottom bunk. "Ask me whatever you want, if it helps to get you back to where you were. I'll answer. Without yelling."

She couldn't think what else to say. His sudden submission brought her up short. But the truth was, he couldn't give her the answers she wanted. Only she could figure herself out.

A wicked look gleamed in his eyes. "I could tell you about how you've always liked it when I—"

She sensed a lascivious comment coming on. Ignoring the pain in her back, she stood to bend at the waist to cut off whatever stupid thing he was about to say with a kiss.

He wrapped his arms around her and returned the kiss, standing and crowding her space until she was forced to step back. The bulkhead pressed against her spine, which hurt like hell, but reminded her that she was alive.

"Don't start something with me just to see if you can," he warned, giving her a hard look. She was tired of him knowing her better than she knew herself. Maybe it was time to change the rules on him.

She wound her fingers into his hair and pulled his head back down to her.

FALLON FELT SQUISHED. Her shoulder ached. She tried to roll over, only to tumble off the bunk and land on her back, which flared with pain. She sucked in a breath and let loose a string of curses.

Raptor roused, sitting up on the bunk with a deep, sleepy breath. Then he saw her and moved to help. "You okay?"

"My back."

He carefully helped her up without touching her most hurty places.

"Wait, are you smiling?" she demanded. "I'm in pain here."

His smile grew into a grin. "Yeah. Bare-assed and previously burned to a crisp, now flopping around on the floor like a fish out of water. It's funny."

She pushed him away. "You were a lot nicer and more sympathetic in the infirmary."

"You were my patient then. Now you're— " he gestured at their mutual nudity, "—not."

"You treat patients better than lovers?" She didn't bother to cover up. She had a strong, healthy body and nothing to hide.

"Seems like it." He continued to grin. "Maybe you made a bad choice."

No. No, she really hadn't. That could work just fine for her, actually. "Could you at least check my back and make sure I haven't done something to make it worse?"

His gentle hands turned her around, then trailed slowly over her skin and down her spine. Her newly regenerated flesh tingled, still painful, but now something else too. She backed up, closing the space between them. She felt his chest against her backbone and his thighs against hers. She rested her head in the junction between his shoulder and throat as his arm curled around her waist, which pinched her skin against her receiver bracelet.

"This is a mistake, you know," he breathed in her ear. "Really stupid of us."

She turned in his arms, letting her hands slide up his stomach to his chest. "Definitely. But I'm writing my own rules from now on."

In spite of Raptor's frequent reminders of their enormous folly, Fallon still didn't feel bad about it when they docked at Dragonfire. He hadn't moved out of her berth, either. That would change when Fallon returned to the executive suite she shared with Peregrine. She wondered if that would change things between her and Raptor.

Her back and lungs both felt better, and she was greatly relieved to know that her darling *Nefarious* would also soon be better, under the tender mercies of Wren's prodigious mechanical skills.

And did Fallon feel bad about her own crossed wires and complicated relationships? Not a damn bit. Actually, she felt pretty good about it. She'd finally taken over the pilot's seat of her own life. The status quo had gotten them all into this situation to begin with. She'd make it all up as she went along, from here on out.

Practice, she thought. *For the work ahead of us.*

The airlock pressurized, and she gave the pilot's chair of the *Nefarious* an affectionate pat before disembarking.

Peregrine went with Raptor to deliver the tech and scientific data they'd stolen from the lab to Brak. That allowed Fallon and Nevitt to have a long-overdue conversation.

Fallon laid it all out for Nevitt. All of the need-to-know information she'd previously withheld now pertained to the captain, and Nevitt listened to everything with a grim but open expression.

"So," the captain said, primly settling herself on the couch in Fallon's suite. "What now?"

"Brak's looking at what we took from the lab. Raptor and Ross are also scouring the data. We're sure it has what we need."

Nevitt shifted, resting one arm along the back of the couch in a much more casual posture. "And if I decide I don't want my station to become the headquarters of a rebel alliance bent on taking down a branch of intelligence I'm not even supposed to know exists?" She arched a supercilious eyebrow.

"Then we'll move elsewhere. But Dragonfire is the perfect location for what we need to do. And I can ensure it's defended."

Nevitt stared her down. "Even against the PAC?"

One of the smiles Hawk hated slid across Fallon's face, in spite of her best intentions. "Absolutely. The connections we have—" She broke off. Nevitt needn't know details about that. She rearranged her face into something less maniacal. "I can make sure we're fortified and protected." She met Nevitt's gaze and stared right back at her.

Nevitt rubbed her thumb over her lower lip, back and forth. Finally she nodded. "This is either going to save the PAC or result in our fiery deaths. But as things stand, our futures don't look good anyway. So I'm in." She narrowed her eyes at Fallon. "And I mean all the way in. I expect to be part of every decision, and kept informed of every development. I realize I don't have command authority over you and your unit, but I'm the authority on this station. Understood?"

Fallon gave a small bow of her shoulders and head from her seated position. A sign of respect and acquiescence. "I expected no less."

Nevitt sighed. "I knew you'd be trouble the first time I saw you." She pursed her lips wryly. "But I never would have guessed you'd bring a Blackout unit here and use my station to stage an insurrection."

"We're not the ones who started the insurrection," Fallon argued. "Krazinski is. The PAC is founded on laws and treaties that he's trampled right over. He's the one putting us on a short road toward galactic war. *We* are the ones protecting the entire PAC."

"From the outside, and in violation of oh-so-many laws and directives."

Fallon smiled. "I didn't say it would be easy."

———

Something tickled her forehead. She lifted her hand to rub at it and heard a chuckle. Opening her eyes, she saw Raptor.

"Glad to see you getting some sleep. You needed it, whether you admit it or not."

Right. After Nevitt had left, she'd gone to bed early. Brak had encouraged her to be well rested for the implant surgery. Fallon struggled to sit up. Her oversized robe had tangled around her. Damn thing. "What's up?"

"Team meeting. Everyone else is already out there."

"Right. I'll throw on a uniform and be out in a minute." She rolled off the bed and untied the belt of the robe.

"Might want to do something about that hair." He pantomimed an explosion with his hands, all around his head.

She threw the robe at his back.

———

"We've located Admiral Colb," Raptor announced as soon as Fallon walked in and half sat on the arm of the couch.

"Alive, I hope." She didn't have great faith in the life expectancy of anyone not under Krazinski's thumb.

"Alive," Ross confirmed. He sat with his right knee bent so that his foot could rest casually on his left thigh. He looked like he was discussing brunch options, rather than planning a precision strike. "We want to approach him in person. Avoid using any long-range transmitters, stay out of the datastream. All that."

She nodded. Of course they didn't want to just call him up, when Krazinski was no doubt listening as hard for them as they were for him. "Plan?"

"Here." Raptor pushed infoboards at her, Per, and Hawk. "All the specs."

Fallon's eyebrows rose as she read the intel. Colb appeared to have holed up on Zerellus, hiding in plain sight. Not a bad strategy if he could manage the details.

"You're sure this is legit?" She worked at committing it all to memory.

"As sure as we can be. Anything can change at any moment, and anything can be planted. But Ross and I agree, this looks like good intel." Raptor stood behind the couch, arms folded.

Hawk and Peregrine nodded as they lowered their infoboards, and all eyes cut to Fallon. Right. Leader. She got the final say.

"Let's do it."

WHILE THE REST of her team made preparations for their trip to Zerellus, which hopefully would be the first step toward taking out Krazinski, Fallon had her own personal mission to attend to.

She walked into Dr. Brannin Brash's infirmary with an odd sense of déjà vu. This was where she'd first woken up on Dragonfire, her memory blanked and her future unclear.

Which now brought her around full circle. She could only hope that the three doctors could give her back what was rightfully hers.

"Fallon," Brannin stepped ahead of the others to greet her with a friendly smile and a bow. His kind, dark eyes welcomed her. "Or can I still call you Chief?"

She returned his bow. "Jury's out on that one. Guess I'll have to ask the captain."

He nodded. "Of course. I'm sure you double-checked it yourself, but all of my staff has been dismissed for the time being, and all security devices blanked. There will be no records of your visit here."

She had, in fact, ensured that, but she only said, "Thank you." She shifted her attention to Jerin and Brak, both wearing surgical scrubs. In spite of the circumstances, she felt a surge of pleasure at seeing them again. The reunion would have to wait, though. "Are we ready?"

Jerin's eyes registered concern. "You're sure about this?"

"Absolutely."

Jerin shared a glance with Brak, who then said, "We're ready."

They guided her onto a techbed and began preparing her. A mild sedative, some synaptic stimulators. More injections that they named, but the medical words slipped past her like encrypted lines of code. Her thoughts had gone elsewhere.

She revisited her life, as she remembered it, all seven months' worth. Plus her recovered memories, which existed in her mind like items on a shelf. Hers, but in a disembodied way.

If the procedure didn't work, and Brak had warned her that it might not, she could lose all of this.

Should she be scared? She wasn't. She had faith in Brak. The technology stolen from the lab on Taravok had further improved Brak's confidence in the procedure. And Fallon had faith in herself, as well. If she lost her memories, she'd be far better off than she'd been the last time it had happened. She'd recorded a series of messages for herself that would explain and re-educate. Plus, she had a lot of people to help get her back up to snuff.

Brannin gently guided a stabilizer around her neck, then closed another one around her temples and forehead. "Ready?" he asked, leaning in so she could see his face. She was surprised to realize she'd missed him. Thus far, he knew nothing of the bigger picture, only that Brak had engineered a treatment for Fallon, and that Jerin had approved of it. What ignorant bliss he lived in, for at least a little while longer.

"Absolutely." She had no doubts.

Jerin's voice floated to Fallon's ears from behind her head. "Administering the sedative now. You're going to sleep through this, Fallon. We'll see you on the other side."

Brak leaned into her field of vision. Fallon admired her draconian beauty—her features and blue-green scales, shining with iridescence. Fallon let out a small sigh. She felt good, and knew that meant she'd be asleep in a moment.

"We're going to do this," Brak said. "Try not to be anxious." She reached for Fallon's hand and gripped it, offering reassurance. Fallon squeezed back, remembering the time Brak had revealed the secret of her prosthetic arms to her. She trusted Brak.

"I'm not," Fallon said. She meant it. All things considered, she should probably be deeply worried, but she had no fears. Only plans for what came next.

FALLON FELT nothing until she found herself in the corridors of her memory. Huh. She hadn't expected to come here. She was pretty sure she should have gone dark. Something was going on. Something important, but she couldn't quite recall what.

She found a tall, rectangular door, the sort she'd learned to prefer. They tended to have the most involved and relevant memories. She reached for its handle, but when she touched it, the door popped like a soap bubble, leaving her in shadow again.

"Well, that was weird."

She moved on, floating past the round and square doors until she found another tall rectangle. A purple one. She reached for it, and it also popped, more like a punctured balloon. An edge of the door slapped her hand before it winked out of existence.

Very weird.

She moved on, faster now, and the little doors began to ripple, falling open and revealing glimpses of lakes, books, glasses of liquid, and other odd assortments. The open doors quivered, as if made of jelly, then became one-dimensional, rolled up into themselves, and dissolved. She started to feel an odd pressure, pushing her down.

Fallon moved around a corner and found a big, glorious rectangle of a door. It glittered with gold, reminding her of Briveen scales. She hesitated, afraid that touching it might make it disappear like the others. But the pressure was forcing her down. Her knees were bending. She'd be on the floor in a second.

She reached for the door and flung it open, and it actually *worked*. She fell through the doorway as the pressure closed in behind her, brushing her heels as it rushed in.

The room was bathed in light. She looked up and saw Brak. The scent of anise assailed her, indicating Brak's concern. Odd. These memories hadn't included much smell before, but this felt really *real*.

"How do you feel?" Brak asked.

Feel? Why? Fallon didn't understand. No one ever talked directly to her in the memories.

Oh. Realization coalesced among her scattered thoughts. "This is real?"

Brak dipped her chin in acknowledgement. "This is real. You're awake. How do you feel?"

The techbed still held her head immobile, but she checked in with her body and found nothing amiss. "Fine. Good."

Brak nodded, presumably to Jerin and Brannin behind Fallon. "We're going to taper off the sedative, and it will clear your system within a few minutes. Just lie quietly."

Sure, no problem. She'd just lie here. She gazed up at the ceiling. She breathed. In, out. In, out. She wiggled her toes.

"Still doing okay?" Jerin's voice asked.

"Yup."

The restraints around her head released and she tilted it from side to side, seeing how it would feel. No soreness.

A minute later, Brannin came into view. "We're going to sit you up now."

The techbed began to shift, moving her into a seated position.

The three doctors faced her, all looking serious. "Can you tell us your name?" Brannin asked.

Her name. Right. She opened her mouth, then paused. "My name," she repeated.

The doctors' eyes lit with worry.

Fallon laughed. "Which one?"

Brak watched her cautiously. "You remember more than one?"

"Oh, yeah. I remember them all. I remember *everything*."

WHEN THE DOCTORS finally released her, with all due caveats and what-to-watch-out-fors, Fallon wasted no time in returning to her team. They'd huddled up together to wait in the small suite shared by Hawk, Raptor, and now Ross too.

Fallon felt silly about activating the chime, but it seemed rude not to. Everyone stared at her in silence as the doors closed behind her.

It was strange, seeing them all again. As if she were looking at them through two sets of eyes. One that showed them from a limited—yet more objective—perspective. And another that revealed all their secrets and idiosyncracies.

She wanted to say something clever. Something funny. But the anxiety on their faces was too intense. She couldn't toy with them.

So she simply said, "I'm back. Intact. All of me."

She hadn't expected the celebratory shout, or the way Hawk knocked his chair over in his eagerness to get to her. He picked her up and swung her around as she laughed, reminding her of their graduation from the academy. The memory of him, young and jubilant, warmed her.

They talked and shouted, asked questions, and Fallon could barely make sense of who was saying what. She tried to answer, and ended up laughing whenever Hawk gave her another twirl, since he hadn't yet put her down. Eventually he handed her off to Raptor, who immediately put her on her feet, but didn't drop his arms from around her.

"Hey," he said softly in her ear, for only her to hear. "Regretting anything now?"

"Not a thing." She leaned out of his grasp, causing his arms to fall away. "Does this change things?"

He looked happy and relaxed. "Nothing. Everything. I have no idea."

"I guess we'll find out."

He grinned. "Right."

Peregrine handed her a glass of champagne that Hawk had poured, then surprised Fallon with a kiss on the temple. "Glad you're back, partner."

The gesture touched Fallon, as she knew Peregrine didn't express affection easily. Her difficult teen years had made her resistant to that sort of sentiment. "Thanks, Per."

Fallon had work to do. She needed to get her ass to Captain Nevitt to make a full report right away, or face the withering consequences of the captain's displeasure.

Then she had an underground intelligence agency to take down and put back together. And a former wife whom she needed to say a few things to.

It would all have to wait. Her team was giving her a proper celebration, and they deserved to enjoy the moment.

"Blood and bone," Hawk announced, raising his glass.

She, Per, and Raptor raised theirs as well, shouting, "Blood and bone!" in return. Ross tilted his glass with a wry grin of not quite fitting in. But he was one of them too, in his way.

"Blood and bone don't quit," Fallon finished, taking a hearty drink of her champagne. The tiny bubbles burst in her mouth, tickling her tongue.

Yeah, she had work to do. A lot of it. But she was going to savor this moment first. She predicted it would become one of her favorite memories. She had so many now. And there were a lot more of them just waiting to happen.

She had her team. She had Dragonfire. And she had her friends on the *Onari*. She laughed. Blackout wouldn't know what hit them.

MESSAGE FROM THE AUTHOR

Thank you for reading!
Please sign up for my newsletter to receive updates on new releases and sales.

Reviews are critical to an author's success. I would be grateful if you could write a review at Amazon and/or Goodreads. Just a couple minutes of your time would mean so much to me.

If you're ready to find out what happens next in the series, you can go straight into *Coalescence*.

In gratitude,
Zen DiPietro

ABOUT THE AUTHOR

Zen DiPietro is a lifelong bookworm, dreamer, and writer. Perhaps most importantly, a Browncoat Trekkie Whovian. Also red-haired, left-handed, and a vegetarian geek. Absolutely terrible at conforming. A recovering gamer, but we won't talk about that. Particular loves include badass heroines, British accents, and the smell of Band-Aids.

www.ZenDiPietro.com

Printed in Dunstable, United Kingdom